INTO THE UNKNOWN

"You're now, as of receipt of this order," his commander, Lieutenant Colnel Kemp, said, "a by-God brevet *captain*."

Benoit opened his mouth to speak but Kemp cut him off. "Explain this!"

"I don't know how to explain the promotion, sir."

"Then how about your transfer," Kemp added grimly.

Benoit was certain he was going to faint. "*What* transfer, sir?"

Kemp looked at him coldly. "Effective one May you're Brigadier General Maurice G. Barksdale's new aide-de-camp."

"Who's General Barksdale?" Benoit asked, puzzled.

Kemp rolled his eyes. "General Barksdale is the new commander of the Ninth Military Department."

"The Ninth! Isn't that in—"

"Fort Macy, New Mexico Territory," Kemp finished for him. "Santa Fe to be exact."

Benoit was sure he had never, in all his life, been so confused . . . "Why me, sir?"

"Ah-ha!" Kemp exclaimed, his eyes bulging. "That's the point! *Why you*?"

BOOKS BY KEN ENGLADE

Hoffa

TONY HILLERMAN'S FRONTIER
People of the Plains
The Tribes
The Soldiers
Battle Cry
Brothers in Blood

NONFICTION
Hotblood
To Hatred Turned
Blood Sister
Beyond Reason
Murder in Boston
Cellar of Horror
Deadly Lessons
A Family Business

TONY HILLERMAN'S FRONTIER

BROTHERS IN BLOOD

Ken Englade

HarperPaperbacks
A Division of HarperCollinsPublishers

HarperPaperbacks
A Division of HarperCollins*Publishers*
10 East 53rd Street, New York, N.Y. 10022-5299

This is a work of fiction. The characters, incidents, and dialogues
are products of the author's imagination and are not to be
construed as real. Any resemblance to actual events or persons,
living or dead, is entirely coincidental.

ISBN: 0-06-101291-2

HarperCollins®, ®, and HarperPaperbacks™
are trademarks of HarperCollins*Publishers* Inc.

Cover illustration © 1998 by Cliff Miller

First printing: March 1998

Printed in the United States of America

Visit HarperPaperbacks on the World Wide Web at
http://www.harpercollins.com

❖ 10 9 8 7 6 5 4 3 2 1

For Trav and Linda

A special message for Rosalie: *Mil gracias*.

BROTHERS
IN BLOOD

Seven minutes, no more. That's how long it should take for the men of C Company to fall in. At least, that's what Benoit demanded. And to make sure they stuck to his timetable he clocked them with the pocket watch that Inge had given him for their first anniversary several months before, the one in the engraved silver case that she had ordered special from New York.

He glanced at the timepiece. A minute and a half since he had sent Sergeant Hampton into the barracks to roust the troops. They wouldn't be happy, he knew, since they were already busy giving the place a good spring cleaning. Too bad. They'd thank him for it later, after Colonel Kemp awarded them the banner signifying they were the best company at Fort Laramie in 1858. It was all part of Benoit's long-range plan to prove beyond a doubt that he could handle the responsibility. Shape up the troops. Get them distracted with one chore, then surprise them with something else, like an unannounced arms inspection. Keep them on their toes. Keep them sharp.

Benoit looked up as two privates came running

out the door, lugging their rifles and strapping on their ammunition pouches. Two minutes. Not bad, he thought.

Impatiently he began pacing back and forth: ten strides to the east, then ten back. When he turned to make the westward leg, he noticed the wind in his face. He stopped and glanced around, his brow furrowed. Here and there across the vast, dusty parade ground, he noted with irritation, several small dustdevils were dancing mischievously about. *"Merde!"* he said half-aloud. "It isn't even midmorning." The wind usually did not begin picking up until the afternoon. Goddamn spring, he thought. He was *really* beginning to hate the season.

This attitude, he would readily admit, was newly developed. When he was growing up in New Orleans, even when he was away at the military academy at West Point, he used to love the spring. In those days he agreed wholeheartedly with the poets who wrote entire sonnets proclaiming the glories of the vernal equinox. It was easier then, he thought, to believe all the words the lyricists wove about spring being a time of wondrous rebirth and rejuvenation. He had been more ready to accept these accolades then because all around him there was evidence to substantiate the claims of the bards. Gentle rain falling from thick, dove gray clouds. Tender new leaves sprouting on once barren trees. Robins singing in the early morning. Dew-sprinkled grass daily turning a deeper, more luxuriant green. And flowers—ah, the flowers—bursting forth from thick, rich soil, promising a display of color that would make even the most insensitive soul soar. But those poets, he reflected wryly, had never been to Fort Laramie. Not one as far as he knew—and he was damn near certain he was correct—had ever trod the Great Plains.

Out west, out here where he and some three hundred other blue-clad men helped protect a steady throng of Pacific Coast–bound emigrants through a harsh and cruel land populated by numerous tribes of increasingly resentful, hostile Indians, the traditional, widely sung benefits of spring were virtually nonexistent. The rain, on the rare occasions when it came, was hardly ever gentle. Instead it arrived in ominous-looking clouds as black as midnight. And it came down not gently but in torrents, accompanied by booming thunder and wildly flashing lightning. Except for the pines and evergreens that grew thick on the nearby mountains, the only trees deserving of the name anywhere near the post were the creaking cottonwoods and supple willows that sprang up along the banks of the North Platte and Laramie Rivers. And these were disappearing rapidly as the emigrants chopped them down for firewood. Grass grew thick and tall on the prairie, but that was utilitarian food-grass, a staple in the diet of the buffalo, the elk, and the antelope. It wasn't lying-on-your-back-in grass; it definitely wasn't making-love-in grass. That kind of grass didn't exist out here. Never had; never would. There was no place here, either, for the flowers of his youth. The wildflowers that grew in the mountain meadows were truly spectacular in their own right—beautiful and lush in their short season, but one had to spend hours in the saddle to see them. On the Plains, where Fort Laramie sat like a wart on a fat man's back, the symbols those who lived back east associated with the season were totally absent.

Not, he thought, that this was not a beautiful

country in its own right. He had never seen a sky as
blue and clear as the western one. The mountains were
not tiny hills, bare undulations on the horizon, but
majestic peaks of black rock with caps of pristine snow
that never melted. Looking to the west, he could see
the fingerlike projectile of Laramie Peak, jutting so far
into the sky that, even at a distance of fifty or so miles,
he could barely take it all in without tilting his head.
The West definitely had its points, he conceded, but
the arrival of spring was not one of them. To him, the
western spring meant one thing: wind. Goddamn,
drive-you-insane, dry-you-out, beat-you-to-death
wind.

In the summer there was the unforgiving sun, but
if one knew what to expect, it was endurable. Besides,
the nights *always* were cool; the temperature invari-
ably dropped thirty degrees or more between the time
the sun went down and the time it rose again. This
was true even in June, which was usually the hottest
month. And for someone who had never seen snow
until he reported for duty at the military academy,
even the western winters were bearable once one
learned to adapt, even if the snow flew from
September through March; even if it piled up in drifts
higher than the tallest buildings along Canal Street. He
could adjust to those seasons. But he had never
learned to adjust to the cursed wind.

It started blowing in March and didn't quit sometimes until July. The western wind was no gentle zephyr,
either. His father, who had been a maritime lawyer and
knew about things nautical, would have classified the
prevailing Fort Laramie springtime "breeze" as being of
the gale-force variety. In other words, on a day-to-day
basis, it was strong enough to make a grown man stagger

like a drunk. And when it really blew, there was no sense
trying to fight it. The solution was just to hole up and
wait until it quit, even though that might be four or five
days, even a week.

What was so infuriating about the western wind,
beyond the fact that it was a constant force to be
combated, was that with it came other unpleasant by-
products. By far the worst was airborne dust and
sand. When the wind blew, the dust climbed up the
nose and clogged the nostrils as if they were plugged
with cotton. It got in the eyes and made them burn as
if they had been rinsed with saltwater. And it
peppered exposed skin, hitting the cheeks and neck
like birdshot. Dust and sand got embedded in your
scalp, lodged between your toes, crept into your
underwear. It covered everything from furniture to
food. Sometimes in the spring, Benoit swore, he was
really dining on soggy sandpaper, not a juicy slice of
buffalo rump.

But to the soldier, the "dust problem," as it was
referred to by some of the emigrant wives, was more
than a nuisance. When dust and sand got into the
working parts of a rifle, it could be disastrous. A man
trying to fight with a sand-fouled weapon might as
well be armed only with a club. Most veteran troopers—those who had been through a western springtime—recognized this danger and took precautions
against it. Usually it was the newcomers who had to
be warned, often several times.

Benoit looked at his watch. Five and a half minutes and all but a few stragglers were there, forming
themselves into a neat formation. Benoit made a mental note that he would need to congratulate them later
on their speed and efficiency. Where in hell are the last

few? he asked himself, looking impatiently at the barracks.

A gust of cool air caught him in the face, causing him to frown. Like a bear seeking a scent, he stuck his nose in the air and sniffed, seeing if he could, like Jim Ashby, actually *smell* a change in the weather.

At slightly over six feet tall, with a deep chest and a short, thick neck that made it look as if his head were resting directly on his powerful, sloping shoulders, Benoit *did*, in all honesty, look somewhat bearlike. Adding to the image were exceptionally long arms that dangled downward so far that he was often teased about being able to scratch his knees without bending at the waist. Unlike a bear, however, Benoit was neither dark nor hairy. His skin was a creamy off white, an apparent gift from an unknown Anglo ancestor—unknown because both his parents and all of the family they could account for came from France and tended to be of a darker complexion. His eyes, unlike those of everyone else in his family, were a startling blue.

He inhaled deeply, wondering how Ashby did it. All *he* smelled was fresh horse manure that was left over from B Company's mounted drill. But the wind *was* coming from the northwest, straight off Laramie Peak, and that was the usual direction from which storms came. Still there was not a cloud in the sky.

"I think they're all present," Sergeant Hampton whispered, hinting to Benoit that he might want to order him to call the men to attention. Benoit looked at his watch. Six and half minutes. Damn good.

The previous autumn, after he was promoted to second lieutenant and given his own command, he had wanted to start immediately whipping the men into what he considered a first-class unit. Some of the other officers, like his best friend, Jason Dobbs, the post surgeon, even suggested that he would probably do better to try to curb his enthusiasm. "You can't treat them like they were seven-year-olds," Dobbs had told him. "You have to give them some leeway; let them do *some* thinking for themselves."

Benoit took the advice to heart. But it wasn't as if he had a lot of choice. By then winter had begun to set in, and for six months everyone on the post had been a prisoner to the weather. In March Benoit was able to get them out onto the parade ground and into the field on a limited basis—between snowstorms, that was. Now that it was April and the weather was beginning to improve, he was hampered by the wind. But rather than being discouraged, Benoit decided to take advantage of the situation. There was no better time than April, he figured, to impress upon the troopers the necessity for making sure their rifles were always clean of windblown sand. It was necessary to his plan. He wanted to make them understand that if an individual trooper sloughed off, he likely would have to pay the price. But in a military group, one man's negligence might affect the others as well. If a man let his rifle get inoperable, he could, in a skirmish, lose not only his own life, but the lives of his fellow troopers as well, since that man's firepower might be crucial to the survival of the entire unit.

At least, that was the way Benoit looked at it. And since he was the company commander, he felt duty bound to make sure such a situation never arose. Not in *his* company. That was why he had called the inspection. In the last two weeks company strength had increased. The unpredictable Cheyenne—after their shellacking the previous summer at the Solomon River—were expected to launch a more aggressive antiwhite offensive as soon as the weather permitted. In anticipation of this, several new men had only recently been sent in from Fort Leavenworth. These were the men Benoit hoped to reach. If they were going to survive to see the next winter, they were going to have to learn how vital it was to maintain their equipment in the face of the elements.

Benoit nodded at Hampton, who called the men to attention. Skipping the preliminaries, Benoit strode forward, heading straight toward the nearest new face. Taking the man's rifle, he was preparing to peer down the barrel so he could see just how dirty it was when he was interrupted by a voice over his shoulder.

"Begging your pardon, Lieutenant."

Benoit turned. Facing him was Corporal Bianchi, the headquarters runner.

"Yes, Corporal," Benoit growled. "What is it?"

"Sorry to interrupt, sir. But the colonel wants to see you."

"Very well," Benoit replied. "I'll be another twenty minutes." He turned back to the rifle, dismissing Bianchi.

"The colonel said 'right away,'" the corporal added stubbornly, standing his ground.

"I just started my inspection, Corporal," Benoit said irritably. "I *said* I'd be along shortly."

Bianchi shook his head "The colonel wants you *now*," he insisted.

Benoit hesitated. It was not often that Colonel Kemp summoned one of the officers in the middle of the workday. And when he did, it was even more rarely termed urgent. To get such a call was not only exceptional, it was alarming. Kemp, known for his hair-trigger temper, never let anything but his anger distract him or his men from a day's labor. And when he was angry, he was a terror. With chest and shoulders as thick as a bull bison's and a tongue as sharp as a filet knife, a rampaging Kemp could strike fear into the heart of the bravest soldier.

Wondering what he could possibly have done to incur Kemp's wrath, Benoit told Sergeant Hampton to finish the inspection, then spun on his heels to follow Bianchi.

"What's the colonel's mood?" Benoit asked as the two of them hurried toward Kemp's office, which was located in a tiny building adjacent to the post's finest structure, a two-story, white-painted, galleried edifice known as Old Bedlam.

Easily the most handsome structure on the entire trail, Old Bedlam had been built in the fall of 1849 as a barracks. The original plans called for an entire company to be housed within its sixteen rooms. But as Fort Laramie grew in size and importance, enlisted men were moved to other quarters and Old Bedlam became Officer Country. On the lower floor, walls were knocked out to make a spacious mess, while on the upper floor the rooms were made smaller, the better to accommodate an increasingly large contingent of bachelor officers.

"I'd say he's pissed off, sir," Bianchi said tactfully, deciding it probably was not wise to tell Benoit that Kemp's summons had been preceded by a shouted curse and the thud of an unidentified heavy object being hurled across the room. Bianchi, as the post's official messenger, did not believe that he should suffer for the bad news he often was required to deliver.

Benoit gave the corporal a sideways look and decided not to push it. He would find out soon enough.

Five minutes later he was standing in front of Kemp's desk. Clicking his heels together smartly, he threw the snappiest salute he could muster. "Lieutenant Benoit reporting as ordered, sir," he croaked, discovering that his mouth had become as dry as last fall's kindling.

Kemp ignored him, concentrating instead on two sheets of paper laid out side by side in the exact center of his otherwise bare desk.

Protocol required Benoit to hold the salute until it was acknowledged. While waiting for the colonel to recognize him, he focused his gaze on the government-issue portrait of an unsmiling President Buchanan that had been nailed to the back wall.

Impatiently, without moving his head, Benoit let his gaze drift downward. The papers were too far away for him to read, but he did notice with surprise that Kemp had a silver dollar-size bald spot. The unreasonable thought flashed through Benoit's brain that it was staring at him like a pupilless third eye.

Being in such close proximity to Fort Laramie's commanding officer was a little unnerving, Benoit reflected. Usually the closest the two came was at mealtime when they met in the officers' mess. But at those times Kemp reigned from the head of the long table while Benoit was relegated to the junior officers' end. From his seat, Benoit had always assumed that Kemp's hair was thick and blond. Up close, he also could see that it was sprinkled liberally with strands of gray.

Benoit grimaced as a cramp began forming in his arm, the result of continuing to hold the salute while waiting for Kemp to recognize him. As the pain increased, Benoit wondered how much longer he could hold out before lowering the extremity. Just when he was about to surrender, the colonel looked up and returned the salute.

Benoit's sigh of relief died in his throat. Kemp's eyes blazed like nuggets of obsidian catching the sun. His lips were clamped together, and his jaw muscles vibrated as he clenched and unclenched his teeth.

Benoit felt his sphincter clench like a baby's fist. "You sent for me, sir?" he asked weakly, wishing he were anywhere else.

"You're goddamned right I sent for you, Ben-oight," Kemp roared.

Benoit flinched, too petrified to remind the colonel yet again that his name was pronounced Ben-wah, with a soft, almost slurred, final syllable. Only ignorant Anglophiles, he had told Dobbs hundreds of times, articulated it with that crude, gruntlike "oight." But a second glance at Kemp's face convinced Benoit that silence was the wiser strategy.

"Tell me, *Lieutenant* Ben-oight," Kemp bellowed loudly enough, Benoit felt, to be heard all the way to Fort Kearny, three hundred miles to the east, "is this you?"

Benoit looked down to see Kemp jabbing at the paper in front of him with a stubby index finger crowned with a thick nail chewed almost to the quick.

Benoit leaned over to see where the colonel was pointing. In bold, black ink he read his name: Jean Francis Xavier Benoit III.

"Yes, sir," Benoit replied uncertainly. "That's me."

"And is this me?" Kemp asked, stabbing at another spot.

Benoit looked. The script read "Aloysius Bradford Kemp."

"Yes, sir, that's you," Benoit confirmed.

"And who is this?" Kemp asked, placing his finger at a signature on the bottom of the document.

Benoit stared. "I think, sir," he said unsurely, "it says 'John E. Floyd.'"

"That's a 'b,' not an 'e,'" Kemp corrected him. "John *B.* Floyd."

Suddenly it dawned upon Benoit. "The secretary of war, sir?" His knees went weak at the thought that he might have done something so egregious that he was personally named in correspondence from the army's second most powerful man, an eminence whose authority over things military was exceeded only by the president himself.

"Yes!" Kemp yelled, slamming his fist on the desk so hard that Benoit half expected it to collapse. "The secretary of war!"

"I don't understand, sir," Benoit whispered.

"Then let me enlighten you," Kemp said brusquely. "But first let me congratulate you."

"Huh?" Benoit squeaked, forgetting he was a junior officer speaking to his commander.

"You're no longer Second Lieutenant Ben-oight," Kemp said.

Benoit looked at him as if he doubted his sanity.

"You're now, as of receipt of this order," Kemp said, letting the document dangle from his fingers as if it were contaminated, "a by God brevet *captain*."

Benoit's eyes glazed over; he felt as dazed and unconnected as he had when he was shot in the chest by Short Hair during the fight at Solomon River. "I don't understand, sir," he mumbled, certain he had misheard.

"Tell me, Ben-oight," Kemp said, tilting back in his chair and looking at Benoit through half-closed eyes, "how old are you?"

Benoit blinked. "I was twenty-six in January, sir."

"And you graduated from the academy when?"

"June 1853."

"And how long were you a brevet before being made a full second lieutenant?"

"Three and a half years, sir."

"How long have I been a brevet lieutenant colonel?"

Benoit frowned. "As long as I've known you, sir. Almost four years."

"And for two years before that. Your friend, Dobbs. How long has he been a first lieutenant?"

"Gee, I don't know for sure. I think because he's a surgeon he was made a first lieutenant when he enlisted. That must have been nearly ten years ago."

"Exactly!" Kemp said emphatically. "My point is, in a peacetime army, promotions are few and far between.

"Yes—"

"But," Kemp interrupted, "you've not only been promoted twice in less than a year, today you've jumped a full grade. Don't you think that's passing strange?"

Benoit opened his mouth to speak, but Kemp cut him off. "Not only that," Kemp added, "but the promotion came outside the usual chain of command. It came directly from the *secretary of war*! It doesn't matter what *you* think, Ben-oight. *I* think it's strange."

Slapping the paper, Kemp turned away, seemingly trying to gather himself.

Benoit felt as if his legs were going to give way, and he was sure all color had gone from his cheeks. Not sure he could trust his voice, he said nothing.

"Tell me, Ben-oight," Kemp said, eyeing Benoit carefully. "Have you been playing politics behind my back?"

Benoit's mouth dropped open. "I don't know what you mean, sir. By—"

"I'll get right to it. Have you been playing footsie with that senator friend of yours?"

"S-senator friend," Benoit stammered.

"Clement Couvillion!" Kemp bellowed. "Ever since that weasel-faced little nincompoop was appointed to fill poor Emile Fontenot's seat he's been nothing but a troublemaker. I've had no use for him since he shot and killed my friend George Teasley, in that duel right out there on the parade ground a couple of years ago in that dispute involving his wife, the woman you were, uh, 'rather friendly' with before you came out west."

"How did you know about Marie?" Benoit asked, forgetting the shock of his unexpected promotion.

"Jesus Christ, Ben-oight, give me some credit. You think I don't know all there is to know about my men? You think I don't make it a point to learn everything I can before I entrust *my* soldiers to every pimply-faced young brevet who shows up at my door?"

"Yes, sir," Benoit said, blushing. "It's just that I didn't think—"

"That's your problem, you don't think enough. You don't presume that when I suddenly get an order from the secretary of war snatching one of my men right out from under my command without so much as a 'please' or 'thank you' or 'what do you think?' that I'm not going to get pretty goddamn riled up about it?"

Benoit frowned. "I'm not following you, sir. I don't—"

"Shut up, Ben-oight. Wait until I've finished."

"Yes, sir," Benoit whispered, his face turning scarlet.

"I've spent a lot of time bringing you along to the point where I finally feel that you know enough to put on a coat before you go out in a blizzard. When I took over the command here, you had as much leadership ability as a half-trained sheepdog. But in the last few years, you've shown remarkable development. I was just getting to the point where I was beginning to have confidence that you were going to be a pretty damn good soldier. And then this happens," he added, thumping the papers. "Explain this, goddammit!"

"I don't know how to explain the promotion, sir."

"Then how about your transfer?" Kemp added grimly.

Benoit was certain he was going to faint. "*What* transfer, sir? You haven't said anything about a transfer."

Kemp looked at him coldly. "You've not only been promoted, Ben-oight, you also have a new posting. Effective one May you're Brigadier General Maurice G. Barksdale's new aide-de-camp."

"Who's General Barksdale?" Benoit asked, puzzled.

Kemp rolled his eyes. "Jesus, deliver me! General Barksdale, you'd better learn damn quick, is the new commander of the Ninth Military Department."

"The Ninth! Isn't that in—"

"Fort Marcy, New Mexico Territory," Kemp finished for him. "Santa Fe, to be exact."

Benoit was sure he had never, in all his life, been so confused. "Let me make sure I understand this, sir. I'm being promoted to brevet"—he could hardly bring himself to say the word—"captain."

"I thought I made that pretty damn clear."

"And, I'm being reassigned to General, uh, General *Barksdale's* staff. . . ."

"That's right."

"At Fort Marcy?"

"God, you sure are a slow learner, Ben-oight. Do I have to repeat everything for you?"

Benoit licked his lips. "Why *me*, sir?" he asked in a low voice.

"Ah-hah!" Kemp exclaimed, his eyes bulging. "That's the point! Why *you*?"

"I don't know what to say, Colonel," Benoit said, shaking his head. "I'm flabbergasted. This comes as a complete surprise."

"Does it now, Ben-oight? Are you *really* surprised?"

Benoit shook his head. "Of course I'm surprised, sir. Why wouldn't I be?"

"That's why you're here. I want to know just how much *you* know about this."

"I don't now know *anything* about it, Colonel."

"I ask you again. Did you ask your friend the senator to push this through for you? Maybe tell him you were tired of chasing Indians across the Plains and he'd be doing you a big favor if he could arrange for some more, uh, *substantial*, duty?"

"He's *not* my friend, Colonel. I grew up with his

brother, but I hardly knew Cle. I *did* have a liaison with Marie, but that was long before she knew Cle, much less married him. And once I left Washington I broke off all relations with her. When she was out here with Cle and her father on that fact-finding mission, I had nothing to do with her. I swear it. If I had, Inge would have killed me. That's the truth. I promise you. And," he added hurriedly, "why would I want a transfer?" He was sure he was beginning to prattle, but he felt unable to stop himself. "I *like* it here. I *like* being a company commander. My wife's here. Her family is here. My best friend's here. Why would I want to go someplace I've never been before to be an errand boy for some general I've never heard of?"

Kemp nodded slowly, the anger slowly draining from his face. "Good answer, Ben-oight. But the response might just be that you're ambitious. Being on a general's staff certainly won't hurt your career. And New Mexico Territory might not be a bad place to be. There's a troop buildup there now; a lot of things are happening. Besides, it has real cities, some form of civilization. . . ."

"None of that appeals to me, sir."

"It doesn't matter whether it appeals to you or not, Ben-oight. If the secretary of war himself says that's where you're going, you will by God *go!*"

"Of course I'll go, sir. That isn't what I meant. I was just trying to explain that I didn't ask—"

"You know what really gripes me about this?" Kemp interrupted. "It's the *way* it was done. Orders like this"—he waved the two sheets of paper—"don't come every week. The secretary of war usually doesn't pluck some shavetail lieutenant from an out-of-the-way frontier post and give him an important new job *and* a big promotion to boot, although I guess one goes with the other. A general really needs a captain to represent him, not some ignoramus wearing a lieutenant's insignia. But jobs like that usually go to the ass lickers around the War Department, a cousin of an influential government official or the son of some widow that a general has been screwing. But that doesn't apply in your case, Ben-oight. Or does it?"

"No, sir!" Benoit said emphatically. "That certainly *doesn't* apply in my case."

"Then we don't know *why* this order came through?"

"I haven't the faintest idea, Colonel," Benoit replied earnestly. "I'm as shocked as you are."

Kemp studied Benoit for what seemed like a long time. "Very good, Lieutenant. That's what I wanted to hear. I didn't want to believe you'd resort to politics. I felt I knew you better than that. But I had to be sure. Know one thing, though: This may be a mystery, but I'm going to try my damnedest to solve it. I haven't been in the army for eighteen years for nothing. I have some friends in Washington who can do some snooping around. Does that knowledge bother you, Ben-oight?"

"Not at all, Colonel. I'd like to know myself. Maybe it's all a mistake."

"It's no mistake. That's your name on the order, sure as hell. Accept it. The army moves in curious ways sometimes. Just learn to think of this as one of those times."

Benoit sighed deeply. He felt exhausted. He also was anxious to get out of Kemp's office; he couldn't wait to be free so he could find Inge and give her the news. "May I be excused, sir?"

Kemp nodded and smiled. His rage spent, Kemp was friendly. Standing, he extended his hand. "Congratulations, Benoit. And good luck."

Benoit felt giddy with relief. "Thank you, sir. By the way"—he grinned—"do you know what you just did?"

Kemp frowned. "I shook your hand."

"More than that." Benoit laughed. "For the first time in memory you pronounced my name correctly."

When Benoit stepped out of Kemp's cramped office he thought at first he had strolled into an icehouse by mistake. In the hour he had been with the colonel, the temperature had dropped forty degrees and the north-west wind that had been slightly gusty when he was summoned was howling at forty-five to fifty miles per hour, hard enough to cause him to brace his feet when he walked, like a sailor trying to negotiate a rolling deck. Looking up, he saw that the once blue sky had turned as gray as a dead man's face, a sure indication that it would be snowing any minute.

Wrapping his arms protectively around his body, he turned left and sprinted the short distance to the kitchen, where the officers' meals were prepared. "Inge!" he yelled, charging through the door. "Inge, where are you? I have some marvelous news."

"Not here," a female voice called from across the room.

"Oh, hi, Holz," Benoit replied, slamming the door against the gale. Pausing to catch his breath, he looked around the room. Near the far wall, leaning over a long table where she was rolling dough for that evening's *Apfelstrudel*, was his mother-in-law, Hildegard Ashby, née Schmidt.

One of the legends of the Oregon Trail, Hildegard was known to thousands of emigrants who had made the long trek from Missouri to the West Coast as a clear example of the brave, unstoppable pioneer woman who could suffer great loss and still come up fighting. In 1854, when she, her husband, Hans, and their two children—Inge and Erich—were heading west, their train was attacked by a group of Cheyenne and Brulé renegades. Hans and several others in the group had been killed. Hildegard herself had taken an arrow in the leg. When the wound became infected, the post surgeon, Dobbs, had to amputate. Since then Hildegard had been affectionately referred to by her family—including her son-in-law—and a few very close friends by a German nickname for someone with a wooden leg, "Holzbein" or, more simply, "Holz." While she was admired far and wide as a paragon of unquenchable spirit, she also was famous closer to home, to the officers at Fort Laramie, for her cooking, especially her baking.

Benoit looked at her tenderly and smiled. The resemblance between mother and daughter had never, not in all the time he had known them, ceased to amaze him. If he had not known better, he would have sworn the two were sisters. In addition to hair the color of cornsilk, both had cheerful turquoise blue eyes and pink cheeks that made them look always as if they had just come in from the cold. Both had rather broad shoulders, ample bosoms, and slim hips. And although he had never seen it, Benoit was certain that Frau Ashby's leg—the surviving one—was long and slender, just like her daughter's.

Watching her, Benoit found he could not suppress a chuckle. Although her blond hair was braided tightly and piled on top of her head, a strand had worked loose until it dangled loosely across her forehead, swinging back and forth in front of her eyes. The fact that her hands and lower arms were coated in flour prevented her from brushing it back into place. Instead she resorted to trying to blow it out of the way with quick, hard bursts that made Benoit think of someone trying to breathe new life into a dying fire.

"Looks like you have a problem," Benoit said cheerfully. Crossing to the side, he brushed back the loose lock, tucking it firmly into place under one of the braids.

"*Danke*," Hildegard said, rewarding him with a huge grin. "It was making my eyes join."

"Cross." Benoit chuckled. "It was making your eyes cross." Her malapropisms were a constant source of amusement to both Benoit and Inge, a subject they often laughed about as they lay on their narrow horsehair mattress in the small bungalow they were allotted at the northern end of the post's parade ground. Since her parents had immigrated to New York a dozen years before heading west, both Inge and the younger Erich had grown up with English and did not share their mother's difficulties with syntax, grammar, and vocabulary.

"Where's Inge?" Benoit asked excitedly. "I have something very important to tell her."

"*Ja, ja, ja,*" Hildegard muttered. "When you are young, *alles* is important."

"No, Holz, this really *is* important. I need to find Inge."

"The sutler's," Hildegard replied. "More *salz* we need."

"I'll go there," Benoit said, turning toward the door. He had his hand almost on the knob when it opened and Inge came bustling in, followed by a blast of cold wind that swirled across the room, sending the flour on Hildegard's table billowing upward in a large white cloud. *"Ach du ßcheisse,"* Hildegard swore loudly.

When Benoit and Inge looked up, Hildegard was white from the waist to the top of her head. Her face was an ivory mask, its chalkiness relieved only by her radiant blue eyes and a red slash they knew must be her mouth.

Both Benoit and Inge burst out laughing, which only made Hildegard angrier.

"You think this is *humorvoll*?" she sputtered indignantly.

Inge covered her mouth, trying to suppress her laughter. Benoit made no such attempt, guffawing loudly. The ridiculousness of the predicament only intensified when Frau Ashby started sneezing uncontrollably, sending up new clouds of white powder.

"You should see yourself, Mother," Inge gasped, grabbing her sides. "Help me, Jean. I can barely stand."

"I don't think I've ever seen anything quite like that," Benoit replied, slapping his thighs.

"Verdammt!" Hildegard cursed, ignoring them. Brushing at her dress only made it worse; the flour just became ingrained.

"Look at this!" she wailed in rapid German. "I am a mess! My dress is soiled beyond redemption! I must go change," she said to Inge. Gathering what was left of her dignity, she stomped across the room, her wooden leg making loud thumping noises as she pounded it on the bare planks.

"Tell her all she has to do is stand outside and the wind will blow it away," Benoit hooted, breaking into a fresh spasm of laughter.

That set Inge off anew, and she threw her arms around Benoit. They sagged to the floor, where they sprawled in a heap, roaring so hard that they could barely sit up.

"*Kinder!*" Hildegard said archly, slamming the door behind her.

"Oh, God, Inge," Benoit said, wiping the tears from his cheeks. "I don't remember when I've laughed so hard."

"Me either," Inge replied. "Mother looked *so* funny. Just like a ghost."

"You think she'll be mad at us for laughing at her?" Benoit said, sobering.

"Oh, no. In an hour she'll see the humor in it herself."

"Here," Benoit said, helping Inge to her feet. "If someone comes in, they'll wonder what the hell we're doing on the floor in the middle of the day."

"Speaking of that," Inge said, looking at him curiously. "What are *you* doing here? You should be working."

Benoit grabbed her hands. "Inge," he said, beaming, "you aren't going to believe this. I've been promoted to captain! Not first lieutenant, but *captain*."

Inge stared at her husband. "Are you joking?" she asked, straight-faced. "If you are, it isn't funny."

"No, I'm *not* joking. I'm as serious as a wooden Indian. The colonel just told me. Can you imagine it? Me, a goddamn captain!"

"That's wonderful!" Inge yelled, convinced it was no prank. "My husband is a captain!"

Clasping their hands together, they did a quick jig around the room, dancing to an improvised chant. "Cap-tain Ben-wah . . . Cap-tain Ben-Wah."

Finally they ran out of breath, plopping again to the floor. "Tell me all about it," Inge gasped. "I want to know *all* the details."

Gulping for air, Benoit related how Kemp had summoned him just as he was beginning his inspection. "I thought sure I was in really serious trouble." Then, like an actor playing two parts in a play, Benoit went through the meeting with Kemp, scowling and pretending to be angry when he recited the colonel's lines, affecting shock and bewilderment when he repeated his own. In no time, Inge was again convulsed in laughter.

"I still can't believe you're a captain," Inge said once she could control her voice.

"Actually, it's *brevet* captain," he explained.

"Brevet schmevet, it's practically the same thing, isn't it?"

Benoit nodded. "Damn near. But," he added, grinning broadly, "that isn't all."

"What do you mean, that isn't all? What else could there be?"

"I mean we're leaving Fort Laramie, too."

Inge gaped, staring at her husband. "Leaving Fort Laramie," she repeated.

"Is there an echo in here?" Benoit joked, looking around the room.

"Jean," Inge said, popping to her feet. "What the hell are you saying?"

"Sit down, honey," he said, steering her to a chair that stood against the wall next to the door. "Let me finish telling you about it."

Sinking to his knees next to her chair, Benoit explained how he was being reassigned to Fort Marcy to be an aide to the man who commanded the entire military district. He was preparing to tell her that Kemp had given his new commander a flattering recommendation when stopped abruptly. "What's the matter, Inge? Are you ill?"

Her face had gone almost as white as her mother's had been, and her lips were trembling. Benoit was sure she was getting ready either to cry or to throw up.

"Has the excitement been too much?"

"You're going to be leaving Fort Laramie," she said so softly that Benoit had to strain to hear her.

"Not me," he assured her. "Us. It's going to be a whole new world."

Inge shook her head slowly, as if she had suffered a blow to the temple. "New Mexico is just a goddamn wilderness."

Benoit was taken aback. "What do you mean, *wilderness*? It's certainly not as isolated as it is here. Santa Fe is a proper city. There will be shops and markets and other women you can socialize with."

"I don't *want* to socialize," Inge said stubbornly, color flowing into her cheeks. "Who cares about shops? We have everything we need here."

"Come on, honey," Benoit said, struggling to control his surprise. "I thought you'd be thrilled."

"I *am* thrilled about your promotion, Jean. I think that's wonderful. But leaving Fort Laramie . . ."

"Aw, Jesus, Inge," Benoit argued, "we knew it was going to happen sooner or later. That's the way life is in the army. An officer is always changing posts. It's the way the system works. You knew when we got married that one day we'd be moving on. Are you upset about the thought of leaving your mother—"

"That's not it—"

"—because if it's an issue, it shouldn't be. She's got a new husband and—"

"It's not *Mutter*, Jean. Not exactly."

Benoit looked at her sternly. "Then what *is* it?"

Inge twisted her hands in her lap. "The timing is bad, Jean. Very bad."

"Inge, now I don't know what the hell *you're* talking about. What do you mean the *timing* is bad?"

"I mean, I'm not sure if this is the appropriate time to leave."

"What's the difference between now and a year from now? Dammit, Inge, sometimes I don't follow you at all."

Inge grabbed his hand and looked into his face. Benoit could see tears forming in her eyes. "Jean," she said slowly, "I think I'm with child."

For the second time that day Benoit looked as if he had been struck. "Holy Mother of God!"

"I didn't say I *am*. I said I *think* I might be."

"Goddammit, Inge," Benoit said angrily. "Why didn't you tell me before this?"

"Tell you what?" she responded crossly. "All I know is what I've just said."

Benoit shrugged. "I guess you're right. It just caught me by surprise, is all. But what if you are? Santa Fe isn't that far. It isn't like you have to go all the way across the country."

"So what if it isn't that far? Do you have any idea where we'll live? Is there housing on the post? Do the other officers have their wives with them?"

Benoit looked bewildered. "I don't know," he confessed. "I never thought to ask Kemp."

"Well, those are some of the things we need to know. Is there a surgeon at Fort Marcy?"

"I don't *know*," he said irritably. "But that shouldn't make any difference. A *lot* of babies are delivered without doctors. That's what midwives are for."

"But there is a *very* good surgeon right here, Jean. Why take a chance on the baby's well-being? You *know* I'd be getting the best care available with Jace. And there's also Mother—"

"Godammit, Inge, that isn't fair. A woman's place is with her husband."

"No, Jean," she said, throwing her arms around him. "Don't misunderstand. I didn't say I *wouldn't* go with you. I just said this might not be the best time for me to go. I could always join you later."

"Later? What's later? After the baby's born? After he's weaned?"

"Jean," Inge said, giving him an imploring look. "Let's don't fight. I still love you and I have no intention of not going with you eventually. This has caught me by surprise, too. This is something we need to give a lot of thought to. I'm delighted about this. I think the promotion is wonderful, and an opportunity like this comes along only once in a lifetime. But it does raise some issues that we have to discuss. I'm so happy for both of us, and I'm sure everything is going to work out. But let's take it a step at a time, all right? We don't have to make a decision right this minute, do we?"

"No," Benoit admitted. "We . . . I . . . don't have to leave for a couple of weeks. Kemp wants to make up a detachment so we can all travel together. He said the War Department is trying to find men who speak Spanish and see that they get to New Mexico.

Apparently, they're building up all the forts down there."

"Then we have plenty of time to iron this out," Inge said encouragingly. "But," she added somewhat hesitantly, "there's one other thing that's bothering me."

"What's that?" Benoit asked uncertainly.

"It may be nothing. . . ."

"Well, come on. What is it? We may as well get everything on the table."

"Well, Jean, I don't want to sound like I'm throwing cold water on this. . . ."

"Inge, for God's sake, spit it out. What's wrong now?"

"Please don't take this the wrong way. I'm not being critical. . . ."

"Jesus, Inge . . ."

"Okay, okay. It's just that something is nagging at me. I mean, Jean," she said, looking at him anxiously, "why *you*? Not that you don't deserve it. Not that you aren't capable . . ."

Benoit's face fell. "I don't know," he confessed. "Kemp asked the same thing. He thought it was because I'd used some influence with Cle Couvillion."

"Oh, Jean, you didn't!"

"Of course I goddamn didn't. But that's the first thing the colonel thought, too. You know how I feel about Cle. We aren't exactly close. Besides, he's been pushing me awful hard to make a decision about resigning my commission and joining the New Orleans militia. But I can't see where this is connected. I wouldn't put it *past* Cle, but I can't see what motive he would have. I can tell you in all truthfulness that I didn't *ask* for it. I swear to you that I didn't ask Cle for *anything.* But to answer your question, I honestly don't know why I was picked. Maybe it will just be a mystery. I mean, who knows why the army does anything?"

"Um," Inge said, nodding. "Maybe we'll never find out." Standing, she shook her head and shoulders, like a dog emerging from a pond. "Right now," she said briskly, "I need to get to work. If dinner isn't on the table, the colonel will be—"

"What's he going to do?" Benoit interrupted. "Send me to Fort Laramie?"

"See, Jean?" Inge beamed. "I knew you'd bounce back. That's one of the reasons why I love you so much."

"I love you, too. Speaking of that," he said, pretending to leer. "Why don't we—"

"Get away from me, Jean Benoit"—she laughed and picked up a large wooden spoon—"or I'll . . ."

"Verdammt nochmal!" Hildegard boomed, rushing into the room. "Is this playtime in *kindergarten?* You two have nothing better to do? Inge," she said accusingly, "is the *Apfelstrudel* ready for the oven? And you"—she turned to Benoit—"why are you still here? Go away. Go to work."

"Okay, okay." Jean laughed. "I'm going." Leaning over, he kissed Inge hurriedly on the cheek. "We'll talk tonight."

As soon as Benoit left, Hildegard turned to Inge. "All right, daughter," she said in German, "what's going on? I can tell by your face that something has happened."

"Oh, you're so right about *that*, Mother. Come on. Let's get dinner ready. I'll talk while we work. I have *so* much to tell you."

Benoit went first to the small room he and Inge were assigned on the north end of the parade ground and dressed himself in warmer clothing. The storm, far from easing off, was growing in intensity, and the wind was blowing so hard that the large wet snowflakes traveled parallel to the ground—never a good sign for Plains veterans. The blessing was that spring storms were usually short-lived. By tomorrow the sky probably would be back to its bright, clear blue, and on the flatlands the snow would be gone in two or three days. The wind, however, might continue for another week.

After bundling up, he scurried across the open expanse to the C Company barracks, where he found the men grouped around the two huge potbellied stoves. Just about every available spot on the bare plank floor was covered with blankets on which the men had placed the parts from their rifles as they took apart the weapons, cleaned them, and then put them back together. The air smelled of old socks, sweat, and gun oil.

"Everything under control, Sergeant?" he asked Hampton, glancing around the room.

"Fine and dandy, sir. The men haven't even complained about cleaning their weapons since it sure beats shit outta being on patrol in this here weather."

"Very good," Benoit replied. Since he was in an expansive mood—he felt he had to do *something* to celebrate his recently elevated status—he decided to give the men a semi-holiday. "Y'all sleep in tomorrow morning. Don't worry about falling in until oh seven hundred."

"Yes, *sir*!" Hampton said cheerfully amid cheers from the men.

Since it was still too early for dinner and he didn't feel like coping with the paperwork that awaited him back at his desk, Benoit tromped across the parade ground yet again, heading toward Old Bedlam. His friend Jason Dobbs had a room on the southwest corner of the upper floor—one of the choice locations, since it had a bird's-eye view of the parade ground and, when the weather was clear, Laramie Peak. If he craned his neck, he could even see a patch of the Laramie River that tumbled cold and clear along the southern perimeter of the wall-less fort. The muddy Platte, cursed by emigrants and soldiers alike as too thin to plow and too thick to drink, ran on the other side of the building.

"Well, look who's here!" Dobbs said merrily when he answered Benoit's knock. "Come in. I was just about to make a pot of fresh coffee. How about it? A good hot cup of java might hit the spot on a day like this."

"Uh . . . ," Benoit stammered. "That's very kind of you, but maybe I'll pass on the coffee."

"Don't be difficult," Dobbs said, pouting. "My coffee making has significantly improved."

Benoit looked at him skeptically. "I've only been trying to teach you for four years. For the life of me, I can't understand why a man of your talents can't learn to boil water."

"You'll hurt my feelings if you don't drink my brew."

"Okay, okay." Benoit sighed and shrugged off his coat. Walking over to the stove, which Dobbs had stoked until it was a cheerful cherry red, he began to warm his hands.

"Don't think this goddamn winter is ever going to end," he said, barely able to restrain himself from blurting out his news. But he wanted to wait a while until the time seemed right. He loved surprises. "I'm not interrupting anything, am I?"

"Not likely," Dobbs said. "The infirmary is empty right now except for a private who got kicked in the head by a horse. Good thing he has a thick skull. I've just been amusing myself with my new hobby."

"Oh, God," Benoit groaned. "What now?"

"Astronomy," Dobbs replied with a grin. "See my new toy," he added, pointing toward the window, where a five-foot-long telescope painted a deep midnight blue rested on a wooden tripod.

Benoit couldn't believe he hadn't noticed it when he'd come in, but then again Dobbs's quarters always looked like a junkyard. Piled everywhere around the room, in boxes and stacks that were almost as tall as Dobbs, who was six two, there were books, magazines, cheap novels with tattered covers, and heaps of old newspapers that were turning yellow with age. The surgeon's taste in reading material, Benoit had learned, was as eclectic as it was compulsive. Dobbs avidly consumed *any* printed material he could get his hands on, everything from medical texts to tracts on architecture and Renaissance art; from current fiction to the classics. Unless his medical duties required him to be elsewhere, Dobbs was always waiting in front of Old Bedlam, as nervous as a kid on his birthday, when the weekly stage was due, unable, it seemed, to curb his yearning to see what new book or newspaper was on board. He also proved to be a merciless scavenger as far as periodicals were concerned; he never let a fellow officer discard anything that could be read, scooping it off the floor where the careless reader had dropped it so he could carry it back to his room like a gift from heaven and pore over it at his leisure.

Scattered among the reading material was the assorted detritus of his previous "hobbies." There were boulders, some of them as large as Benoit's head, from the time he was interested in geology, and bottles of mysterious powders from when he'd decided he might want to start a subspecialty as an herbalist. There were broken pots from the time he was fascinated with archaeology, and a large box of drafting instruments he had left over from his passing fancy with engineering. "It's a damn good thing you never were attracted to music or you'd have an organ in here," Benoit had told him once. Dobbs had taken the comment as a challenge. The next day he had ordered a harmonica from a firm back east and for months bored everyone silly with endless, inept renditions of Stephen Foster medleys, including "Old Folks at Home," "My Old Kentucky Home, Good Night," and "Old Dog Tray."

"Certainly you aren't seeing much through a telescope in this weather other than snowflakes," Benoit teased.

"No, not today. But I've been working on some star charts I just received from a colleague in Maryland. Would you like to see them? They really are engrossing."

"Uh, no thanks," Benoit said quickly. "But on second thought that coffee sounds pretty good."

"I knew you'd see things my way." Dobbs laughed. "Won't take but a moment. The instruments are all laid out," he said, pointing across the room. On a tiny table that stood against a far wall was the long-necked, French-style coffeepot Benoit had given him as a Christmas gift two years before, plus a battered copper kettle, a large, heavy spoon, a black cast-iron skillet, and two demitasse cups, one of which was badly chipped, which he had taken in payment from a passing emigrant in return for performing minor surgery on an ingrown toenail. "Would you like to assist?"

"No"—Benoit smiled—"this is your show. Prove to me you can do it."

Ever since they had come west together in the same group that included the Schmidts, Benoit had been trying to teach Dobbs how to make New Orleans–style coffee. But when it came to transforming ground beans into a drinkable liquid, the man who could seemingly master so many trades was notoriously incompetent. No matter how hard he tried, Dobbs's coffee always ended up tasting like medicine.

As much as he dreaded facing another cup of Dobbs's concoction, Benoit was delighted to find his friend in such good spirits. It didn't seem so long ago that he had worried about Dobbs taking his own life.

The previous autumn, Dobbs had been seriously hurt in an incident that had also involved himself, a berserk captain named Harrigan, and a woman named Ellen O'Reilly, the well-liked and much respected madam of the only whorehouse in the territory, an establishment called the Hog Ranch, located just a few miles south of the post.

What a catastrophe that had been, Benoit recalled. It was bad enough that Harrigan had gone mad, but it got worse when he tried to take his anger out on Ellen, who also happened to be Dobbs's fiancée. Both he and

Dobbs had been at the Hog Ranch when Harrigan had shown up and burst into Ellen's office. In the confusion, Ellen had pulled a pistol out of her desk drawer, intending to shoot the wild-eyed captain, who was holding them all at gunpoint. Harrigan had fired first, killing Ellen instantly. When the unarmed Dobbs had tried to jump the insane captain, Harrigan had hit him behind the ear with his Colt. Benoit, who had scooped up Ellen's pistol, had shot and killed Harrigan, but Dobbs had been grievously injured. Harrigan's blow had damaged a nerve behind the ear, leaving Dobbs with half of his face paralyzed. His right eye was frozen open and teared constantly, impairing his vision to the extent that he was unable to practice as post surgeon. Colonel Kemp had had no choice but to place him on medical leave, reluctantly telling him that if his health did not return, he would have to process him for discharge.

Dobbs had taken it hard. Although he could cover the staring eye with a patch, there was little he could do about the steady stream of saliva that flowed out of the paralyzed side of his mouth. Unable to drink from a cup, he had to use a straw fashioned from a hollow reed. Wherever he went he had to carry both the reed and a supply of fresh handkerchiefs to mop his chin.

Embarrassed by his condition and aware that his presence at the officers' mess made the others uncomfortable, Dobbs retreated to his quarters, becoming a virtual hermit and admitting no visitors other than Benoit, Inge, and Frau Ashby, who brought him food he had no appetite for and could barely taste anyway because of the paralysis.

Under the best of circumstances, the six-foot-two Dobbs, naturally lean and reedy, looked slightly

underfed and malnourished. When the injury took
away both his ability to eat comfortably and his desire
for food, his weight dropped precipitously; his
appearance degenerated from what might have been
called "lanky" to "cadaverous." Benoit and Inge often
lay abed at night discussing how to prevent their
friend from starving himself to death. But the problem, Benoit and Inge knew, extended beyond Dobbs's
physical condition; Ellen's loss also was taking its toll
on his psyche.

Even more tragic for Dobbs than the trauma of
witnessing the murder of his fiancée was the fact that
it was the second woman Dobbs had lost. His wife,
Colleen, had died while Dobbs was off in Mexico during the war, leaving two young children who now
were being raised by her relatives in New England.
Dobbs himself knew it was irrational for him to feel
guilty about Colleen's death, but that knowledge was
not enough to stop the nightmares. Ellen, on the other
hand, had represented a new start for the surgeon. The
decision to ask Ellen to marry him and risk the censure
of his fellow officers, perhaps even the end of his
career, had not been an easy one. Then, when Ellen
was killed, the guilt over Colleen's death had
returned.

The way Dobbs coped with his physical and psy-
chological demons was with laudanum. Benoit was
aware that the drug was a near universal medicament;
just about everyone he knew had used the drug at one
time or another for everything from a pick-me-up to a
balm for a toothache. Benoit had taken laudanum
more than a few times himself when he had been
injured. But once his wounds improved, his need for
the nostrum disappeared. Benoit's insides, however,

were not being gnawed away by guilt, justifiable or not. While Benoit and hundreds of thousands of others were not affected by laudanum's addictive qualities, Dobbs increasingly came under its grip. At one point Benoit broached the issue to Dobbs only to be told emphatically to mind his own business.

Just when things seemed darkest—Benoit in fact was on the verge of appealing to Kemp to place Dobbs under a suicide watch—the surgeon's health began to improve. Given time, the damaged nerve began to heal on its own. As it did, the paralysis gradually disappeared. First, Dobbs began swallowing with less difficulty and his appetite came back. He began to regain some of his lost weight, and there was more color in his normally pale cheeks. Over a period of weeks his vision returned, and the once dreadful-looking eye shrank to its normal size and shape. As he got better physically, Dobbs's mental state also began to recover. He returned to take his seat at the officers' dinner table, and his once vibrant sense of humor showed signs of resurfacing.

The disability period had lasted, Benoit calculated quickly, some five weeks. Now, almost eight months after the incident in Ellen's office, Dobbs seemingly was back to normal. Except for the laudanum. On several occasions Benoit had seen his friend nipping at a quart-size bottle and knew instinctively what the dark liquid was. Tempted as he was to lecture on the subject, Benoit bit his lip and kept his silence. If it helped Dobbs regain his sense of equilibrium, who was he, Benoit figured, to make an issue of it.

Infused with joy over his friend's apparent recovery, Benoit, smiling to himself, wandered over to the telescope and stood looking at it, his brow creased in perplexity.

"Don't touch it!" Dobbs shouted in warning from across the room.

Benoit jumped as if the instrument were a coiled rattlesnake. "What's the matter?" he asked anxiously.

"Nothing's the matter." Dobbs laughed. "I've just spent several hours aligning it precisely to an area I want to view as soon as this storm blows through. I don't want to have to do it all over again."

"Okay, okay." Benoit sighed and moved away. "How's that coffee coming?"

3

"Am I doing this right?" Dobbs asked, pouring water into the cast-iron skillet until it was about a quarter of an inch deep. "Now this," he added, setting the coffeepot precisely in the middle of the skillet.

"That's right," Benoit said encouragingly. "Now wait for the water to boil and *spoon* it—whatever you do, don't pour it—over the grounds."

"Got it," Dobbs said enthusiastically, rubbing his palms together briskly.

Pale and thin, with wispy blond hair that barely covered his massive head, Dobbs looked like everyman's idea of the mad scientist, especially when he got excited about a project. At times like that, his blue eyes gleamed with an inner light that signaled either genius or madness. In his eagerness to articulate his thoughts, his mind tended to outrun his tongue so that his sentences came out as a series of seemingly disconnected, slurred phrases. A stranger might think him mentally unstable; someone who knew him recognized the need to listen carefully. Benoit and a handful of others at Fort Laramie understood Dobbs's mannerisms and simply rolled their eyes when the surgeon stuttered and sounded like a man whose rationality had deserted him.

"What's gotten into you?" Dobbs asked, glancing at Benoit, who had begun to pace about the tiny room in quick, short strides. His voice was pleasantly deep and contained only a hint of a Massachusetts twang. "You have someplace to go or something?"

"Oh, just nervous, I guess," Benoit replied, anxious to tell Dobbs about the day's developments but trying to postpone it until the coffee was ready to pour.

"About what?"

"Work. Thinking about the army. One thing or another."

As Benoit passed by Dobbs's worktable he glanced up and noticed the calendar fixed to the wall with a horseshoe nail. "By God!" he said, snapping his fingers. "It just occurred to me. What's today?"

Dobbs, who was watching the kettle, waiting for the water to boil, replied distractedly, "Oh, hell, I'm not sure. Tuesday?"

"No, Jace," Benoit said with exasperation. "It's Wednesday. But I mean what's the *date*, not the day of the week."

"I don't know," Dobbs said, shaking his head. "Two or three weeks before payday, I guess. If the pay wagon's on time."

"It's April seven," Benoit said firmly.

Dobbs shrugged. "So?"

Benoit laughed. "You sentimental old fool, you. Come next Thursday, it'll be exactly four years ago that we left Independence."

"Who cares?"

"Well, I certainly think *you* should. A lot has happened since then."

"It sure has," Dobbs agreed. "For one thing, I've learned to make *real* coffee. You ready for a cup?"

"You didn't *learn*, you big ox. I tried to *teach* you."

"We'll see if you *taught* me correctly." Dobbs grinned as he topped off the cups with boiling water from the kettle. To his own cup, he added a dollop of dark liquid. "Here's looking at you!" he said cheerfully.

Benoit lifted the cup and studied it carefully. As with wine, the benefits of a good cup of coffee rested in near equal proportions to taste and aroma. And Benoit wanted to enjoy both. Sticking his face directly over the cup, his nose a mere three inches above the jet black liquid, he sniffed like a hound on the trail. "Ah," he sighed. "Ambrosia."

"Usually," Dobbs said pedantically, "the word 'ambrosia' is used to refer to flavor rather than fragrance, but I guess you could use it that way. How is it?" he asked anxiously.

"So far, so good," Benoit replied, cupping his free right hand around the cup and his nose, trapping the vapor. "How's your bean supply holding out?" he asked, his voice distorted by his hand so that he sounded like someone with a bad cold.

"Getting a little low. I hope a new package from Marion is on the next stage."

Benoit's sister, Marion, posted both of them a fresh supply of beans from New Orleans every three weeks, using her contacts with their late father's clients along the docks to get the best available of every new shipment that arrived from South America. Despite her diligence, less than half of the packages of the freshly roasted beans, which were as precious as nuggets of gold deep in Indian country, successfully completed the journey to Fort Laramie. The others either were lost en route or were stolen by coffee lovers who somehow managed to divine the contents despite Marion's attempt to seal them tightly enough so the smell wouldn't be noticeable.

Smacking his lips in anticipation, Benoit took a small sip. Immediately he regretted it. Smothering the urge to spit it out, he struggled to keep his expression impassive. Fearful of hurting Dobbs's feelings, he forced a smile. "You're getting better," he mumbled, hoping his tone was sufficiently noncommittal.

"You don't like it?" Dobbs asked, sounding crushed.

"I didn't *say* that, Jace."

"You don't have to say it. I can tell."

"Jesus, you sound like a woman who's just discovered her husband has been unfaithful."

"You *could* be a little more tactful. I have a reputation to uphold, you know."

Benoit could not keep from chuckling. "What kind of reputation is that?"

"You see these hands?" Dobbs asked, shoving his long, pencil-thin fingers almost in Benoit's face. "They're the hands of the most gifted surgeon in the entire Third Infantry, maybe the whole damn army. You think I want to risk having people laugh behind my back, saying, 'He may know how to doctor a broke leg, but he can't fix coffee for horseapples'?"

"Nobody's going to say that, Jace, especially not me," Benoit said placatingly.

"I would *hope* not," Dobbs said with a sniff.

"Jace," Benoit said hurriedly, eager to change the subject, "I have all the respect in the world for your abilities. The depth of your competence never ceases to amaze me."

"I don't mean to sound like a prima donna. . . ."

"I know that, Jace. I didn't mean to insult you. It's just I have something else on my mind."

Dobbs looked carefully at his friend. "That wound isn't giving you trouble, is it? The one you suffered in that fight with the Cheyenne last summer?"

"No, it isn't that."

"The broken arm? From that incident at Fort Kearny?"

"No," Benoit said. "It has nothing to do with my health."

"It's not Inge, is it? Your sister? You've had bad news from New Orleans?"

"No, it's none of that."

"Then what the hell is it?" Dobbs asked impatiently.

"We've been friends for a long time, haven't we?" Benoit asked slowly. "I've always confided in you."

Dobbs nodded. "Yes, you have."

"I've always welcomed your advice. Maybe because you're nine years older . . ."

"Eight and a half."

"Okay"—Benoit chuckled—"eight and a half. But just because you were older didn't stop us from being friends."

"Right."

"In fact—"

"Come on, Jean," Dobbs interrupted. "What's on your mind? You have something you want to ask me? Or tell me?"

"Both."

Dobbs nodded gravely. "Okay, both. Why don't you start by *telling* me."

"I've been promoted to brevet captain," Benoit blurted.

Dobbs almost dropped his cup. "That's great!" he shrieked. "That's wonderful! But—"

"The promotion is only half of it," Benoit said hurriedly.

Dobbs paused. "Oh?" he said, looking at him quizzically.

"I'm also being sent to a new post."

"*¡Por Dios!*" Dobbs exclaimed, reverting as he sometimes did to one of the expressions he'd picked up in Mexico during the war.

"It's ironic that you should respond in Spanish," Benoit said, surprised.

"Why? I speak a bit of the language. I find it very expressive."

"It's strange because I'm being posted to Fort Marcy."

"Marcy!" Dobbs said, shocked. "In Santa Fe? In New Mexico Territory?"

"That's right."

"You lucky dog," Dobbs said enviously. "It's beautiful country."

"Have you ever been there?"

"No, but—"

"Then how do you know it's beautiful?"

"That's what I've read and heard. What's the matter? Aren't you happy about it?"

"Yes and no," Benoit said evenly. "I'm going to be aide-de-camp to General Barksdale. . . ."

"I've heard good things about him."

"That's what Colonel Kemp says. But I'm also worried."

"Worried, for God's sake! About what?"

Benoit rose and resumed his pacing, clasping his hands behind him. Excitedly he told Dobbs about his session with Kemp, enriching the tale with the same animation he had used when telling Inge and her mother about the meeting. Purposely he omitted Inge's suspicion that she might be pregnant and might want to remain at Fort Laramie until after the baby was born.

"That's the funniest goddamn story I've heard in a long time," Dobbs said when Benoit had finished. "Too bad you can't take it on the stage."

"You may think it's funny, but I can see a big problem. Several problems, as a matter of fact."

"Like what?"

"Like, for starters, I don't speak any Spanish."

"Don't worry about that. You speak French and you have a facility with languages. Spanish will come easily. In two months you'll be talking like a native. I promise you. What else?"

"I don't know a damn thing about Fort Marcy or New Mexico."

"Well, maybe I can help you there," Dobbs said, rising and walking over to a stack of newspapers. "Now where did I see that?" he said absently, shuffling through the pile.

"See what?"

"Ah, here it is," Dobbs said triumphantly. "I knew I'd seen something recently. Here"—he thrust the periodical into Benoit's hand—"read this while I do some more digging."

Benoit looked at what Dobbs had handed him; it was a three-month-old edition of the *St. Louis Chronicle*. He had no trouble identifying what Dobbs was talking about; it was the only story on the front page.

PLANS FINALIZED FOR OVERLAND MAIL, the headline read in black, inch-tall letters.

Benoit began reading the story:

Mr. John Butterfield, founder and president of the Overland Mail Company, has announced plans for the initiation of the long-awaited service that will link the East, via terminals at St. Louis and Memphis, to the rapidly growing West via the already famous California city of San Francisco.

Following a meeting with company principals earlier this week, Mr. Butterfield said the service will commence simultaneously from St. Louis and San Francisco on September 28, 1858, with stages leaving both cities, one eastbound, one westbound. Each is expected to complete the 2,795-mile trip in less than a month.

The announcement has been eagerly anticipated for more than a year, ever since Postmaster General Brown and Congress authorized the establishment of the service despite vehement objections from those pessimistic naysayers who wanted the route to be oriented in a more northerly direction. According to authorized plans, the St. Louis leg will pass through Tipton, over the Ozark Mountains, and on to Fort Smith, Arkansas, which lies on the Canadian River. There it will be intersected by a route that runs eastward to Little Rock and Memphis. From there, the route will plunge in a southwesterly course across Texas to the Río del Norte and through the Mexican city of El Paso del Norte, where it will turn more westerly, running across the territory of New Mexico and on to San Diego, California. At that point, it will veer decidedly northward toward San Francisco.

The finalization of plans that has resulted in a target date for the beginning of service has been impatiently awaited by all of St. Louis ever since Mr. Butterfield first proposed the plan. The 18-month gap which will have occurred since the plan was announced and the actual commencement of service has been filled by the organization of details required to actually put the plan into operation. Over the months, Mr. Butterfield has had to recruit and hire some 800 men who will run the service. In addition, he has had to arrange for the placement of more than 1,000 horses and 500 mules, which will be used to propel the 250 coaches, primarily Concords, which are produced by the Abbot-Downing Company of Concord, New Hampshire, and will make up the Overland fleet.

As part of the concerted effort to launch the system, widely viewed as a precursor for a railroad linking the United States to California, the War Department also has announced plans to open several new forts along the route to provide protection against hostile nomads who still roam the area, mainly in Texas and New Mexico. . . .

"That's what Kemp was talking about when he said that the army was building up the manpower in the territory. That's why," Benoit said excitedly.

"Precisely!" Dobbs called from across the room. "At least one of the reasons. Look here," he said, scooping up an armful of books and a large rolled document that looked like a scroll. "Here's some more material." After bounding to Benoit's side in three long strides, he put the books on the plank floor and extended the scroll. "Even found a pretty good map."

"Where in hell did you get that?" Benoit asked, amazed at his friend's resourcefulness.

"One of the members of the geological survey team that went through here last spring left it. Said since they had already used the pertinent portions he didn't want to tote it all over the West. I was happy to take it off his hands."

Carefully Dobbs unrolled the chart and spread it on the floor, anchoring two of the corners with their coffee cups, the other two with the coffeepot and the bottle that contained the laudanum. Together they kneeled on the floor and began to study the document.

"Look," Dobbs said rhapsodically, "it even shows the existing forts. Damn, those survey people do good work. Here's where you'll be." He pointed to a small dot labeled "Fort Marcy," barely readable because of a series of wavy lines in which "Sangre de Cristo Mountains" was written in.

"Sangre de Cristo?" Benoit asked, puzzled.

"Blood of Christ," Dobbs translated.

"That's a hell of a name for a mountain."

"A chain, actually," Dobbs pointed out. "The southern end of the Rocky Mountains."

"But *Blood* of Christ, for Christ's sake?"

"Called that because they turn a bright red at sunset. Look," he said, moving a bony finger down the map. "Here's the Sandia Mountains and the Manzanos."

"So?"

"Sandia means 'watermelon,' also called that because of the red hue they take on when the sun goes down. Same thing for the Manzano Mountains; manzano means 'apple.'"

"What does 'Santa Fe' mean?" Benoit asked, jabbing at the letter just above the spot identified as Fort Marcy. "I've never heard of a Saint Fe."

"It means 'Holy Faith.'" Dobbs chuckled. "Santa Fe is the City of Holy Faith."

"Isn't that a strange name for a city?"

"Not when you consider the background. The first Europeans known to have seen New Mexico were the Spanish *Conquistadores*. Here," Dobbs added, grabbing one of the books and flipping it open. "History records that the first white men into the area was a group led by Francisco Vásquez de Coronado. After conquering Mexico—or Méjico, as they called it, and Perú—they started looking to the north, where it was rumored that there existed seven cities so rich that the streets were paved with gold. The Spaniards' first name for that unknown area was *Nueva Méjico*. That's *nueva*, with an 'a.' That means 'another.' It was only later that it became known as *Nuevo*—with an 'o'—*Méjico*, or a 'New' Mexico."

"That's fascinating, Jace, but—"

"Don't interrupt me, Jean. You said you wanted to know more about where you're going."

"I do, but—"

"Then keep still and listen. Drink your coffee."

Benoit looked distastefully at his cup. "Okay, go ahead." He sighed, reluctantly lifting his cup, replacing it as a paperweight with a jar of salt from the table.

"Coronado's exploration took place from 1540 to 1542," Dobbs continued, warming to the subject. "He got almost as far north as we are now," he added, running his finger down the page as he read.

Benoit glanced at the title on the book's spine. *A History of the Great West* by Alexander Baughman. "Did he find those cities of gold?" Benoit asked with a smile.

"Not likely." Dobbs chuckled. "New Mexico is one of the poorest places on the continent."

"Well, what did he find?"

"According to this, lots of Indians."

"So what's strange about that? We've got lots of Indians right here."

"But not like the ones in New Mexico," Dobbs said. "The Spanish found whole tribes who lived in established communities called *pueblos*. The Franciscan friars just loved that because they were easier to convert if they weren't constantly on the move, like the Sioux and the Cheyenne and the other tribes we have around here."

"You mean there aren't any Plains tribes in New Mexico?"

Dobbs turned a couple of pages. "Not at all. It says here there are Comanches, Apaches, a tribe called the Kiowa-Apaches, and a few Utes and Cheyenne. But the *pueblos* are thrown in to complicate the issue."

"And they're hostile?"

Dobbs grinned. "The Plains tribes sure as hell are. In Spanish, they're called *los bárbaros*, the barbarians or savages. I remember reading somewhere else that they've been pretty quiet of late, but that doesn't mean they'll stay that way, though, especially if the army moves in and starts building new forts. That'll stir 'em up good."

"But the pueblo Indians . . ."

"No." Dobbs shook his head. "They were pacified long ago. Except for a revolt in, let's see, 1680, in which they ran the Spanish out for a dozen years or so, they haven't given anyone any trouble to speak of. They converted to Catholicism, at least nominally, and settled down. Speaking of that, you're Catholic, aren't you?"

"Of course I am," Benoit said. "Very few Frenchmen aren't. But I'm not a zealot. God, I don't even remember the last time I went to Mass."

"How about confession?" Dobbs asked, his eyes glinting mischievously.

"That's pretty personal, isn't it?"

"Just checking." Dobbs laughed. "I figured whatever you'd have to say would sizzle some poor priest's ears. Anyway, this new posting will give you the chance to reestablish your contact with the church. The ties to Catholicism aren't as strong as they were when the territory was controlled by the Spaniards—in those days the church *was* the state—but the church is still very strong. You'd best go back and read your old missal or whatever."

"Thanks tremendously for that advice," Benoit said dryly. "How about specifics? Is there anything in that book about Fort Marcy itself?"

"Strange you mentioned that," Dobbs said, setting aside the volume. "Nothing in that book, but there *is* something in this document that came along with the map I got from the survey team."

Dobbs opened a folio that had been sitting on the floor with the books and thumbed through it. "Fort Marcy . . . Fort Marcy . . . Fort Marcy," he repeated tonelessly, searching the document. "Oh!" he said in surprise. "Here's something I didn't know."

"What's that?" Benoit asked.

"As of when this was written, which I guess was

at least a year ago, there were eleven military facilities in the territory."

"Eleven! That many?"

"Yep." Dobbs nodded. "It surprises me, too. Damn near seventeen hundred men, too."

"*Sacré merde!*" Benoit mumbled. "No wonder they have a brigadier general commanding. What about Marcy?"

Dobbs flipped a few pages. "Here's Fort Marcy. Okay, let's see . . . Established 1846 near the site of what previously had been known as the *Presidio* of Santa Fe—"

"What's a *presidio*?" Benoit interrupted.

"A Spanish fort."

"Oh," Benoit said sheepishly. "Sorry."

"As I was saying. Established in 1846. Named for William L. Marcy, who was secretary of war at the time. The fort itself is built in what this document calls 'an irregular shape.'" Dobbs paused. "That's unusual. I guess it was constructed to conform with the contour of the land, since this says it is on a knoll that commands a view of Santa Fe's central plaza. By the way," he continued, "did you know that Santa Fe was established as the capital of the territory way back in 1610? That's amazing. That was almost two hundred and fifty years ago—*ten years* before the Pilgrims landed at Plymouth Rock."

"I'm impressed," Benoit mumbled. "Go on about Fort Marcy."

Dobbs sighed. "Don't you have *any* sense of history, Jean? Anyway," he continued, shaking his head, "Fort Marcy itself is just a fortification. . . ."

"What do you mean, *just* a fortification?"

Dobbs looked up. "It's just a walled enclosure to

be used in case of an attack. According to this report, the barracks, corrals, officers' quarters, and all other facilities are about a third of a mile away, where the old *presidio* is."

"Isn't that strange?"

"Not necessarily, given the conditions. I gather that Fort Marcy is basically an administrative post. That's why General Barksdale is there and it's the command post for the entire Ninth Military Department. Apparently the real work is done out of Fort Union, which"—he turned two pages—"is northeast of Santa Fe, near a community called Las Vegas. There are roughly one hundred and fifty men there, and that's where the patrols operate out of to protect the Santa Fe Trail."

"Santa Fe isn't on the Santa Fe Trail?"

"It's at the southern end of it," Dobbs explained. "Understand that the Santa Fe Trail is not an emigrant track, like ours. It's almost exclusively a commercial route, a way to bring merchandise to an area that has been almost totally isolated for two and a half centuries. The trail itself didn't even exist until after Mexico won its independence in 1821. Before that, under the Spanish, trade between New Mexico and the United States was prohibited."

"You mean the people in New Mexico had no contact at all with the outside world?" Benoit asked, flabbergasted.

"Damn near," Dobbs said soberly. "Only with Mexico. What provisions and supplies there were came northward along what is known as the Chihuahua Trail, which has its northern terminus at Santa Fe. That's one of the reasons for the military headquarters being there rather than at Fort Union. It's the junction of the only two major trade routes through the territory."

"Is Santa Fe a city of some size?" Benoit asked.

"A hell of a lot larger than Fort Laramie," Dobbs said, laughing. "About four thousand people, according to this report. But there are about sixty thousand in the territory, about two-thirds of whom are Indians. The rest are Spanish speakers—descendants of the *Conquistadores* or Mexicans who came in after the Spanish left in 1821. They're mainly farmers and ranchers, living for the most part along the Río del Norte valley."

"No white people?"

"You mean Americans?"

"Of course I mean Americans."

"Very few," Dobbs said. "It's only been under U.S. control since 1848 after the Treaty of Guadalupe Hidalgo ended the war. It just became a territory eight years ago."

"All that history is going to confuse me, Jace."

"I know." Dobbs chuckled. "You need to take this material with you and read it over. You have a lot to learn."

"Let's go back to Fort Marcy for a minute. You said there were a hundred men at Fort Union. . . ."

"A hundred and fifty, give or take."

"Okay. Then what's the complement at Marcy?"

Dobbs consulted the document. "Says here sixty-seven."

"Sixty-seven! That's all?"

"But it's the brain for the whole territory."

"Still, it doesn't sound very interesting," Benoit said dispiritedly. "I mean, what the hell am I going to *do* there? I won't even have my company to command."

"At the risk of sounding facetious," Dobbs said somewhat tersely, "I'd say you *do* whatever the hell the general wants you to do."

"Oh, you're a great help."

"Be realistic, Jean. You're probably going to be traveling a lot. Barksdale can't be everywhere at once, and as an aide-de-camp you'll be his representative. That's probably why you were promoted to captain. It gives you more authority; it strengthens your position when speaking on the general's behalf. Remember, the territory of New Mexico is a damn big piece of ground, stretching from the Texas border to California. According to this report, it's some two hundred and forty thousand square miles, which is roughly the size of Texas."

"Phew," Benoit whistled.

"Phew is right. If I were you, I wouldn't worry about not having enough to do."

"Wait a minute!" Benoit said, wrinkling his brow. "If the territory isn't part of Mexico anymore, the Spanish are gone, and there are no Americans, who in hell is running the place?"

Dobbs grinned broadly. "¡A la Virgen! By gosh, you catch on pretty quick. No one is running the place. That's what makes your job so interesting. Right now, the army represents virtually the only authority. Until the Mexicans took over, the Franciscans—that is, the Catholic church—controlled everything. But when the Mexicans got their independence and the Spanish left, so did the Franciscans. The church remained a dominant force. But now that New Mexico is a territory of the United States, Washington won't stand for a church-run state. So there's what you might call a power vacuum. For the last eight or ten years, it's been rather chaotic. What a challenge you face. ¡Mal ajo!" he

said with a wink. "That means 'confound it.' I wish I
were going with you."

"I do, too, Jace. I really do. I don't know anyone
there. I wish you were along to watch my back."

"You don't need me, Jean. You'll have Inge."

Benoit blushed. "Well," he sputtered, "maybe not
for a while."

Dobbs's eyebrows flew up. "What in hell do you
mean by *that*?"

"I didn't know until this afternoon."

"Didn't know *what*?"

"That Inge is with child. At least she's pretty sure
she is."

"Holy Mother of God!" Dobbs ejaculated. "That
does put things in a new light. You mean she doesn't
want to go?"

"Maybe not right away," Benoit said sadly. "She
says it might be better if she stayed here until after the
baby's born. You know, where she can have you and
her mother to fall back on."

"Ummm," Dobbs said, rubbing his chin. "That's
an interesting perspective."

"From what you just told me, there's probably no
post surgeon at Fort Marcy."

"You're probably right. But certainly they have
civilian doctors in Santa Fe."

"Ones who speak English?"

Dobbs nodded. "That's a good point. I doubt it."

"You see what the problem is? What Inge's object-
ing to?"

"Sure, I see. Her argument has value."

"Well, what do *you* think? Should she go with me
or wait until after the baby is born?"

"Oh, no!" Dobbs said, waving his arm in front of

his face. "You're not going to get me involved in *that*. That's something between you and Inge. I'm going to stay the hell out of that discussion, thank you very much."

"I don't blame you," Benoit said, shaking his head. "I think you're smart. I just wish I knew what was the right thing to do."

"You and Inge are both intelligent people. You'll figure it out," Dobbs said encouragingly.

"I wish I were as confident," Benoit said unhappily.

"Cheer up!" Dobbs said, slapping his friend on the shoulder. "I'll give you a quick Spanish lesson."

"Oh, yeah," Benoit said, unconvinced. "What's that?"

"A proverb I learned when I was there. *'Si tú mal tiene remedio, ¿para qué te apuras?'*"

"And what the hell does that mean?"

"If your sickness can be cured, why worry?"

"What else would I expect from a doctor?" Benoit laughed. "If treatment doesn't work, try words."

"And take these books with you," Dobbs added, stacking them. "Read them and learn as much as you can before you go. As they say in Spanish, *'Saber es poder.'*"

"And that means?"

"Knowledge is power."

"That figures."

Dobbs shook his head. "In your case, I probably should have said, *'Ni con agua bendita.'*" He grinned and held up his hand. "Before you ask, that means 'Not even holy water will help.'"

Benoit stood with his right hand against the wall, leaning forward until his nose almost touched the cracked pane that covered the single window in the small room he and Inge were allotted. When he exhaled, a small frosted spot appeared on the glass—the only thing, Benoit reflected, that kept the cursed wind from roaring into the room. By craning his neck slightly, he could see, off to the south some one hundred yards, the post's flagpole, which was bent at a noticeable angle by the gale. There had been no flag on the pole for the last three weeks, not after the wind had shredded the last one in just a little over forty-eight hours, turning it into a tattered piece of multicolored cloth not fit for further duty. After that, Colonel Kemp had ordered that the officer of the day would proceed with the mandatory flag raising and lowering ceremonies each morning and evening with one significant modification: there would be no flag. Fort Laramie, Kemp explained in frustration, was down to its banner, and replacements would not be available until the next supply train arrived from Fort Kearny. But no one knew when that would be; it already was two weeks late because of the spring storms that swept in one after the other, like little ducks following the mama duck to the edge of the lake.

Sighing, Benoit drew back from the window and ran his hand through his hair. He was not surprised to find his scalp encrusted with grit. "This goddamn sand gets into *everything*," he said half-aloud.

Turning to Inge, he looked at her sadly. "Are you sure this is what you want to do?"

Inge sighed. "We've been over this a dozen times," she said tiredly. "I thought we'd agreed that now that I'm positive I'm pregnant, I'd stay here until the baby is born."

"That won't be until late October or November," Benoit argued weakly. "Then you won't be able to get out of here until the next spring. We're probably talking close to a year before you can join me."

"What's a year, Jean? I mean, in the scheme of things. Look at Colonel Kemp. His wife is *still* back east and he's been out here for five years."

"Four."

"All right, four years. You see my point."

"But he's an old man. He's been married forever. It doesn't make any difference to him whether his wife's here or not. He probably can't perform more than once a month anyway."

Inge tried to keep from laughing. "Yeah, I guess it isn't any fun anymore once you pass forty."

"What if there's some problem or something? With the delivery, I mean. I'll be way to hell and gone in New Mexico and you'll be here."

"So will Jace," Inge reminded him. "And *Mutter*. What could you do if you were here, anyway? If there was a problem, that is. Jace says I'm fine; that he's never seen a healthier mother-to-be."

"What else would Jace say?" Benoit complained. "He doesn't want me to go off worried."

"I don't want you to go off *at all*," Inge replied, crossing to his side and stroking his shoulder. "But we both know we don't have any choice in that matter. You *have* to go. Besides, it will be better in the long run. It's a step up the ladder for you."

"It might be a bigger step if I just resigned my commission and joined the New Orleans militia like Marion and Francois want me to do. Take a commission there and then transfer to the Confederate Army once war comes."

"You still think there's going to be a war?" Inge asked, frowning.

"Absolutely. I can't see any way around it. All those problems they're having in Kansas; that's just the beginning of what we're going to see on a nationwide basis once the Southern states decide to secede. I wish I knew what was going on back home. It seems like months since I've heard from my family."

"They've been occupied, Jean. Francois is finishing his second year at the Naval Academy. His studies keep him busy. And Marion, I'm sure, is knee deep in wedding plans. The big day's only three weeks away."

"My sister the social belle."

"Don't be critical, Jean. She's marrying a doctor from a prominent family. She's obligated to make it a big event. I'm just glad we didn't have to go through all that."

"Me too." Benoit nodded and plopped onto the bed. "God," he said, lifting his hands and brushing them together, "even the bed is covered with sand."

"It comes in through the cracks. I can't help it."

"That wasn't a reflection on your housekeeping, Inge. But this damn wind is going to drive me crazy."

"It's getting to everybody. Even Jim, who's been out here for something like thirty years, says he's never seen the spring winds blow so long or so hard."

"Speaking of Jim, how's he feeling?"

"Not too good. The gout gives him problems from time to time. When an attack comes on you should see his big toe. It looks awful."

"It's no fun getting old, is it? I wonder how my mother has changed, what with my father's death and all. I sure would like to see her. I haven't been home since the summer before I came out here. And that's been almost five years. Francois was just a kid, following me everywhere I went. And Marion was a gigantic pain in the butt. I guess older sisters always are."

"Careful," Inge teased, sitting next to him.

"I mean *most* older sisters," Benoit said quickly. "I don't think Erich feels that way about you."

"He'd better not. At least he'd better not *tell* me that. I'll spank his bottom."

Benoit laughed. "That would be a sight to see. He's what, eighteen now? And damn near as big as I am. I'd love to see you try to give him a spanking. He'd probably take that big knife he carries and skin you alive."

"What is it about you men that make you feel you're so tough?" Inge said, letting her hand rest on Benoit's thigh. "Most of you are so controllable."

"Are you talking about me?"

"Of course I'm talking about you, silly," Inge said, increasing the pressure on the inside of his leg. "What other man would I know as well as I do you?"

"No one, I hope," Benoit said, finding his breathing growing deeper. "But you think I'm controllable?"

"I can make you do anything I want." Inge smiled, moving her hand upward.

"Oh!" Benoit sighed. "You just think you can. I happen to have a tremendous amount of willpower. I can resist anything."

"You can, can you?" she said, slowly massaging his crotch.

"Inge, you're taking advantage of me," Benoit squeaked.

"You're damn right I am," she agreed, leaning over and blowing gently in his left ear.

"That doesn't bother me a bit," Benoit said, squirming.

"I know it doesn't. It must be that pistol barrel you've stuffed down your trousers that's causing you all this difficulty."

"Oh, God, Inge, don't do that!"

"Do what?" she asked innocently. "You mean put my tongue in your ear? Like this?"

"Not that. The other."

"Oh, you mean this?"

"Inge, for God's sake. What if someone knocks on the door?"

"Who's going to be knocking this late in the afternoon? Who's going to come out with the wind blowing like this? You have some time off because of the storm, you may as well put it to good use."

"That's not a bad idea," Benoit said, easing his hand under her skirt.

"Oh, no," she said, pushing it away. "You're the tough guy. You can resist anything."

"I *can*!" he said stoically, throwing himself

backward on the bed and crossing his hands behind his head. "Whatever you do, it doesn't bother me at all."

"That's good," she said, unbuttoning his shirt. "Just don't pay any attention to me. Just lie there and think about clean rifles or your horse or whatever it is you soldiers think about."

"For your information, I'm thinking about a huge platter of boiled shrimp. I can't even remember the last time I had boiled shrimp."

"I'm thinking about shrimp, too." Inge chuckled throatily as she began to undo her husband's trousers.

"Just what are you trying to tell me?" Benoit said, bolting upright.

"Lie back," she said, pushing gently on his shoulder. "Can't you take a joke?"

"That isn't funny."

"It certainly isn't," Inge replied, gripping him tightly with her hand. "I certainly don't see any humor at all in this. It's all red and swollen. Not a bit funny."

"With lots of cold beer," Benoit gasped. "And lemon. Plenty of lemon juice."

"Lemon, eh," Inge said. "Doesn't that make your mouth pucker? Like this?"

Benoit groaned. "Steamed *sac à lait*? Perch fresh from Lake Pontchartrain. A big filet. Nice and hot."

"Umm," Inge agreed. "This is certainly nice and hot."

"French bread! A crusty baguette."

"Don't flatter yourself."

"I'm completely oblivious of what you're doing, Inge. It doesn't do a thing for me. I think I'll close my eyes and take a little nap. I think . . . I think . . . I think . . . Oh, my God!" He shuddered. "Oh, my God!"

"See?" Inge grinned. "You just think you're tough."

"More *Bienenstich*?" Hildegard Ashby asked, holding the knife poised over the round of honey almond cake.

"Oh, no," Benoit said, patting his stomach. "I couldn't eat another bite."

"Jim?" she asked, turning to her husband.

"Not for me."

"I'm not bashful," Erich piped up, extending his empty plate.

"My son is always hungry." Hildegard grinned. "I knew more he would took."

"*Take*, Mother. You knew I would *take* some more."

"*Ja*. Your appetite is, how you say, *kräftig*."

"I think 'strong' might be an understatement." Inge laughed. "My *little* brother can eat enough for any two people I know."

"I'm a growing boy," Erich replied, flexing his biceps. "I have to eat a lot to stay healthy."

"Growing boy, my foot." Benoit laughed as he studied his brother-in-law. Although a tad shorter than Benoit, Erich Schmidt, not yet nineteen, outweighed him by a good twenty pounds. With huge shoulders, a thick chest, and thighs the size of telegraph poles, he was, at least in Benoit's view, an intimidating physical specimen. Handsome, too, Benoit conceded. Erich's hair, as fair and light as his mother's and sister's, had remained uncut for so long that it reached to his shoulders. When he was around the post, he wore it loose, letting it dangle over his collar and down his back. But when he was out on the

Plains, where its blond flamboyance stood out like a mirror flash on the ocher-hued background, he wore it braided Indian fashion and tucked it under a dark slouch hat—the better, he said, to conceal his presence. The Schmidt bloodline also was evident in his twinkling blue eyes, turned-up nose, and lips as red as if they had been rouged. But his fair skin was tanned three shades deeper because of his almost constant exposure to the elements—the result of his profession, which was that of scout-hunter-guide, chief assistant to his stepfather. "If you grow any more," Benoit teased, "you're going to be a giant."

"Speaking of eating," Erich said, shoveling another forkful of *Bienenstich* into his mouth, "what would you like for your farewell dinner? I know you're partial to backstrap. But it's just as easy for me to get some buffler liver or a nice, tender antelope steak."

"Too early for good buffler," Ashby interjected. "They ain't had time to fatten up much yet."

"That's okay," Benoit said. "Backstrap sounds good to me. Besides, I don't know if I'll be able to get much elk in New Mexico."

"Up in th' mountains you ken," said Ashby. "'Least that's what I been tole."

Physically, Benoit noticed not for the first time, Ashby and Erich were about as dissimilar as two people could be. Ashby was short and wiry, with leathery, wrinkled skin the color of good bourbon and eyes that were an unfathomable black, almost as dark as Colonel Kemp's. When he walked he rolled like a sailor fresh ashore from a six-month voyage, a condition, Benoit knew, that resulted mainly from having lost three toes to frostbite. Withdrawn by nature—as opposed to Erich, who was about as gregarious as anyone Benoit knew—Ashby preferred to let his actions speak for him. Totally uneducated, Ashby nevertheless was fluent in Arapaho, Cheyenne, and Sioux; knew enough French to communicate readily with the Canadian trappers who still roamed the Plains; and could get by in Crow and Pawnee. Ashby was as illiterate as a grizzly, but he could read a trail as well as Benoit could a newspaper—and draw more from what he had ingested.

Despite their physical differences, Erich, ever since he had informally signed on with Ashby as an apprentice during the trip west in 1854, had done his best to imitate his mentor's dress and mannerisms. When Erich, clad in buckskin and loaded down with the weapons of the Plains hunter—tomahawk, general-purpose knife, and battered, large-bore rifle—performed even some simple task, such as scratching his ear, it was like looking at Ashby. One thing Erich could not emulate, however, were the tattoos that dotted his mentor's chest, a series of mysterious gravings put there by Ashby's first wife, an Arapaho named White Deer who had died of cholera years before.

So alike were the pair's mannerisms that when Hildegard Schmidt married Jim Ashby the previous summer, she told her daughter that it was almost like having twins underfoot, except the twins were thirty years apart in age.

"I'd better head out in the morning, then," Erich said. "The wind's been down for two days. No telling how much longer it's gonna be quiet."

"I reckon it's gonna be dandy for 'nother three, four days," said Ashby. "An' I ain't usually wrong about the weather."

"It's gonna seem strange me going off without you, Jim," Erich said.

"You don't need me," Ashby replied. "You know what to do. After all these damn storms, the elk'll be on the move, headin' to high ground. Jes' check the meadows. An' watch out for injuns. They gonna be out lookin' for fresh meat theirselves."

"Only ones I have to worry about are the Crow," Erich said.

"Don' be too sure about that," Ashby cautioned. "After that fiasco on the Solomon last year the Cheyenne might not be feelin' too friendly neither. Bes' thang to do is be wary of 'em *all*. You see any injun sign, you fergit the backstrap and get yore ass back to the fort. You un'erstan'?"

"'Course I do, Jim. I ain't no greenhorn no more. You got to figure I learnt something from you after all these years."

"I jes' hope you learnt enuf. You wanta take one o' th' soljers with you, jes' in case?"

"I don't need no soldier, Jim. He'd probably just mess up everything. I reckon I can do better by myself."

Ashby nodded slowly, spitting a stream of tobacco juice with incredible accuracy into a nearby spittoon. "Tha's pr'ly true enuf. A soljer who don't know his way 'round the forest might jes' make things worser."

"You leaving on Sunday, right?" Erich asked, turning to Benoit.

"Right. *Early* Sunday. I'm allowing four days for me and the men to get to Fort Marcy. That's not an absolute schedule—it won't matter much if we're a day or two later, but that's the current schedule."

"Well," Erich said, calculating quickly. "Today's Monday. I'll leave early in the morning and probably be back tomorrow night, Wednesday morning at the latest. That'll be plenty of time. Might even have time to pick a batch of fresh onions if they're up yet."

"Too early," Ashby said sagely. "Need another two weeks."

"Okay." Erich laughed. "Forget the onions."

"Where you planning to go?" Ashby asked.

"Reckoned I'd head up Fish Creek, see what I can find."

Ashby pondered that. "Might do better goin' up the Laramie," he said. "Them Crow like the east side o' Laramie Peak."

"So do the elk."

"My advice is try the Laramie."

"Aw, hell, Jim. Let me do this on my own. I can try Fish Creek, and if I see any injuns, I'll just back-track a bit and head south to the Laramie."

Ashby grinned. "You be right, boy. You gonna hafta do it the way you reckon is bes'. Jes' keep a sharp eye. Not only for injuns, but for storms. You watch for the signs like I learned you. If it looks like the weather's gonna change, despite my readin' of it, you fin' a nice, warm, dry place to duck into. Ain't no sense you gettin' froze jes' to make it back in time for Jean's dinner. He ain't gonna fret none if there ain't no backstrap on the table."

"Yes, sir," Erich said, throwing Ashby a mock salute. "Your wish is my command. Is that the way you say it to Colonel Kemp, Jean?"

"Not exactly." Benoit chuckled. "But it's close enough."

"In that case," Erich said, rising, "I guess I'd better

get some sleep if I'm going to be out of here before dawn."

"You want to say good-bye now," Benoit said, also rising. "In case you get stuck in the mountains by a storm."

"I ain't much on good-byes," Erich mumbled.

"Neither me," Benoit said, betraying his New Orleans heritage with his odd phrasing. "Besides, it isn't really good-bye. I imagine you'll be coming down to New Mexico with your sister next spring."

"Wouldn't miss it for the world." Erich grinned and threw his arms around Benoit, giving him a crushing embrace. "I want to see if them *señoritas* is really as pretty as they say."

"I don't plan to investigate that," Benoit said, giving Inge a sideways glance.

"You'd better not," Inge said. "Or *Mutter* won't be the only one in the family with an amputated appendage."

"I'm really going to miss all of you," Benoit said sadly as he and Inge strolled back to their room. For the first time since the previous fall both were without coats, taking advantage of the almost balmy night. Although they knew every inch of the parade ground by heart and could traverse it blindfolded, Benoit carried a lantern borrowed from his in-laws. As they walked, its light cast an eerie, dancing glow across the space, which was as barren of vegetation as the face of the moon, its surface littered with clods of mud thrown up by the horses during the daily drills ordered by Kemp.

"It's going to seem really strange without you being around," Inge agreed. "But you're going to be so busy you probably won't be giving us a second thought."

"That isn't true and you know it," Benoit said, sounding hurt. "What really bothers me is I'm not going to be here when our son is born."

"What if it's a daughter?" Inge smiled.

"It can't be. You know the rule: The firstborn is always a son."

"That wasn't true for your mother or mine."

"Well, as of right now the son rule applies." Benoit laughed and threw his arm around his wife. "Jean the fourth is going to demand it."

"I'm right glad I talked you out of Jeanette if it's a girl." Inge laughed.

"And I'm just as glad I talked you out of Hildegard."

"I think Katherine with a 'K' is a good compromise."

"A new name to both families," said Benoit.

"Oh, look," Inge said excitedly as they approached their door. "The mail's been sorted."

Benoit looked at the small pile of envelopes that had been placed neatly on their stoop. "It's a damn good thing the wind has stopped or they'd be back in Kansas City by now."

The stage had arrived earlier that morning, after being infuriatingly delayed by the series of spring storms, bringing mail and fresh newspapers. Lieutenant Grant, who acted as part-time postmaster, had separated the mail and seen to its delivery. There still was no sign of the supply train, but Kemp had announced at dinner that he had decided to take a chance and allow the hoisting of the last remaining flag, pending the approach of a new storm.

"Here's one from Francois," Inge said, holding up an envelope with a United States Naval Academy return address. "And two . . . no, three, from Marion. But one looks like an invitation. That was sweet of her. One from your mother."

"What else is there?" Benoit asked, peering over her shoulder.

"One from my cousin Karl in New York."

"Cousin Karl?"

"Father's sister's son. The clock maker. You remember me mentioning him."

"Oh, yeah," Benoit said. "It rings a bell. What about the other one?"

Inge looked at the envelope, then quickly clasped it to her bosom. "You sure you want to know?" she asked, lifting an eyebrow.

"Of course I want to know," he said, reaching for it.

"I'm not sure you do," Inge said, moving it out of his grasp.

"Come on, Inge, quit playing games."

"Okay," she said, handing it to him. "But don't say I didn't warn you."

Benoit stared at the seal of the United States Senate, surmounted in an elaborate hand by a name: "The Honorable Clement Couvillion, Senator, State of Louisiana."

"Oh, *that* son of a bitch," Benoit said with distaste.

"Are you sure you don't dislike Cle because he married your old sweetheart?" Inge asked. "Maybe there's a touch of jealousy there?"

"You're damn right I'm sure. Marie's part of the past, but Cle's just a goddamn fool."

"Do you miss her?" Inge asked, trying to keep her voice light.

"Miss who? Marie?"

"And who the hell else were we talking about?" Inge asked peevishly, throwing open the door.

"Aw, God, Inge, let's don't go through that again. Marie doesn't mean a thing to me anymore."

"She's still your sister's best friend, isn't she?"

"That's Marion, not me. I haven't heard from Marie since she and Cle left here, what was it? Two and a half years ago?"

"Two years eight months," Inge said smugly.

"Jesus, how do you remember all that?" Benoit asked, impressed.

"A woman always remembers those kinds of things. Aren't you going to open the letter? Maybe she and Cle are coming back out west. Another fact-finding trip for some committee or other."

"And maybe he just wants to pester me some more about resigning my commission and joining the New Orleans militia," Benoit said, stuffing the envelope in his rear trouser pocket. "He's beginning to get on my nerves about that."

"Open it!" Inge commanded, crossing her arms across her chest.

Benoit looked at her and smiled. "Are you going to stomp your foot, too?"

"You're damn right I am," she said, stomping her foot. "Open it!"

"Okay, okay." Benoit sighed as he pulled out the envelope and ripped it open. "Let me turn up the lantern," he said, crossing to a small table on the south wall and twisting the knob that lengthened the wick, throwing more light into the room.

"Well?" Inge said impatiently.

"I haven't read it yet. Give me a chance," Benoit

said, unfolding the two sheets of fine paper covered in a neat, masculine script. As he read, his eyes began to bulge and his face turned as red as if lit by an inner flame. "That bastard!" he swore. "That *espèce d'enculè!*"

"What is it?" Inge frowned. "Is there something wrong?"

"Here!" Benoit said, crumpling the letter and thrusting it into her hand. "You read it."

"You know I have trouble reading other people's handwriting, Jean," Inge said, blushing. "I haven't had your education. Read it to me." She handed it back.

"Okay," Benoit said, his lips set in a straight line. Smoothing the paper, he glared at Inge. "He calls me his 'dear t-Jean,' but I'll be damned if I'm his 'dear' anything."

"Read the letter," Inge said. "Save the comments until later."

"All right, all right." Benoit shrugged. "'My dear t-Jean,'" he began, clearing his throat. "'By now, you're probably wondering why you were selected for promotion and a new posting to the territory of New Mexico. Wonder no longer. You can thank me and Jeff Davis. I know I've been putting a lot of pressure on you to give up your commission and join the Confederates, but I realize, after a long session with Jeff, that it probably is better if you don't do that right away. As you know, Jeff was elected to the Senate after he was replaced as secretary of war by President Buchanan. Since then, the two us and a few other Southern sympathizers here in Washington were able to convince the President to appoint John Floyd as Jeff's successor. John, you may not realize, is a Virginian and very *sympathique* to our cause. Actually, this all is working out much better than we anticipated. Jeff has been working for months on a master plan that the Confederacy can follow once the decision has been made for the Southern states to leave the Union. After secession, our army will be moving quickly to consolidate, in the process grabbing as many fortifications as we can. It suddenly dawned upon us that it would be tremendously advantageous to the Confederacy if we had people in strategic locations so they could be ready to move when the time comes. That's where you fit in. New Mexico will be important as one of the westernmost areas the Confederacy will need to control. With our troops operating from there, we can put the U.S. Army in an uncomfortable position, forcing it to fight on yet another front. Since you were already on the frontier, it made sense to position you in New Mexico. This was, in my own humble opinion, a stroke of genius. General Barksdale was no impediment since he is a close friend of John Floyd's; they grew up on adjoining plantations. When John submitted your name to the general as an aide-de-camp, Barksdale was all too happy to agree. Be assured that New Mexico is only one of several targeted areas—the others I cannot divulge to you for security reasons. It will, nevertheless, be vital to our plans.'"

Benoit paused for breath. Glancing at Inge, he noticed that she had paled. He continued: "'By the way, I'm not worried that you will disclose any of what I'm telling you in this letter to your commanding officer, or anyone else, for that matter. You see, I have a firm written commitment to join our forces from your younger brother, Francois. So if you expose us, you will be exposing him as well and subject him to whatever punishment the navy wishes to impose. I

think the authorities probably would consider it trea-
son. If tried and convicted of that, as you know, he
could be hanged. Besides, I know in my heart that you
are with us; you just have to convince yourself of that.
We're not asking you to make any blatant moves—no
spying in the strict sense of the word. We want you to
do nothing except absorb as much information as you
can. Learn *everything* about existing fortifications,
manpower deployment, battle plans—whatever
details come your way. All of this will come in very
handy once war is declared. If you unwisely decide to
stay with the U.S. Army, which I don't think you will
once you come to your senses, we have lost nothing.
But if you choose to join us, we will have gained a
great deal.

"'Think about it, *mon ami*. It's the opportunity of a
lifetime. I wanted to make you a full captain rather
than a brevet, but Floyd felt that would be pushing
things too far. When you decide to join the
Confederacy, we will, of course, promote you again.
How does Colonel Jean Benoit sound? Someday you
will thank me immensely for all that I've done for you
and your career. Do not bother to respond to this; the
less we have in writing, the better. I suggest, in fact,
that you destroy this as soon as you have read it.
Marie sends her love. I remain, as always, your faithful friend. . . .'"

"That . . . that . . . *schwachsinnige*!" Inge yelled
when Benoit finished. "That arrogant *arsch*! That . . ."

"All that and more," Benoit agreed. "The question
is, what do we—rather, what do I—do about it?"

"Oh, Jean," Inge said, sinking to the bed, "this is
terrible. It's just what Colonel Kemp feared. He felt all
along that Cle was involved in this."

"Except he was wrong by suspecting I also played a part. This letter makes it clear that I had nothing to do with it. *That* is very important. I'm just a pawn in Cle's deadly little game."

"Yes, but will the colonel believe that?"

Benoit shook his head. "He'll never know."

"Jean!" Inge said, amazed. "You mean you're not going to tell him?"

"How can I?" Benoit said angrily. "Cle's right. He's a son of a bitch, but he's also a smart son of a bitch. If I share this with anyone, I'll endanger Francois. I can't be responsible for subjecting my brother to the threat of being hanged."

"But the letter shows he was duped."

"Who would believe me? It would be my word against that of the secretary of war and two United States *senators*, for Christ's sake."

"But the letter . . ."

"Cle could say it was forged, that I had someone write it as part of a malicious attempt to punish him for marrying Marie. John Floyd, of course, would deny all of it. And so would Jeff Davis. I'm in a real bind. I don't see where I have any choice but to keep my mouth shut."

"Open Francois's letter," Inge said abruptly. "Maybe *he* says something that will help."

"Good idea," Benoit said, reaching for the envelope from his brother. He ripped it open and began reading it to himself.

"Nothing so far," he said, glancing down the page, "just the usual crap about his studies and the navy. . . . Wait, here's something." He paused, then began reading aloud: "'I've been in touch lately with your friend Clement Couvillion, the Senator. He must have gotten my address from Marion. He said that he has been communicating with you and that you have given your word that you will resign your commission and join the Confederate forces at the appropriate time. Although I'm a little surprised, since I had always thought you totally dedicated to the Union Army, I think your decision is a wise one. My inclinations also have been to do likewise. I believe that the South has legitimate complaints that are not being properly addressed and that the only way this situation will be remedied is through war. A lot of my classmates feel the same way, and I am amazed at how many of them share my sympathy for the South. In view of all this, it was not a complete shock when I heard from the Senator that you, too, were of like mind. He asked me for a commitment in writing, which I was only too happy to supply since I knew you already had done the same. Just yesterday, I received my instructions: Do nothing for the time being. Continue to let the Navy educate me so I can be as knowledgeable as possible when the split actually comes. So, for the present, at least, I'll continue to do exactly as I've always done. I realize it might be difficult for you to share your orders with me, but please tell me what you can. Meantime, life continues to be hectic. Surely you remember what it was like to be a cadet. . . .'

"That's it," Benoit said, scanning the remainder of the letter. "The rest is just telling about life at the academy, how he's looking forward to being home for the summer, the usual things."

"Oh, God," Inge said, sinking her face in her hands, "it really is a predicament, isn't it?"

Benoit nodded. "It certainly is."

"What can we do, Jean?" she asked, looking up.

Benoit saw that tears were beginning to roll down her cheeks.

"For the present, nothing," he replied grimly, putting his arm around her and drawing her close. "The worst thing we could do would be to act without thinking. The only choice we have is to continue as if we know nothing. Given time, I'm sure I'll think of something. Cle thought he was being very clever by pushing my promotion and my new posting, but that may, in fact, be his downfall."

"What do you mean?"

Benoit shook his head. "I don't know, Inge. I really don't. But as a brevet captain I'll certainly have more authority than I would as a lowly second lieutenant. I'll report to General Barksdale as scheduled. I'll go ahead as if I had never heard from Cle and wait for an opportunity to present itself. In the meantime, I won't tell anyone about what I know. The same has to apply to you. Not a word," he cautioned her sternly, "not even to your mother."

"I understand." Inge nodded solemnly. "What about Jace?"

"Oh, God," Benoit groaned. "Jace least of all. We've already had one major argument about the secession issue. I thought our friendship was going to end right then and there. I *absolutely* can't give him even a hint of what's happening."

Inge stood and began unbuttoning her dress. "It's strange, isn't it, about how much our lives have changed in just the last few weeks. First, we get all excited about your promotion and a new posting. Then I discover I'm pregnant. And now you learn that you're being used against your will as a spy. I certainly hope this is the last of our major surprises."

After pulling her dress over her head, she shed her petticoats and then climbed nude into the bed.

"What else *could* happen?" Benoit asked, holding Couvillion's letter above the top of the lantern until it burst into flames. "Besides, there's one good thing to come out of all this."

"Oh, yeah?" Inge asked, her tone skeptical. "What's that?"

"At least the mystery has been solved," Benoit said, tossing the burning paper to the floor and stomping on it. "We don't have to go around any longer wondering why I was chosen out of all the officers in the army."

"That's true," Inge agreed. "Good news is where you find it. By the way," she said, brightening, "I have one other piece of good news for you."

"Tell me quick," Benoit said, pulling off his boots. "I need some cheering up."

"I changed the sheets," Inge said, forcing a grin. "No more sand."

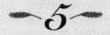

Benoit and Second Lieutenant Joseph Battaglia were on their knees in a corner of the room set aside for all the officers to use on the second floor of Old Bedlam, poring over stacks of paper that were too voluminous to spread out on the tiny desk assigned to company commanders, when they heard a muffled voice from the other side of the door.

"Jean," Inge cried, "please let me in."

"Sorry," Benoit said, scrambling to his feet. "I didn't hear you."

"This is the third time I've called," Inge replied somewhat peevishly. "I can't open the door with a tray in my hands."

"We were concentrating pretty hard," Benoit said. "I've been filling Joe in on what his duties will be when he takes over command of the company on Saturday. What do you have there?" he asked, lifting a corner of the napkin that covered the tray.

"Oh, great," Battaglia said enthusiastically, eyeing the small mound of sandwiches and pitcher of cold milk. "We got so carried away, we forgot to come to lunch."

"I know." Inge smiled. "That's why I figured I'd better bring you something."

"How did you ever land a woman like this?" Battaglia asked Benoit, grinning.

"My irresistible charm," Benoit said, reaching for a sandwich. "Either that or my family fortune."

"That'll be the day." Inge laughed, watching as the two men attacked the food. She waited for them to finish their first sandwich and start on the second before speaking again.

"Jean," she said, "I'm worried."

Benoit looked up. There was no laughter in her eyes, and her lips were set in a grim line.

"What is it?" he asked, feeling a knot form in his stomach. "Are you feeling all right? Is it because of your condition?"

"No, it has nothing to do with that. It's Erich."

"Erich? What about him?"

"He hasn't come back yet."

Benoit paused, digesting the information. "What time is it?" he asked, concern evident in his voice.

"Almost midafternoon. Remember, he said he'd be back either late yesterday or early today."

"Maybe he had more trouble than he thought finding an elk."

"Then he would have come back empty-handed. He knows better than not to be back when he said he would be."

"That's a mortal sin out here, I'll grant you that," interjected Battaglia.

"Maybe he got turned around?" Benoit offered hopefully. "You know, lost?"

Inge shook her head. "Erich? Lost? Come on, Jean, you know Erich better than that."

"Maybe he had trouble with his horse."

"And *maybe*," Inge said emphatically, "he ran into a bunch of hostile Indians."

"Why would you think that? Just because he's a couple of hours late, that doesn't mean it's a catastrophe."

"Jim's worried, too," Inge said resolutely.

Benoit looked up in surprise. "Did he say that?"

"No," Inge admitted, "but I can tell. He's acting real distracted. *Mutter* had to ask him twice if he wanted more dessert. And he kept looking out the window, toward the stables."

Benoit rubbed his chin. "Look, Inge, I don't want to make light of this, but it's a little early to get too distressed. He's only a couple of hours late and—"

"But that's not like Erich," Inge protested. "He's always so . . . so *dependable*."

"I know he is," Benoit said soothingly. "But sometimes things happen that no one can foresee. Just because he's a little late, that doesn't necessarily mean that something really bad has happened."

"Oh, yeah," Inge said skeptically. "Like what else?"

"Oh, God, I don't know! A hundred things. Maybe he just wounded the elk and then had to track it down to kill it. Maybe he spooked the herd. . . ."

"Not Erich."

"Okay, that was a bad example. Maybe his horse stepped in a hole and hurt itself or even broke its leg. Maybe he's having to walk back."

"How long would that take?"

"I have no idea because I don't know where he might have been."

"Jean," Inge said, crossing her arms over her chest, "I want you to do something!"

"Well, hell, Inge, what do you want me to do? I can't just go out and saddle a horse and ride off into the mountains."

"Why not? That's probably what Jim is working up to."

Benoit sighed. "Jim doesn't have a reason why he has to stay here. I do. I'm supposed to be leaving on Sunday, and I still have a lot to do—"

"Don't worry about me," Battaglia interrupted. "I'm not exactly ignorant about the operation here. I can handle it."

Benoit shot him a hard glance. "Okay," he said to Inge, "I'll tell you what. Go tell Jim not to do anything yet. Then if Erich isn't back by this evening, I'll ask Colonel Kemp for permission to go looking for him."

"What if he says no?"

"He won't. Besides, if he does, Jim can go anyway. He doesn't need Kemp's approval. It's too late for him to get started now, anyway. It'd be dark before he could get very far. It'd be better to go off early tomorrow, before dawn. That way we'd have the whole day to look." He put his hand on her shoulder and squeezed. "Is that okay?"

"I guess so," she said uncertainly. "What you say makes sense."

"You want me to go talk to Jim?"

"No, that's okay. I'm sure he'd agree, too. It's just that Mother and I—"

"I know," Benoit said. "I understand. But let's wait until tonight before we start to panic. In the meantime, Joe and I need to get back to work."

"All right," Inge said, gathering up the tray. "I'll go talk to Jim."

"Thanks for lunch, Inge," Battaglia called as she

went out the door. "It was great. You're a heck of cook. . . ."

"Don't overdo it, Joe," Benoit cautioned. "She doesn't even have a sister."

"Well?" Inge asked anxiously when Benoit returned to their room late that evening. "What did the colonel say?"

"He said okay. I knew he would. He's not really happy with the situation, either. The last thing he wants is to lose a man."

"So what are you going to do?"

"I talked to Jim. We're going to leave about four A.M. and head toward Fish Creek. That's where Erich said he was planning on going, didn't he?"

"That's where *he* wanted to go; Jim wanted him to go up the Laramie."

"Well, knowing Erich, I'd say he went to Fish Creek. He's damn near as headstrong as you are."

Inge looked at him sharply. "Are you trying to start a fight?" she asked testily.

"Oh, God, no," Benoit replied quickly. "I was just teasing you a bit."

"I'm in no mood to be teased."

"Inge, you can't get that upset. We still don't know that anything *happened* to Erich. As I said this afternoon, there are plenty of reasons for him to be late. . . ."

"Not this late."

"Okay. Okay. It's unusual, but not unprecedented. Remember when he and Jim went out to meet that group of emigrants we feared. . . ."

"But Jim was with him then," Inge said. "This time he's all by himself."

"He's not a child anymore, Inge."

"I know that," she replied, collapsing on the bed. "I don't worry about him when he's with Jim. But when he's out by himself . . ."

"He has to venture off on his own sometime."

"Mother and I are very much in agreement about this," Inge said abruptly.

Benoit frowned. "What do you mean?"

"Our intuition tells us both that something bad has happened."

"Inge, you can't let your emotions get out of control on this. There's absolutely no factual basis—"

"Facts be damned!" she said angrily. "We *know* something has happened."

"Okay." Benoit shrugged. "I can't argue with that."

"I'm not trying to argue."

"Oops, wrong choice of words. I don't know what to say when you get in this kind of mood. We're going to do everything we can. Jim and I and two troopers are going out tomorrow to search for him. If something's happened, we'll know soon enough. Personally, I think there's nothing to get upset about. We're going to find Erich fat and sassy and loaded down with fresh meat. He probably decided to bring back more than the backstrap, which is why he's late. He took the time to butcher—"

"I hope you're right," Inge said, throwing her arms around her husband. "Hurry up and get into bed. I need a cuddle."

"Sounds good to me," Benoit said, grinning lasciviously.

"Not tonight, Jean. I just want you to hold me."

There was a crescent moon dangling over Laramie Peak when the four men mounted their horses and headed them northwest, away from the fort.

"It looks like the moon is dripping cream onto the peak, doesn't it?" Benoit asked no one in particular, pointing at the lower part of the crescent that appeared close enough to touch the tip of the snow-topped mountain.

Ashby grunted noncommittally, and the two troopers made no response at all, sitting slumped in their saddles and rocking slowly with the movement of their mounts. With their hats low over their eyes, Benoit was unable to tell if they were asleep or awake. They'd probably been up all night playing poker, he thought.

All four men were heavily armed, prepared for, if not exactly expecting, a skirmish with bloodthirsty Indians looking, perhaps, for fresh scalps they could pridefully display at the forthcoming sun dance ceremonies.

It was curious, Benoit reflected as they climbed slowly upward into the pines and evergreens, how each man's choice of weapons was an accurate mirror of that individual's personality. He himself was deeply attached to his Model 1853 Sharps, a somewhat cumbersome, single-shot, .52-caliber breechloader. Every time he fired it, he had to manipulate the trigger guard operating lever that opened the block so he could insert a fresh linen cartridge before he could fire again, but as far as he was concerned that was no great disadvantage. Very few of the tribesmen against whom he might have to use his Sharps were equipped with rifles, so accuracy, not rapid-fire capability, was his primary concern. He had bought the Sharps just before leaving Washington and had guarded it carefully on the long trip down the Oregon Trail, letting it out of his sight only when he had loaned it to Erich so the youth could hone his marksmanship.

Once Erich went to work for Jim Ashby and began earning a little money on his own, he had begun to save for his own rifle. A couple of years before, he had walked into Sevier's store and plunked down his hoard for a .50-caliber Hawken that he had been eyeing for months. Erich's choice had been guided by the philosophy that if he hit something, whether it was a charging grizzly or a war-painted hostile, he wanted it to drop. "If I shoot something, I want it to stay shot," Benoit remembered him saying with a grin. The Hawk was renowned for its stopping power—a weapon, Erich swore, that was capable of dropping a buffalo bull dead in its tracks at 350 yards.

Ashby, on the other hand, favored a .52-caliber Model 1819 Hall, a near ancient firearm for which he took much ribbing since it had only one-third the stopping power of most other muzzle-loading muskets. But to the veteran scout, whose philosophy was opposite Benoit's, the benefit of the Hall was that its cap-lock design allowed it to be fired more than twice as quickly as most other Plains rifles. He valued the Hall because in a fight with Indians, he reckoned that if he could throw out a virtual wall of bullets, his foes might think twice about pursuing the attack.

The two enlisted men accompanying Benoit and Ashby had little choice about their rifles since they carried what they were issued—Model 1842 cap-lock muskets known as Yaeger rifles.

Rifles were not the men's only weapons, however. Around his waist Benoit wore a .36-caliber

Navy Colt revolver. One of the troopers, a newly arrived corporal named Smithers, also carried a sidearm—an old .31-caliber five-shot Colt commonly called a Baby Dragoon. The other trooper, a twenty-two-year-old private from Tennessee named Hendrickson, shunned a revolver, preferring instead a tomahawk that he had taken in trade from an Arapaho. Hendrickson, who topped out at six feet four and weighed upward of 250 pounds, had a reputation on the post as a brawler, a man who preferred to do his fighting face-to-face, depending on cunning and brute strength rather than firearms. Because of his pugnaciousness, Benoit had hesitated about choosing Hendrickson for the team, but he relented after telling himself that the exercise in discipline he could get on the mission would be good for the young farmboy. Ashby, too, disdained a sidearm, electing to place his trust in his fearsome-looking broadax-style tomahawk and a knife with an eight-inch blade that he kept honed to a razor's edge.

Except for their weapons, the men traveled lightly, carrying only enough rations to last them a day. That was Ashby's idea. The scout reckoned the mission was not a complicated one: they would go out until they found Erich and then come back, no more than a half day's ride in each direction. If they failed to find him in that time, they would come back to Fort Laramie and reconsider their options, since Erich was not *supposed* to have wandered any great distance. The only way he might be farther than that was if he had been captured and spirited off by a passing group of warriors. If that was the case, more than four men would be needed to get him back. It was not, however, the practice of the Plains tribes to take captives;

they preferred to leave their victims dead and hair-less.

Ashby pointed his swaybacked pony toward Laramie Peak. "Lookit," he said. "See that slight haze up near the crest? You ken see it because of the moon-light."

Benoit grunted in acknowledgment.

"That's wind blowin' the snow. Don' like that much. Means we might be in for 'nother storm 'fore nightfall."

"I thought you said that the good weather was going to hold for several days," Benoit said somewhat irritably.

"I said I *reckoned* it would," Ashby said dryly. "I ain't God. I can't make the weather."

"Well, I guess it doesn't matter. If the storm holds off till dark, that's all the time we need."

"Tha's an estimate, too," Ashby added. "Might be midafternoon. Might be tomorrow morning."

"Well, we can't let that stop us." Benoit sighed. "If worse comes to worse, we can always hole up some-place."

"Don' think that'll be necessary. It be too late in the sprang for a mean 'n."

"You think we're likely to see some injuns?" Hendrickson asked, speaking for the first time since they'd left the fort.

"Hard to tell," Ashby said. "If I had my druthers, we won't."

"I'd be tickled to git me a scalp," Hendrickson said. "That shore would be sumthang to show aroun' Cabot's Cove."

"Scalpin' be fine as long as it be someone else's scalp you collectin'," Ashby said. "Mite be a differen' story if some injun went back to his camp with *your* scalp."

"I ain't worried about that," Hendrickson said. "I ain't yet seen an injun I couldn't whip hands down."

"Could be a different story if'n they ain't anxious to fight your way," Ashby said. "An injun from fifty yards don' hardly miss with his bow. An' their arrows got enough force to go through your horse."

"You trying to scare me, Jim?" Hendrickson said with a smile that made his teeth glow in the moonlight as if they were lit from within.

"Hell, no," Ashby replied. "Reckon the firs' time an injun comes after you, you'll be scared enuf to shit yore pants without me needin' to say a thang."

"I'd like to see an injun go up agin this," Hendrickson replied, lifting a ham-sized fist. "I reckon lead'd be better than an ol' arrow any day."

"Provided you get a chance to use it," said Ashby. "Most o' the injuns I know don' think much about sluggin' it out when an arrow or a war club'll do the trick."

For the next hour the men rode in silence, climbing straight toward Laramie Peak. At sunrise they burst through the towering trees, emerging into a large clearing from which they had a spectacular view of both the mountain in front of them and the rolling plains behind. By mutual agreement they reined in their horses and remained where they were, watching appreciatively as the snow-capped peak turned pink and then blinding white.

"I don't think I've ever seen a sight quite so beautiful," said Benoit. "I'm sure going to miss this in New Mexico."

"They got right pretty scenery there, too, I be told," said Ashby.

"You know where we are?" Benoit asked. "Or do I need to dig out my map?"

"Sheeet," Ashby said, sounding insulted. "I know this country better'n I know ever' scar on my body. Once we git in the woods yonder we be pickin' up Fish Creek. Then all we gotta do is follow it upstream."

"How far?" Benoit asked.

"Depends. Don' know how up the elk've gone so far. There's a right nice meadow just about an hour's ride away. If'n we're lucky, that's where Erich spotted a herd. If not, we jes' keep goin' up until we fin' either him or the elk. It ain't—"

"Over there!" Smithers yelled excitedly, interrupting Ashby. "Injuns!"

Pointing with one hand, the trooper fumbled with his rifle with the other, yanking the Yaeger out of its scabbard and lifting it to his shoulder.

Ashby swiveled to face the direction where Smithers was pointing. A hundred yards away, on the far side of the clearing, a lone Indian was sitting astride his pony just inside the trees. "Cheyenne!" Ashby said instantly.

"A dead Cheyenne," Smithers mumbled, leveling his rifle.

"Hold it!" Ashby barked, knocking Smithers's rifle aside just as he was preparing to squeeze the trigger.

"What in hell'd you do that for?" the trooper asked indignantly.

"He ain't after us," Ashby said calmly. "Look. He ain't displaying a weapon; he ain't wearing no war paint."

"I think I know him," Benoit said. "I think I remember him from around the camp when Dobbs and I were with the Cheyenne a few years ago."

"Put tha' damn rifle away," Ashby told Smithers. "Thar'll be no shootin' 'less we're shot at firs' or unless the lieutenant orders you to. You un'erstan'? Both of you?" he said, looking from Smithers to Hendrickson, whose eyes were as large as silver dollars.

"I get you," said Smithers, slipping the Yaeger back in its case.

"Me too," echoed Hendrickson, his cheeks flaming, apparently embarrassed because he had been so slow to react.

"Who is he?" Benoit asked Ashby.

The scout squinted and stared across the open space. "Tha's Trembling Leaf," he said after several moments. "He's a warrior from the Aorta band."

"What you figure he wants?" Benoit asked curiously, never taking his eyes off the Cheyenne.

"Reckon I won't know till I go ask him," Ashby said, moving his pony forward. "Figger it'd be smart you and these two trigger-happy soljers stay here whilst I go see."

Ten minutes later, after considerable gesturing and head nodding, Ashby—to Benoit's surprise—rode alone into the trees, leaving the Cheyenne exactly where he had been when they'd first seen him. Just when Benoit was beginning to get anxious, Ashby reappeared. Then he and Trembling Leaf turned their ponies and began slowly approaching Benoit and the two troopers. As they came forward, a half dozen other Indians emerged from the trees.

"What th' hell's goin' on?" Hendrickson asked nervously.

"I don't like this worth a shit," Smithers said, slowly running his palm over the butt of his rifle.

"Keep calm," Benoit ordered brusquely. "Don't make a move until I tell you to."

Turning his attention toward the approaching group, Benoit was startled to see that the last horse was pulling a travois. Strapped to the rude frame was an indistinct figure covered in robes.

When the Indians got close enough to be recognizable, Benoit's face erupted into a large grin.

"Dah-veed!" he yelled excitedly, urging his horse forward. "David Legendre!"

His enthusiasm evaporated, however, when he saw that the figure on the travois was Erich.

At first, Benoit thought he was dead. His face was completely without color and his eyes were wide, staring straight up into the sky. When he got closer, however, Erich swiveled his head until he was facing his brother-in-law. "Hi, Jean," Erich said weakly. "You're a sight for sore eyes."

"Oh, God," Benoit breathed in relief. "What a scare you gave me. I thought you were dead."

"Might as well be," Erich said quietly. "My legs're dead. I can't walk."

"Can't walk?" Benoit gulped. "What the hell happened?"

"He got throwed," Ashby said quietly, joining Benoit at Erich's side. "He was gettin' the backstrap when he got surprised by a group of Crow. He was smart enuf to know he couldn't fight 'em all, so he jumped on his horse and was gettin' the hell out of thar when the Crow shot his horse out from under him. Trembling Leaf and th' others was nearby, an' when they heard Erich's rifle, they came to investigate the noise. Reckon they were pretty happy when they discovered the Crow; them two tribes have been enemies forever. As it turns out, they got thar jes' in time. Them Crow was mighty surprised to fin' themselves facing a passel of Cheyenne, so they took off. I reckon they'll be back, though. Soon's they get their courage up."

"What's going on?" Smithers asked anxiously. When he and Hendrickson saw Benoit galloping toward the Indians they had followed, arriving just as Ashby was finishing his explanation. "He don't look so good," he said, nodding at Erich.

"You wouldn't neither, you couldn't walk," Erich answered righteously, giving the trooper a dirty look.

Benoit looked around him. Except for Trembling Leaf, they were all youths in their mid-teens. Budding warriors, he figured, out on a hunting expedition with an experienced teacher.

"How are you, David?" Benoit asked in French, nodding at the youth. He was the son of the trapper, Etienne Legendre, who had been killed by a group of Brulé renegades the previous summer.

David looked confused, trying to understand a language he had long since ceased to use. "I . . . am . . . well," he said ponderously, groping for the correct words.

"They was gonna bring Erich to the post," Ashby interrupted. "But then they met us firs'. I tole Trembling Leaf we much appreciated his kindness, but we could handle it from here. He said he reckoned he and his would-be warriors would ride with us for a spell, jes' to make sure we got outta here without them Crow comin' back. I figger it'd be smart if we don' stan' around gabbin'. I figger them Crow ain't finished for the day."

"Then let's get going," Benoit agreed, swinging onto his horse.

Slowly the group began moving toward Fort Laramie, Benoit and Ashby in the lead, followed by Trembling Leaf and the young Indians. Smithers and Hendrickson, looking nervously over their shoulders, brought up the rear.

After a few minutes Benoit dropped back to talk to Erich. "Don't give up," he said, hoping he sounded encouraging. "In a couple of hours we'll be back at the post and Jace will have a look at you. Maybe it ain't as bad as it seems. Remember how he recovered from that blow to the head that left half his face paralyzed? To look at him now, you'd never know he was in such bad shape just a few months ago."

"I know you mean well, Jean," Erich said slowly, almost totally without emotion. "But I think this is different. I felt a twinge in my back when I hit the ground. I'm scared I ain't never going to get any better."

Benoit looked closely at his brother-in-law, not knowing how to respond. "I'm not a doctor," he said after a long pause. "I can't say for certain what happened or what's going to happen. But don't get depressed. At least wait for Jace to examine you. You comfortable?"

"Being toted like a load of buffler meat ain't too bad," Erich said, forcing a weak grin. "I ain't never ridden on a travois before. It's kinda like being in a buggy 'cept I can't see where we're going."

"We'll be home in a couple of hours," Benoit said, forcing a smile himself. "Why don't you just try to relax and not worry too much. At least wait until we've seen an expert."

"I hope that's all there is to it," Erich said. "But I do feel right tired. You won't mind if I try to take a little nap?"

"'Course not." Benoit nodded. "I'll be sure and wake you up before we get there."

Benoit continued to ride beside the travois until Erich closed his eyes and his breathing grew deep and regular. He urged his horse forward until he was riding beside the youth he had known as David Legendre.

"How are you doing among the Cheyenne?" he asked in French, trying to speak slowly, enunciating his words carefully.

"I am progressing in good fashion," David replied stiltedly. "Next year I will be old enough to join the warriors on a horse raid."

"Time really flies," Benoit said, more to himself than to the youth.

"Pardon?" David asked, raising an eyebrow.

"Nothing," Benoit said, shaking his head. "I was talking to myself. The last time I saw you, you were called Plays With His Toes."

David laughed. "That is a child's name. Now I am known as Little Wolf."

"I definitely can see you are no longer a child." Benoit smiled, noting how David had his father's broad shoulders and deep chest. Even as a teenager he was large—almost, Benoit guessed, as tall as he was. "And how," he asked guardedly, "are Werner and Wilhelm?"

David looked puzzled. "Oh," he said in recognition, "you mean Magpie and Puma?"

It seemed strange to Benoit to hear the two German children referred to by their Cheyenne names.

He still remembered them as they were on that day almost four years before when they had been captured on the raid on the wagons, the same day his mother-in-law had lost her German husband and her leg.

"They are . . . uh . . . *progressing* as well," David said, unable to find the words he wanted. "Puma is now this long," he added, lowering his hand until it was about five and a half feet off the ground, "and Magpie has a chest like this." He took a deep breath and expanded his own sizable upper body. "Soon they also will take adult names and begin training as warriors."

"Are they happy?" Benoit asked anxiously, knowing his mother-in-law would grill him closely on the subject. Frau Ashby had never adjusted to the reality of the two boys being adopted into the tribe, taking it as a personal campaign to try to bring them back to live among the whites.

"Oh, yes." David nodded eagerly. "They have already forgotten they could ever speak anything except Cheyenne. Their memories of life among the whites has all but faded."

"And yours?" Benoit asked, looking at him closely.

David paused, searching his faded French vocabulary. "I miss my father," he said slowly. "I will never forgive that devil Blizzard for taking his life in such a horrible fashion. I regret that Blizzard also now is dead because I would like nothing better than revenge. But, yes, I am happy. The Cheyenne are my people. They have taken good care of me. Despite the parts of me that still look white, my soul is Cheyenne. I will live as a Cheyenne and I also will die as one."

Not knowing how to respond, Benoit said nothing. Instead he nodded solemnly at David and dug his heels gently into his horse's sides. A minute later he was riding alongside Ashby, neither talking, each lost in his own thoughts.

The attack came twenty minutes later, totally without warning. Benoit was sipping from his canteen, mentally calculating how far they were from Fort Laramie, when he heard a solid thud, followed by a surprised grunt. Turning quickly, he saw Smithers grabbing his leg, where an arrow protruded from his thigh. As Benoit watched, Smithers's horse reared once, then dropped, killed instantly by an arrow through its neck.

"Crow!" Ashby cried, reaching for his Hall.

Benoit was about to issue a command to run for it when he suddenly remembered Erich and the travois. "Dismount!" he yelled instead, pulling his Sharps free and jumping to the ground. "Take cover!"

He was running to get behind a large Ponderosa when he looked up to see Hendrickson charging in the direction from which the arrows had come. Bellowing like a wounded bear, Hendrickson had drawn back his lips in a terrible grimace, and his eyes flashed wildly. "Where are you, you motherfuckers?" he screamed.

Before Benoit could yell a warning, an arrow pierced Hendrickson's right leg just above the knee. Staggered by the force of the blow, he spun halfway around, then righted himself and returned to his original course, dragging his wounded leg limply at his side.

"Where's my rifle?" Erich hollered. "I can shoot, goddammit."

"Here," Benoit said, tossing him his Hawken, which Trembling Leaf had given him earlier. Hauling on the reins of the horse that was pulling the travois, Benoit moved deeper into the forest, hopefully to safety.

"Come out, you sonsabitches!" Hendrickson screamed to the trees. "Come out and fight like men."

In response there was a flurry of arrows, all aimed at the monstrous target. One hit Hendrickson in his left shoulder, causing him to jerk backward as if he had been kicked by a horse. In quick succession, even as he was turning, another arrow struck him between his shoulder blades, and another struck just above his right kidney, burying itself up to its feathers. Without much more than a gurgle, Hendrickson toppled forward like a giant tree being felled by a lumberjack, hitting the ground face first with a noise that sounded like a bale of hay being tossed out of a loft.

Benoit calculated his position. To his right, Ashby was crouched behind the stump of a lightning-killed pine, firing into the trees as rapidly as he could reload. To Ashby's right, Smithers, the arrow still sprouting from his thigh, was hiding behind a small boulder, trying to control his shaking hands enough to pour the black powder into his Yaeger.

"Not so much powder!" Benoit yelled as he watched Smithers tip his flask and hold it there.

The warning came too late. Ignoring Benoit, Smithers lifted the Yaeger to his shoulder and pulled the trigger. There was a boom and a bright flash, then Smithers tumbled backward as if he had been shoved by a giant. "Oh, my God!" he screamed, grabbing his right eye and curling into a ball. "Jesus help me," he yelled, rolling in the dust. "I can't see! I can't see!"

Benoit ran to his side. Flipping him over, he took one look at the injured soldier and knew immediately what had happened. The skin on the right side of the soldier's face looked like a piece of steak seared over a flame. Already the skin was blistering; the right eyebrow and eyelids were burned off, and the eye itself looked like a chunk of raw buffalo liver.

"You dumb son of a bitch," Benoit cursed softly. "You stripped the nipple, didn't you?"

Smithers nodded quickly. "I didn't report it to the armorer," he said in a quaking voice. "I was afeared you'd give me extra duty."

"And this is the price you paid," Benoit said sadly, shaking his head. "A stripped nipple is *always* going to blow sooner or later. If infection doesn't set in and you live, your army days are over. Maybe, just maybe, Lieutenant Dobbs can save your other eye."

Ripping a piece off the wounded man's shirt, Benoit fashioned a crude bandage, wrapping the entire right side of Smithers's face.

"I think they're gone," Erich yelled.

Operating clumsily from his supine position, he had been loading the Hawken as rapidly as he could, firing blindly into the forest.

Suddenly Benoit was aware that he, Ashby, Erich, and the wounded Smithers were alone in the small clearing. "What happened to everybody?" he asked Ashby, looking around anxiously. "Where're the Cheyenne?"

"They went off in the woods," Ashby replied. "Takin' the fight to them fuckin' Crow."

As if to emphasize his words, Benoit was suddenly aware of the muted sounds of battle coming from deep in the trees. There was no gunfire; apparently neither group of Indians had firearms. But there were loud whoops and bloodcurdling screams that made the hair rise on the back of Benoit's neck. He could hear the twang of bowstrings, the whine of arrows flying through the air, and the crunch of war clubs smashing on flesh and bone.

"Hold your fire," he commanded Erich, who was lifting his newly loaded Hawken to his shoulder. "You might hit one of the Cheyenne."

"You're right," Erich replied, lowering his weapon.

As quickly as it started, it was over. Despite the sound of his own blood pumping furiously in his ears, Benoit was suddenly aware that everything was quiet, that the battle had either moved on or was over. Then the Cheyenne began emerging from the forest. Trembling Leaf came first, grinning broadly despite the fact that his left arm was dangling at his side, the result of a blow from a fiercely swung club. Still grinning, he lifted his good arm and raised two fingers, telling Ashby in Cheyenne that he had killed two Crow.

Almost on his heels was Little Wolf, the youth Benoit knew as David. Blood was running down his left leg from a knife slash across his thigh, but in his right hand he held a dark bundle that was dripping crimson onto the fresh pine needles. Benoit had to swallow when he saw the scalp, praying that he would not embarrass himself by throwing up.

When it was all sorted out, Ashby explained that the Cheyenne had killed five Crow while suffering one dead and two badly wounded. They did not, of course, count the dead and wounded soldiers as *their* casualties.

"Those Crow bastards won't be back," Ashby said with finality after he had heard the battle report. "By now they're probably halfway home, dragging their sorry asses behind them."

"Then let's get out of here ourselves," Benoit said briskly. "You okay?" he asked Erich.

"Let's go home," the youth replied solemnly.

"How's Smithers?" Ashby asked Benoit.

"Better than he deserves to be," Benoit grumbled. "He's lucky to be alive."

Quickly they transferred Erich's travois to Hendrickson's horse and threw the dead trooper's body over the horse's back.

"You ride my mount," Benoit said, boosting Smithers into the saddle. "I'll walk a spell. We don't have that far to go.

"Jim," he said, turning to Ashby, "tell Trembling Leaf again that we appreciate his help. Now let's get going before the weather turns really nasty."

During the skirmish the sky had clouded over, and small, white flakes were now flying in the swirling wind.

"It ain't going to last long," Ashby predicted as the small group split in two, the white men heading southeast toward Fort Laramie while the Cheyenne disappeared into the forest. "Too late in the sprang for a real blow."

Benoit dragged his bedroll off to the side, just far enough from the other men to insure himself some privacy. After digging in his saddlebags for his writing implements, he propped the folio that Inge had given him years before on his knee and began to write.

Along the Canadian River
5 May 1858

My Darling Inge,

Finally, I have had time to sit down and pull out my pen. The last three days have gone by in a blur since we have been traveling hard, trying to make up for the time we lost while I was engaged in the search for Erich and the subsequent confusion. You don't know how much it pained me to have to leave in such circumstances, what with you being pregnant and Erich bedridden, perhaps for life. No matter how hard I try I cannot erase from my memory the sight of him lying forlornly in bed, propped up by sandbags. Thank God for faithful, attentive Jace. Much of his medical lingo was lost on me (I'm still not sure I understand exactly what an "afferent sensory nerve" is and how it differs from an "efferent sensory nerve"), but the gist of what he said is frightening, the fact that Erich's paralysis is the result of an injury to his lower back, probably a compression of the spinal cord, and may be permanent.

As always, I am in awe of the courage displayed by your mother. Rather than falling apart as many others in her situation would have, she was incredibly resolute. In the four years since that fateful day along the Platte, my memory has dimmed and I had forgotten just how stoic she had been in the face of the loss of her husband, and later, in the knowledge that her leg would have to be amputated. I wish all my soldiers could be as brave. Erich obviously inherited the family trait; how he managed to remain in good spirits throughout the early days of his ordeal I'll never completely understand. I fear if it were me and I were faced with the prospect of going through the rest of my life as a cripple, I'd be sorely tempted to put my pistol to my head. As it is, I feel like a coward running from the scene of a fight, abandoning you in a time of personal crisis. It is my deepest wish that you will find it in your heart to forgive me. My guilt magnifies when I am forced to remember that it will be at least a year before I see you again, and when I do our lives will have been changed forever by the arrival of the baby.

Undoubtedly you can tell how weary we all are by the tone of this correspondence. We should be jolly, rejoicing in the fact that tomorrow we will be in Fort Union, and from there it will be only a relatively short journey to Fort Marcy. In a way, when I can shove my exhaustion aside, I'm excited about the prospect of what the future holds. Just a few weeks ago it never would have occurred to me that I'd really be leaving Fort Laramie, perhaps never to return. But now that reality is starting to sink in, I can't help but feel a tingle of excitement. So far, the journey has been long but uneventful. The Canadian River, alongside which we are camped tonight, is running very high and fast with snowmelt and it will be difficult to cross, but that is practically the only danger we have faced so far in the trip. Yesterday, we crossed paths with a civilian who begged to be allowed to travel with us since there are rumors of Comanches roving in the area. He is a very unusual-looking man, short and very dark with shiny black hair and huge, soulful brown eyes. He dresses in trousers made of goatskin, dyed a faded red. They are not nearly as handsome as the elkskin favored by the Cheyenne and Arapaho, but undoubtedly very serviceable. His blouse is made from inferior wool obviously loomed by his wife, and rather than a coat or a jacket, he wears a home-weaved blanket with a hole cut in the center for his head. Naturally he speaks only Spanish, which makes me realize yet again how necessary it will be for me to learn the language.

So far, language has not been a problem, however, because my traveling companions all speak one dialect or another. That very facility, you will remember, is why they are making the trip. There is a desperate need, I am told, at the New Mexico installations for soldiers who are able to communicate with the residents. Sergeant Wade, my highest-ranking enlisted man, claims to be more fluent than any of the others, and he has been my main interpreter. The sergeant's father is a merchant in a city in southern Texas called Brownsville, and his mother is a Mexican from a fairly well-to-do family. As a result, he grew up not only speaking Spanish, but having a good deal of exposure to the written language as well.

Have I told you the name of this poor traveler? I think not. In any case, and I hope I am getting this right, it is Porfilio Rodriguez, and he hails from a village deep in the mountains in the northern part of the territory. When Sergeant Wade told me the name of the village, I at first did not believe him; it was simply too many words. But the sergeant assures me it is correct. Earlier this evening I had him write it down for me so I could communicate it to you. The village is formally called—and here I am relaying Sergeant Wade's exact words—Santo Tomás Apostal del Río de las Trampas, or, in English, Saint Thomas the Apostle of the River of Traps. Commonly it is called Las Trampas. According to Sergeant Wade, *trampas* means "traps," but I am not sure of the precise connection between these "traps" and the name of the village and a river. I can only assume it once was a popular camping ground for the trappers who previously frequented the vicinity. I can see, though, that I have much to learn about this new place and its people.

Señor Rodriguez (the sergeant assures me that this is the proper form of address) is small and very dark with kinky hair, totally unlike that of the Plains Indians or any Spanish people I have met previously. Given Señor Rodriguez's complexion, I asked Sergeant Wade to inquire into his paternity. What we learned is that he is a direct descendant of a man named Sebastian Rodriguez, an African who came to New Mexico as a drummer boy with the Conquistador Diego de Vargas more than 150 years ago. That Rodriguez was later freed and became one of the pioneer settlers of the village where the family still resides.

Another interesting thing about Señor Rodriguez is his profession. Although most of those in his village are poor farmers, he is an artisan, a carver of religious figures. In Spanish, he is known as a *santero*. All winter, he told Sergeant Wade, he works on his statues and plaques, and in the spring and summer he travels far and wide, selling them. At present he is journeying to Santa Fe, where he hopes to do a good business in the marketplace. He has shown me some of his works, and I must admit that they are quite beautiful in their own rustic way, remarkably different from the holy figures that I grew up with in New Orleans. It is obvious that his models were fellow villagers because they all have the same general features of the Spanish and do not look at all like the northern Europeans which you and I are accustomed to seeing in religious paintings. At the risk of ruining the surprise, I purchased one of his small carvings for you. That is all I am going to tell you about it; I want to wait and let you see it.

If there was ever any doubt in my mind that things were going to be different in the New Mexico Territory, the mere presence of Señor Rodriguez has dispelled it. It is not only that he dresses strangely and speaks a language I cannot as yet understand, but his lifestyle, too, is unlike anything you have ever been exposed to. A deeply religious man, he unabashedly kneels to pray in the morning and the evening, and food never passes his lips without a prayer of thanks. The men, probably because of their exposure to the customs of other Spanish speakers, do not seem to find this in the least unusual, although I myself have been a little taken aback. The obsession with prayer reminds me very much of my childhood with the Jesuits, an experience I thought I had left far behind me.

While we have taken our meals almost entirely on the move, the fare has been our usual: dried meat and quickly boiled beans. Señor Rodriguez, on the other hand, seems to exist almost entirely on an item called—again I rely on Sergeant Wade—*atole*. Personally, I find it very unappetizing, maybe because I'm unsure if it's supposed to be a food or a beverage. Basically, it is a powder composed of ground meal with some local nuts called *piñon* mixed in. Its consistency resembles that of water from the Platte during the period of heavy flow, although it can be made thick or thin, depending on how much water is added. Despite its slightly revolting appearance, I am dying for a taste, but I fear I don't know the poor traveler well enough to ask.

In the beginning, I was worried about letting Señor Rodriguez join us because I thought he would slow us down, traveling as he is without a horse. The favored local mode of transportation, Sergeant Wade tells me, is the ass, which is usually referred to by its Spanish name, *burro*. Señor Rodriguez must make a tidy living as a *santero* because he has *two burros*—one of which he rides upon and one that he uses to carry his trove of carvings. I need not have worried about him not being able to keep the pace because his *burros* are capable of moving along quite rapidly. Perhaps they, too, fear the Comanches since Sergeant Wade tells me the nomadic tribes in this region—lacking access to the large herds of buffalo and elk that so predominate around Fort Laramie—like nothing better than to dine upon *burro,* mule, and horse, all of which, of course, they steal from villagers. After eating many a meal of fat puppy during my time with the Brulé and Cheyenne, I do not find this particularly unusual or unsettling, although the men seem to find it disgusting.

What I find most amusing about Señor Rodriguez—and I am sure he is unaware that he is acting for my amusement—is the way he guides his *burro*. Lacking a saddle, bridle, or halter, he uses instead a small club, really no more than a trimmed branch. When he wants his *burro* to go to the right, he taps it on the right side of the head with the cudgel. When he wants it to go the other way, he smacks it on the left.

Even as I write this, the good Señor
Rodriguez is deep in loud prayer, singing his sup-
plications to the stars. Every now and then I catch
a word I understand, which gives me hope that I
eventually will master the language. Witnessing
such an open and fervid display of faith makes
me realize how negligent I have been in giving
thanks for my own good fortune in having full use
of my arms and legs, not to mention how blessed
I am to have a beautiful wife who loves me. With
those thoughts fresh in my mind, I think I will
crawl under my blanket and try to drift quickly
into sleep, hoping you will visit me in my dreams.
I trust I'll be able to post this at Fort Union. I'm
told the mail service is quite good from there to
Missouri, then back to you via the Oregon Trail. I
will write again as soon as I get to Fort Marcy and
give you my first impressions of our new home.
With all my love, your devoted husband,

Jean

"It looks pretty barren to me," Sergeant Wade
declared, standing in his saddle and gazing across a
seemingly limitless open space, where the only colors
were green and blue—newly emerged spring grass
and the vast sky. Since crossing the Canadian early
that morning, the group had been traveling almost
due south, traversing a broad prairie that reminded
Benoit of Fort Laramie. Although they could see
mountains in the distance, the southern end of the
Rockies that Benoit knew were called the Sangre de
Cristos, this territory was relatively flat, consisting pri-

marily of treeless hills rolling off toward Santa Fe, a hard day's journey to the southwest.

At midmorning they spotted a sizable herd of antelope grazing on new shoots off to the west, but when Benoit agreed to let one of the privates pursue them in hopes of bagging fresh game, the animals dispersed quickly, disappearing over the horizon before the soldier could fire a shot.

"Don't worry too much about it, " Benoit said consolingly. "We'll have a feast once we get to Fort Union."

A little after noon, after stopping alongside a small creek that ran fresh and cool through a cut in the hills so everyone could gobble a quick lunch of buffalo jerky and hardtack—except for Rodriguez, who stuck to his *atole*—they intersected a well-traveled path that wound as far as they could see in a northeast-southwest direction.

"The Santa Fe Trail, I imagine," Benoit said, noting the mule and horse droppings and the deep ruts worn down to the underlying rocks by the passage of uncounted wagons.

"Look!" shouted Sergeant Wade, pointing down the trail. "Dust!"

"Let's catch up," Benoit yelled, spurring his horse forward. Eagerly the men followed him, leaving Rodriguez flailing his *burro*, cursing loudly.

"Blue shirts," Benoit said excitedly ten minutes later when they got close enough to see the group ahead. "Must be a trail patrol."

"That's right, we're from Fort Union," the young brevet second lieutenant confirmed after Benoit and his men had joined the two dozen travel-worn troopers. "My name's O'Hara," he said, offering a sunburned hand. "Sean O'Hara. Dayton, Ohio."

O'Hara was painfully thin, with reddish blond hair and a mass of freckles. Benoit wondered if he actually was old enough to be in the army.

"So you're bound for Fort Marcy?" O'Hara asked after Benoit introduced himself and his men.

"After we refresh ourselves at Fort Union," Benoit said, nodding.

"We can use some refreshing ourselves." O'Hara smiled. "We been on the trail for two weeks. It's going to feel real good to have a bath and a beer."

"I know what you mean," Benoit said sympathetically. "Tough patrol?"

O'Hara shook his head. "Just boring. The men on the Mountain Branch are getting most of the action these days. The Cutoff's been real quiet."

Benoit looked confused. "I don't understand," he said. "What's the Mountain Branch and the Cutoff?"

"You really are new to the territory, aren't you?"

"Fill me in, why don't you?"

"At Cimarron, in Kansas just west of Fort Atkinson, the trail breaks into two branches," O'Hara explained. "One heads almost due west, then turns abruptly south, coming through the dreaded Raton Pass and straight south to Fort Union. The other heads southwest out of Cimarron, meandering through a bunch of nothing. It joins the Mountain Branch just south of Fort Union. That's the one we're on now."

"Why *two* trails?" Benoit asked. "Funny I never heard of but one."

"It's not two trails," O'Hara said patiently. "It's two *branches*. The Mountain Branch is about a hundred miles longer."

"Well, if it's longer, how come any people use it at all?"

"The Cutoff has hardly any water, so it's a long stretch for wagons and mules. If someone gets delayed for some reason or falls behind schedule, they could be in real trouble. Some merchants would rather take the longer route and not worry about their mules dying of thirst before they can get to Santa Fe. Besides, the Cutoff used to be the dangerous route, back when the Kiowas and Comanches were all stirred up. But they've been pretty quiet of late, confining their activities to raids on the settlements. Stealing a few horses, women, children, that kind of thing. But it's the Utes, the Jicarilla, and the Navajos who've been acting fierce lately. The Mountain Branch is in their area."

"That's interesting," Benoit said. "I didn't think Indians were much of a problem in the territory anymore."

"They're not, really. The main problem right now is trying to convince the greasers that they're Americans."

"The who?"

"The chili-bellies. About ninety-nine percent of everybody in the territory who isn't an Indian is either Spanish or Mexican. It's been that way for such a long time, they're having trouble adjusting to the fact that now this area is part of the United States. They don't want *gringos*, us white Americans, here. They make that pretty plain. To them, we're just *extranjeros*, foreigners."

"Is there any real trouble?"

"Depends on what you call real trouble. About ten years ago, I've been told, some greasers got the Pueblo Indians at Taos, which is west of here, all fired up, and they had a minor revolt. The governor, Charles Bent, the man the fort's named after, was unlucky enough to be visiting there at the time. The injuns snagged him and scalped him while he was still alive and then shot him when he tried to escape. Then they nailed his scalp to a board and carried it all around the village, showing it off like it was something to be real proud of. Then they went on and grabbed several more Americans, torturing them, scalping them, and eventually killing them, too. One of 'em was a federal district attorney named Leal. They really worked him over. Stripped him nude—and this was the middle of winter, mind you—and marched him through the streets while they poked at his face with lances. This went on for a long time, him begging them to kill him. Finally, they threw him in a ditch and left him there for several hours to see if he'd freeze to death, I guess. When they came back, he was still alive, so they finished him off. Then they cut up his body and fed it to the hogs."

Benoit gave him a horrified look. "Are you making this up?"

O'Hara shook his head solemnly. "I swear it's true. I didn't see it, but I heard it from some who did."

"Then what happened?"

"Oh, they killed six or seven more Americans at a place called Arroyo Hondo, and a couple more at Red River. All told, I think, there were a dozen murdered."

"What was the final resolution?"

"The commander at Santa Fe, a Colonel Price, went after 'em with three hundred and fifty troops and four mountain howitzers. By the time he got to the place where they decided to fight, a town called Santa Cruz, there were about two thousand of 'em. They fought all of one afternoon before the rebels broke and ran. Price went after 'em. Five days later, they fought again near a place called Embudo, means 'funnel.' It's a narrow canyon, vaguely shaped like a funnel. Again, Pierce made 'em retreat. Pretty soon the rebels found themselves back in Taos, where Price opened up on 'em with the howitzers. Caught 'em in a crossfire from four hundred yards while they were holed up in the church. Finally, the howitzers blew a hole in the wall of the church, which was three feet thick. It was a real fight; the church was totally destroyed. Price suffered ten men killed and fifty-two wounded, but the rebels had one hundred and fifty men killed and at least that many wounded."

"And it's been quiet since then? Between the Spanish and Mexicans . . . what do you call them?"

"I call them greasers."

"What *else* are they called?" Benoit asked sternly, adding the word, "Lieutenant."

"Hispanos," O'Hara replied, seemingly only mildly chastised.

"So the Hispanos have been peaceful?"

"No, there's always talk of another revolt, but there hasn't been anything major. In Santa Fe, though, there are a lot of young . . ." He paused. "Hispanos, who make it clear they don't like Americans, especially American soldiers. About once every couple of weeks they find the body of a trooper who's wandered off alone in the back streets and been murdered by local thugs. They never find out who did it; civilian law enforcement is a joke. But remember when you get there: Be careful where you go."

"Is the city really that bad?" Benoit asked, wondering what he might be bringing his wife and child into.

"Not at all!" O'Hara said brightly. "You'll like it. There's a lot to do. Plenty of good whorehouses . . ."

"I'm married."

"Oh, well. In that case, there are the gambling halls. Open twenty-four hours a day, every day."

"I'm not much of a gambler, either."

"You don't have to be. There's some pretty good entertainment at the halls. When you get there, be sure and visit a place called La Estrella. It means 'The Star.'"

"What's so special about it?"

"It's run by a woman named Doña Rosalia. You'll fall in love with her, I guarantee it."

"That's just what I need."

Ortiz laughed. "She must be sixty years old. Short and ugly, but she sings like an angel. And she's the best monte dealer in the whole damn territory."

"Monte? What's that?"

O'Hara laughed. "You'll find out. Also, you'll like the Santa Fe restaurants. They have several good ones."

"Restaurants!" Benoit said, feeling his mouth begin to water. "I haven't eaten in a restaurant in more than four years."

"Something else to look forward to. I predict you'll enjoy New Mexico. There are a lot of attractions there that you probably don't find on the Plains. Fort Laramie must have been a real hellhole."

"It has its points." Benoit laughed. "How about Fort Union?"

O'Hara shrugged. "It's not bad. The work is dull and it's frustrating being posted off in the middle of nowhere, but it has advantages. Is today Saturday?"

Benoit thought for a minute. "Yeah. Must be."

"Good. You picked a fine time to show up. Saturdays are extraordinary. That's when Captain Lang—"

"He's the commander?"

"Yeah. John Lang. You know him?"

"I went to the academy with a Lang, but his name was Albert. I wonder if that was his younger brother. I remember Al saying he had an older sibling who was already in the army."

O'Hara shook his head. "I've never heard him mention a younger brother. Still, he's a good man. He takes care of his troops. He knows none of us are too happy to be isolated up here instead of in Santa Fe, so he tries to make it as enjoyable for us as he can."

"Why *are* you up here? Couldn't you ride patrol on the trail from Santa Fe just as easily?"

"Sure we could. Fort Union was Colonel Sumner's idea. He hand-picked the location specifically to get the troops out of Santa Fe, which he called, and I quote, 'a sink of vice and extravagance.'"

Benoit laughed. "I didn't realize ol' Bull o' the Woods was a prude."

"I can't speak for him personally," O'Hara said tactfully, "but he sure wanted his men to be chaste. You met him?"

"I was on the Cheyenne expedition last year," Benoit said, unconsciously rubbing the scar on his chest, the result of a near fatal wound suffered at the hands of a warrior named Short Hair. "I'm not likely to forget that campaign." Then he added bitterly, "And neither will the Cheyenne."

"The way I hear it," O'Hara said, looking at Benoit with newfound respect, "is y'all really laid it on them injuns."

"Ummmm," Benoit grunted noncommittally. "But you were saying about Saturday nights?"

"Oh, yeah," O'Hara said brightly. "On Saturday nights the captain lets us cut loose."

"Cut loose?" Benoit laughed. "What do you do? Screw sheep?"

"Sheep might be an improvement over some of the whores at the Loam."

Benoit wrinkled his brow. "The Loam?"

"Short for Loma Prada." O'Hara chuckled. "It's a little village to the south, mostly whorehouses and bars, that sprung up when Colonel Sumner moved the fort. But that's not the point. On Saturday nights we all get together, officers and men. Out on the parade ground, if the weather's nice. If it's not, we move the bunks out of Company A's barracks and gather in there. Then we have a little *entertainment*."

"What kind of entertainment?" Benoit asked, raising an eyebrow.

O'Hara shrugged. "Whatever's available. Or I should say, whoever's available. We've got a private named Calhoun who can play a fiddle so sad you'll want to cry. One of the officers, Lieutenant Hapworth, can recite Shakespeare like you wouldn't believe. . . ."

"You mean the enlisted men happily listen to the Bard?" Benoit asked in disbelief.

"You bet," O'Hara replied cheerfully. "They love it! Can't get enough of it. I think their favorite passage is the one from *Twelfth Night*. 'What is love? 'tis not hereafter; Present mirth hath present laughter. . . .' You know how that goes?"

"It's been a long time," Benoit said, chuckling. "But it rings a faint bell."

"Some of the men are pretty good gymnasts, too, and every couple of weeks or so they put on an exhibition. During the summer, the captain gives us the whole afternoon off and we hold *burro* races around the parade ground or there's a rooster pull—"

"A what?" Benoit interrupted.

"Basically, a horsemanship contest," O'Hara said, laughing. "What you do is bury a rooster in the sand until only its head is sticking out. Then the men take turns riding by at full gallop and try to pull its head off. . . ."

"No kidding," Benoit said. "I'd bet a Cheyenne or a Sioux would be able to do it every time."

"I don't know about them," O'Hara said, "but for us it's a real contest. When the captain sends out word there's going to be a rooster pull, men come from as far away as Alburquerque and Taos."

"So what's on tap for tonight?"

"Don't know," O'Hara said. "We've been out for two weeks, so there's no telling what the men have planned. You can count on one thing, though."

"What's that?" Benoit asked.

"You'll be asked to perform."

Benoit yanked on his horse's reins. "Me!" he cried, shocked. "What do you mean?"

"It's tradition." O'Hara grinned. "Visitors are always asked to contribute."

"I have no talent," Benoit said, looking worried. "I can't do a damn thing except make a great cup of coffee."

"Well, you'd better get ready for it. If you don't do *something*, you have to buy a round for the whole house. And there's a hundred and fifty men on the post, give or take."

"Well, I guess there's always *one* thing I can do," Benoit grumbled.

"Oh, yeah. What's that?"

"Screw a sheep."

O'Hara noticed the shocked look on Benoit's face when they rode into the wall-less Fort Union, passing the ordnance department, an enlisted men's barracks, and a row of small, cabinlike structures reserved for officers.

"Pretty dilapidated, isn't it?" O'Hara asked, smothering a grin. "It looked this way when I came here a year and a half ago. Only a little better."

"How old did you say this place was?" Benoit asked.

"Built in 1851. Seven years ago. Hard to believe, huh? Considering its condition, I mean."

Benoit studied one of the officers' homes, its raw pine logs already showing major signs of deterioration, its walls sagging inward, seemingly in immediate danger of collapsing. Would I want Inge and my son living in a place like this? he asked himself.

"Don't worry," O'Hara said cheerfully, as if reading his mind. "Fort Marcy is much better."

"Why is this so, uh, run-down?"

O'Hara shrugged. "Built in a hurry by people who didn't really know how to build. Colonel Sumner was just anxious to get it up and get the men the hell out of Santa Fe."

"Is it as bad inside as it looks on the outside?"

"Worse," O'Hara said, nodding. "The roofs leak and vermin are a real problem. Mice, rats, the occasional snake. They're already talking about building a new fort, several miles east of here, smack on the Cutoff instead of on the Mountain Branch."

"Looks to me like they could have done it yesterday," Benoit said caustically.

"Well, you know the army. They've been here seven years, and it's taken the brass that long to decide the current location is not totally defensible. Too close to the mesa or something. Sounds like hogwash to me."

"What's there to defend against? I thought you said the Indians aren't that belligerent anymore."

"Who's talking about injuns? The worry these days is the Confederates. The muckety-mucks in Washington reckon when war comes, Fort Union—and all the forts in New Mexico, for that matter—will be prime targets for an enemy moving out of Texas."

Despite himself, Benoit felt his interest rise. "Why do they say that?"

O'Hara shrugged. "Who knows why high-ranking officers say anything? Historically, though, it wouldn't be the first time Texans invaded New Mexico. No matter what uniform, if any, they're wearing."

"Is that right? I didn't know that had been a problem before."

"Let's just say it's a continuing fight," O'Hara said with a smile. "After they won their independence from Mexico in 1836, Texans decided that all the territory up to the eastern bank of the Río del Norte, which would include where we are right now, belonged to their republic. But they didn't try to do anything about it until 1841, when a ragtag army of three hundred men marched in to try to enforce the claim by capturing Santa Fe. The attempt failed, of course—the mercenaries were captured long before they got to the capital and were marched off as prisoners to Mexico—but it helped build a distrust of Texans in the New Mexicans' minds."

"That doesn't have anything to do with Confederates."

"No, except the people here might have difficulty making the distinction. Texans are Texans. I personally agree with those in Washington who believe that when war comes, the New Mexico forts will be at definite risk."

"*When* war comes. Not if?"

"When," O'Hara repeated. "I saw a Memphis newspaper last week in Fort Atkinson, and even granted the fact that it would naturally be pro-Southern, the war drums seem to have increased in volume."

"Why, what's happening?" Benoit asked, hoping his anxiety was not reflected in his voice. "Is there something going on that I don't know about? I've been out of touch."

"No," O'Hara said, shaking his head. "Just the same old thing. Hell is still being raised over President Buchanan's proposal to admit Kansas as a slave state and salvage the Lecompton constitution. Stephen Douglas is campaigning against it, but nothing solid. Don't worry yet, the South still hasn't seceded."

To his own surprise, Benoit felt a tremendous sense of relief. Each day without a major event meant one more day when he would not have to make a final decision about where to place his loyalty.

"Well," O'Hara said, reining his horse before a building that looked even more ramshackle than the others, "here we are. The abode of the commanding officer, Fort Union, territory of New Mexico. If you want to go on in and report to Captain Lang, I'll have my sergeant arrange for quarters for your men. See you at the festivities this evening? Dinner begins at five-thirty, and the activities at seven o'clock."

"Soon as I get a bath and a fresh uniform," Benoit said, dismounting. "I enjoyed the conversation. You know quite a bit about local history."

"Hobby of mine," O'Hara said lightly. "Don't forget that you have to prepare something for this evening. Either that or bring plenty of money."

Benoit grinned. "I'll think of something."

"I'm sure you will. By the way," he added with a grin, "do you like your sheep shorn or unshorn?"

Benoit was amazed at the amount of preparation that had gone into the operation. When he walked into the barracks after a large but unimaginative meal of stewed beef and boiled potatoes, he was surprised to see that decorations of brightly colored paper hung on the walls and large groups of lanterns had been spaced around the sizable room in an attempt to give it a theaterlike atmosphere.

Over the meal, his table companion, the Bard-quoting Lieutenant Gerald Hapworth, had explained that the Saturday night festivities were still being held indoors because May nights in the mountains tended to be chilly, with the thermometer often dropping into the thirties. But the literature-loving officer had said nothing to indicate to Benoit just how seriously the men of Fort Union regarded their weekend galas.

In one corner of the room, lanterns had been laid in a semicircle to delineate the area reserved for the "band," in this case a bugle, a fiddle, a triangle, two guitars, a kazoo, and a snare drum. Along each of the two long walls of the rectangular room were tables that served as makeshift bars. Captain Lang, Benoit had learned, was more liberal in his treatment of the troops than most commanders. After making it understood that drunkenness and brawling absolutely would not be tolerated, he permitted beer drinking on post at the Saturday night activities as long as the privilege was not abused.

Drawing a beer from one of the two kegs that had been set up behind the bars, Benoit took his glass and found a spot on the fringe of the crowd, not too close to the "stage," but not too far away, either.

Sipping the bitter, locally produced brew, Benoit studied the crowd. The men, enlisted and officers alike, were in shirtsleeves, apparently in deference to the steamroomlike quality that would permeate the room as the evening wore on. They were all, Benoit noticed, exuberant without being boisterous, cheerful and expectant, but not clamorous.

Lieutenant Hapworth, the unofficial master of ceremonies, strode confidently to the center of the room and raised his arms for silence, the signal that the night's entertainment was about to begin.

Without fanfare, Hapworth introduced the first performer, a private from C Company, who marched onto the stage, grinning happily, his teeth shining from a face blackened with ash. Brandishing a scarred banjo, the private launched into a spirited rendition of "Oh! Susanna!" It was obviously one of the troopers' favorites, for they cheered lustily when it was over.

Less well received, perhaps because of the political overtones, was an A Company corporal's off-key delivery of "Darling Nelly Gray," a song designed to arouse sympathy for the slaves.

Benoit's riding companion, Lieutenant O'Hara, gave a passionate reading of the poem "Maud Muller" from John Greenleaf Whittier's book, *The Panorama*, and a C Company sergeant named MacLean was good-naturedly booed off the stage—apparently a staple event, Benoit deduced—after only a few opening notes on a battered, screeching bagpipe. While the sergeant was vacating the stage, Hapworth explained to Benoit that the instrument had been purchased in Santa Fe from an *arriero*, a Hispano muleteer, who had lugged it all the way from Chihuahua City. The fact that MacLean had not the slightest idea how to play it helped account for his rude reception and quick removal.

After the unfortunate MacLean retreated to the beer keg, three bare-chested young troopers from Company B bounded into the center of the room in a series of leaps, flips, and somersaults. For the next twenty minutes they put on an exhibition of gymnastics that left the crowd whistling and stomping.

By popular demand, Lieutenant Hapworth surrendered his emcee hat to render a scene from Shakespeare's satire on love and war, *Troilus and Cressida*, ending with the memorable quote from the character Thersites: "Lechery, lechery, still wars and lechery! Nothing else holds fashion."

"That just about sums up our situation as well,"

he said, taking a deep bow while the soldiers clapped wildly.

"Okay," a beaming Hapworth told Benoit softly with a wink and a leer. "It's your turn. Or would you rather buy the beer?"

"With a newly pregnant wife, the last thing I want to do is spend money on other men's drinks," Benoit said happily, and strode to the center of the stage.

While the soldiers were settling down, Benoit beckoned to three men in the front row and whispered something in their ears. Then he asked for a fresh glass of beer.

"I'm going to tell you a story that's oft repeated in the city I call home," he said loudly after he had the troopers' attention. "But first I'm going to introduce you to a song that was popular among my peers. It's a drinking song called '*Si Je Meurs*,' 'If I Die.' I'm going to sing it first in French, which is the only proper way for a Creole to do it. Then I'll repeat it in English. Do what I do."

Clearing his throat, he adopted a solemn expression and lifted his beer glass to eye level.

"*Si je meurs, je veux que l'on m'enterre,*" he began in a trembling baritone.

> *Dans la cave, où il y a du vin,*
> *Le deux pied contre la muraille*
> *Et la tête sous le robinet.*

Lifting his glass above his head, he tipped it until a few drops fell into his open mouth.

> *Si il tombe quelques goutres*
> *Ce sera pour me rafraichir,*

Si le tonneau se défonce
Qui j'en boive à ma fantaisie.

When he finished, he again lifted the glass over his head and poured the remainder of the beer in a steady stream down his throat.

"In English! In English!" the troopers chanted.

"Okay." Benoit grinned. "But I need a new glass of beer."

Immediately one was passed to him, hand to hand, freshly drawn from the keg on his right. He again cleared his throat and stared gravely into the near distance.

"If I die," he began, then paused. "Does everyone have a beer?" he asked jocularly.

"Go on! Go on!" the troopers yelled.

Grinning, he started over.

If I die, I wish to be buried
In the cellar, where there is wine,
Both feet against the wall
And the head under the faucet.

"Now just a little beer," he instructed the crowd, lifting his glass and letting some drip into his mouth.

If a few drops happen to fall
It will be to refresh me,
But if the barrel opens up
I will drink all I want. . . .

Having concluded, he poured the beer into his open mouth.

When the troopers tried to imitate him, half of

them missed their mouths with the stream of beer, splashing it in their faces or down the front of their shirts.

"It happens all the time," Benoit laughingly told Hapworth. "It takes quite a bit of practice and a hell of a lot of beer to learn how to hit your mouth. I haven't done it in a long time, and I was worried I might screw it up."

"They love you now," Hapworth said, mopping his chin, "but they're going to hate you in the morning when they have to scrub the floor."

"You promised us a story, too," called a frail-looking corporal in the front row.

"Story! Story!" the troopers began to chant, picking up on the prompt.

Benoit nodded to the three men he had whispered instructions to earlier. At his command they quickly went around the room, lowering the flames in the lanterns until it was almost dark.

"This is a ghost story," Benoit said loudly when the troopers began to look questioningly at one another. "I need the right atmosphere."

"Ah," they sighed. "Ghost story! Ghost story!"

"As all of you undoubtedly know," Benoit began, "New Orleans at one time was under the king of Spain, just as the New Mexico Territory was not many years ago. In those days, not far from where my family now lives, there was a large building that served as a barracks for several companies of Spanish soldiers. One day, an order came down from the general which said that troops were needed in the Floridas, so all except one company of the troops marched away to fight the Indians. Now," he went on, "this building also served as the paymaster's headquarters, and as such, a considerable amount of gold was kept there to pay the troops. . . ."

"I wish they'd do that here," a voice called from the rear of the room.

"Quiet," another voice said. "Don't interrupt."

"After most of the troops marched away," Benoit continued, unfazed, "those in the remaining company suddenly realized they could be very rich if they could steal some of this gold and hide it. That way, even when the theft was discovered, no one would know who took it or where it went. But"—and he emphasized the word—"there was a problem."

"There's *always* a problem," the same voice called from the rear.

"Shut up, Hardy," one of the troopers yelled. "Or we're going to throw your butt out of here."

"What was the problem?" another soldier yelled.

"The problem"—Benoit smiled—"was that some of the troopers didn't want to go along with the theft."

Ooohs and ahhs echoed around the room.

"So what did they do?" Hardy called.

"They stole the money anyway," Benoit said. "But since they didn't want those who refused to go along to turn them in, they knew they were going to have to take care of them."

"What does that mean?" a soldier wanted to know. "You mean the thieves killed them?"

"Yes." Benoit nodded. "Slowly and deliberately. They murdered them in a very horrible fashion."

"You mean like the Comanches and the Navajos do to their captives?" yelled Hardy.

"Worse," said Benoit. "What they did was hang them on spikes driven into the wall, as if they were beef carcasses."

"That's pretty grim," said one of the troopers, grimacing.

"But that wasn't all," Benoit said. "To make sure the men's weight didn't pull them to the ground, thereby killing them instantly, they drove spikes through their feet. In essence, they nailed them to the wall."

"Like Christ on the cross," offered one of the troopers, a sallow-faced youth with long blond hair that dangled in his eyes.

"Those bastards," another began.

"Hold on!" Benoit said, raising his arms. "That's still not all. To make sure they died slowly and painfully, the thieves tied huge rats to their stomachs, knowing that when the rats got hungry they would begin gnawing on the meat in front of them. That is, the condemned men's bellies."

"That's terrible."

"It's inhuman."

"Barbaric."

"Did the men die?" asked the wide-eyed blond-haired soldier.

Benoit nodded. "This is a not a story with a happy ending. The men died very painfully. And it took them a long time."

"What about the thieves?" Hardy yelled.

"Yes!" the soldiers yelled. "What about the thieves?"

"They got away with it completely," Benoit said, shaking his head. "Some of them, the tale goes, invested their money wisely and became very wealthy and influential. Some of them returned to Spain as rich men. But several of them actually stayed in New Orleans, where their descendants are today regarded as prominent citizens. Of course, no one can *document* the source of their wealth; there's no *proof* they were thieves. There are only rumors."

"But what about the ghosts?" Hardy persisted. "I thought you said this was a ghost story."

"Ah-ha!" Benoit laughed. "Indeed it is. There are many people—I know several of them personally—who swear that the barracks, before it was torn down a few years before I was born, virtually reverberated with moans and shrieks, supposedly the agonizing cries of the men who died there. In addition, those who dared venture into the building after dark say the tormented faces appeared on the wall where they were impaled and murdered, glowing like dim lanterns.

"And the rats!" Benoit added loudly. "For years, rats as large as hound dogs were said to materialize as if from thin air. Those who saw them said they simply emerged out of the wall, then gathered in the nearby courtyard, where they romped and played like bear cubs. Some people tried to lure the rats away with food, but the beasts would never touch anything that was offered. It was as if they had eaten enough to last them through eternity."

"That stuff about rats is all nonsense," the trooper called Hardy yelled. "We have enough rats around here to know they'll eat anything, anytime."

"And how much do *your* rats weigh?" Benoit asked.

Hardy shrugged. "I don't know. Two or three pounds, maybe?"

"And if you picked one up, you wouldn't be straining yourself?"

"No, I don't think so," Hardy said, smelling a trap. "Not that I'd want to."

"Well," Benoit said, "one of my father's friends was a physician, and I heard him telling my papa one day about a man he had treated a number of years before."

"Treated him for what? A rat bite?" Hardy scoffed.

"No," Benoit said solemnly. "For an arm that was broken in so many places that it had to be amputated."

"What'd he do? Fall out of a tree?" Hardy asked sarcastically.

"No," Benoit said. "The patient said he was watching the rats at play and something inspired him to try to join in the game. Squatting on the ground, he held his arm out in front of him and one of the rats ran up it. He told the doctor he was sure the rat weighed at least a thousand pounds because his arm was crushed so badly, it looked as though it had been run over by a beer wagon."

The men began cheering.

"Good story!" the blond youth yelled. "You know any more?"

"I know *lots* of ghost stories," Benoit said, nodding. "New Orleans has hundreds of spirits. Some of them much more dreadful than those poor soldiers."

"Tell us!" the troopers chanted.

Benoit smiled. "Not tonight," he said. "I'd probably scare myself so badly I wouldn't be able to sleep."

"Aw, go on!" the blond youth guffawed.

Lieutenant Hapworth jumped into the open space in front of Benoit. "That's enough for tonight, men. Captain Benoit will be back—we hope with some more stories. Now the band has been waiting patiently. Let's dance!"

While Benoit watched in amusement, half of the

men whipped out bandannas, which they tied around their left arms to signify they would be the "women" during the dance. The following week, Hapworth explained, the roles would be reversed. Tonight's "women" would be the "men" at the next dance.

"Sounds fair to me," Benoit said, straight-faced. "But I still keep hearing rumors about sheep."

Benoit, feeling somewhat tipsy as a result of the unaccustomed alcohol, was chatting with Hapworth when Captain Lang approached. In his late thirties—about Dobbs's age, Benoit guessed—tall and slim, with broad shoulders and a thick chest, he could easily have passed for Benoit's brother, except that Lang was a blond.

"You put on a good show," he told Benoit, slapping him vigorously on the shoulder. "I'm sorry I didn't catch it all. I came in just at the end of your song. Would have been here sooner, but I was stuck at my desk. You wouldn't believe the paperwork that Washington is demanding these days. I also apologize if I seemed rather abrupt this afternoon. I had a lot on my plate when you first came in."

"Think nothing of it, Captain."

"Call me John," Lang said with a grin. "You're a captain just like me."

Benoit blushed. "N-not exactly," he stammered. "I'm only a brevet. And the promotion came so recently, I still have trouble remembering that I'm no longer a lowly lieutenant."

Accepting a glass of beer from the private tending the keg, Lang locked eyes with Benoit and motioned with his head. "Why don't we go get some fresh air?"

Benoit frowned. "Sure," he said. "Mind if I bring my beer?"

"By all means," Lang replied, turning and working his way through the crowd.

"Ah, this is better," Lang said, stretching and taking a deep breath. There was no moon, so the sky seemed blanketed with stars. A faint breeze blew from the east, carrying the smell of burning *piñon* from the cook shack. "I truly love it out here. I'd have a hard time if I ever had to go back to Illinois."

"Is that your home?" Benoit asked.

Lang nodded. "Springfield. Born and raised there. Hope I don't have to die there, too."

"I knew a Lang at the academy," Benoit said. "His name was Albert. But I think he was from somewhere in Massachusetts."

"Never heard of him. But I do know your old commander, Captain Kemp. I was a young officer in his command at Fort Leavenworth years ago."

"It's Colonel Kemp now. He's a brevet light colonel."

"Good. He deserves to be promoted. Tough but fair, which is what I think makes a good officer. I hope my men think of me that way, too."

"You seem to have good troopers."

"They are," Lang agreed. "By and large. Have a few troublemakers, just like everyone else. But so far no major problems."

"I'd bet one of them is that private named Hardy."

Lang laughed. "Herman Hardy, the old Pittsburgh Pounder. Known far and wide for his proclivity to engage in undisciplined fisticuffs. Yeah, he can be a handful sometimes. Been in the army longer than I have. He's been busted more times than my aunt

Jane's china. Every time he makes corporal, it seems as
if he can't stand the responsibility and does something
stupid to have his stripes taken away. He's what I call
a fighting soldier: a good man to have on your side in
a skirmish; a pain in the ass when there's no action."

"I've seen a couple like that myself," Benoit nodded.

"Let's sit," Lang said, pointing at a large boulder a
few feet away. "I'll give you a quick read on the situation in the territory."

Benoit sipped his beer and remained silent, waiting for Lang to continue.

"You know anything about the history of the
church in New Mexico?" Lang asked several minutes
later.

"A little," Benoit said, struggling to recall what
Dobbs had told him and what he had read. "The
Franciscans came up with the *Conquistadores*, didn't
they?"

"That's right." Lang nodded. "Then when Spain
turned the territory over to Mexico, the Franciscans
were replaced with home-grown priests."

"I understand that," said Benoit, "but what does
all that have to do with us?"

Lang smiled sardonically. "It's complicated and
rather subtle. But here's the basics: The church is still
the major power in New Mexico—"

"But it's now a territory, for God's sake," Benoit
interrupted. "Part of the United States. You know, sep-
aration of church and state and all that."

"A *new* territory," Lang corrected. "These people—the Hispanos, I'm talking about—have been living this way for two hundred and fifty years. They're
not going to change just because they're told they're

now under the jurisdiction of some government in some place they've never heard of. Most New Mexicans—excluding the Indians, of course—are simple farmers. For two and a half centuries they've led very tough lives. Madrid didn't give a shit about them. And neither did Mexico City. Once the Spanish found out that New Mexico didn't have cities with streets of gold and that there was no Northwest Passage on the other side of the Sangre de Cristos, they lost all interest. They left the New Mexicans to fend for themselves. And since the people didn't have a strong government to unite them, they fell back on the one thing on which they could rely: their faith. The church."

"The people in Louisiana are very religious, too. . . ."

"No," Lang said, waggling a finger. "This isn't just about religion. It's about organization and authority as well. The Franciscans told the people how to live their lives, threatening them with religious retaliation if they didn't listen. You're a Catholic, aren't you?"

"Yeah, but—"

"I'm an Episcopalian myself, but that's a cousin to a Catholic, so I can understand strong ties between the people and the church. I'm not saying that the Franciscans were wrong. Far from it. From my point of view, they created a viable society where none would have existed without them. But they also forged a very strong bond between church and state that just doesn't work under our form of government. You follow me?"

"Sure, but—"

"Okay. So we had the Franciscans setting a pattern of reliance on the church that was ingrained in the people over two hundred years. But when they left in

1821, there was a hell of a vacuum. The church in
Mexico, which also had been a creation of the Spanish,
proved itself incapable of extending its authority way
up here. The bishop in Durango—you'll undoubtedly
hear more about him; his name, let me see if I can get
it right, is José Antonio Laureano López de Zubiría y
Escalante, otherwise known as Bishop Zubiría—
thought he could solve the control problem by recruiting New Mexico men, then sending them through the
seminary at Durango, where they could be indoctri-
nated into the Mexican way of thinking. That way, in
theory, when they came back to New Mexico, they
would feel obligated to his authority. It didn't work.
Zubiría's arm wasn't long enough. The men he
recruited and educated, for the most part, have proved
corrupt and very political. Do you know anything
about that revolt in Taos in 1848?"

"Lieutenant O'Hara told me about it."

"Good. He's a fair historian. For an amateur.
Anyway, it is widely believed that one of the master-
minds behind the revolt was one of Zubiría's priests, a
Father Antonio José Martinez. He's still in Taos, by the
way."

"What do you mean, 'corruption'?" Benoit asked.

"Oh, the usual things." Lang shrugged. "There's a
popular priest in Alburquerque, a Father José Manuel
Gallegos, who's said to be too worldly. He likes to
gamble. He likes to live well. And he has in residence
in his rectory a very beautiful woman who, rumor has
it, was previously the mistress of two Mexican army
officers. No doubt Father Gallegos is interested in her
soul. He's also very political. A few years ago he
served a term as New Mexico's delegate to Congress in
Washington. He was elected to a second term, but the

House refused to seat him. That's another story, though. Other priests, it is said, are making a tidy living by levying extortionary charges for common services, such as weddings, funerals, and baptisms. Others are rumored to be openly supporting mistresses and various illegitimate children."

"Forgive my ignorance," Benoit interrupted, "but I don't see what this has to do with me."

"Ah, but it does," Lang said ponderously. "Let me continue."

"Okay. I didn't mean to break your chain of thought."

"That's all right. Anyway, shortly after New Mexico became part of the United States, following the late, great war, the American clergy decided that the new territory should be under the spiritual care of an *American* rather than a Mexican. Rome agreed, and they made the territory a new archdiocese, which I gather is our equivalent of a state. And the pope named someone to run it, thereby cutting Zubiría out altogether. Only the new bishop isn't exactly an American. His name is Jean Lamy and he's a Frenchman by birth, although he had been working in a mission in the States—in Ohio, I believe—when the appointment was made. His chief assistant, kind of like your position vis-à-vis General Barksdale, is another French priest named Joseph Machebeuf. Both of them are very competent men. I know Don José— that's Machebeuf—much better than I know the bishop. He's a good man. You'll like him."

"I still don't—"

"Dammit, Jean, let me explain in my own way. Sometimes I take the long way around, but I eventually get there."

"You sound like Colonel Kemp now." Benoit chuckled. "I tend to get impatient."

"Curb it, my boy. This is New Mexico. Not for nothing is it called Mañanaland. As I was saying, when Lamy and Machebeuf came in about seven years ago—it was before my time—the first thing they wanted to do was enact a number of reforms. Not surprisingly, this hasn't sat well with the entrenched clerics, priests like Martinez and Gallegos, not to mention Zubiría, who, from what I gather, is being a real horse's ass about the whole matter. In short, it hasn't been easy for the new regime, and things are still far from settled. Martinez and Gallegos are fighting Lamy and Machebeuf as hard as they can. There's a real war going on."

He paused and took a sip of beer. Benoit bit his tongue and held his silence.

"You see," Lang continued, "it's mostly the political activism by priests like Gallegos and Martinez and their followers that promises to cause problems for you."

"Not me," Benoit said, unable to remain quiet. "I'm just going to be a damned aide."

Lang shook his head slowly. "No, you're going to be the general's right hand. Believe me, more responsibility than you can imagine right now is going to fall on your shoulders."

Benoit opened his mouth to ask a question, but Lang held up his hand.

"Nope," he said firmly. "I'm not going to get into that. There are some things you're going to have to figure out on your own. I just want to give you some background because no one else is likely to do it. The commander at Fort Marcy, Major McNamara, is locked in a power struggle with General Barksdale. They're too busy fighting with each other to pay much attention to anything else, so a lot of problems they should be handling are going to be dumped on you."

He stopped and studied Benoit. "When you showed up in my office this afternoon, I didn't intend to tell you all this. But after watching you tonight and seeing how you handled the situation with Hardy and the other men, I think you're an intelligent, conscientious officer. You're going to want to do the right thing. At the same time, you need to know what you're getting into. I'm putting my ass on the line by opening up like this, but I think it's information you need to have. Besides, what's going to happen if I'm wrong about you? They going to send me to Fort fucking Union in the middle of the mountains? I'm not worried. War is going to come sooner than most people realize, and when it does, the army is going to wipe all its slates clean. They're going to need every officer they can get. When the bullets start flying, no one is going to care what I have or have not told you."

"I appreciate your being so candid with me," Benoit said softly.

"The thing is," Lang said, "I *care* about New Mexico. I like the people. I like the country. I even like Fort Union. I want to see Bishop Lamy and Don José get the civilian mess straightened out. Remember, they're fighting the same kind of battle with Zubiría and his priests that Barksdale and McNamara are fighting in Santa Fe. Power is what it's all about, and the people are caught in the middle. Right now, they may be a little anti-American, but I reckon that's natural. They see their very existence threatened. Their lives are wrapped around their religion, and they think the United States is a nation of godless heathens who are going to start throwing them to the lions any day now. Once they learn that nobody in Washington is going to tell them what they have to believe, things will get better. Unfortunately, it may take a while for this to sink in. So you're going to *have* to learn some patience, buckaroo."

Benoit sighed. "Patience is a trait I don't think I'm ever going to acquire."

"It comes with age and experience." Lang smiled. "May I offer you some advice? I mean, in addition to subjecting you to my speech?"

"Sure," Benoit said, nodding.

"Okay. Here goes. Get to know Don José. Make a real effort. By scratching each other's backs, you can get a lot accomplished. Leave the big things to Barksdale and Lamy. You two will be the out-front representatives of the two reigning powers: church and state. It will be a lot better if you can work together."

"How do I do that? Get to know Don José, that is?"

Lang nodded. "Good question. It may be much easier than you think. It's customary in New Mexico for ranking military officials to present themselves to the bishop and his top aide when they arrive. I know a brevet captain isn't what most people consider a *ranking* officer, but your position opens the door. If Don José doesn't invite you to dinner, make it a point to ask *him*. Take him to the best restaurant in town, order some good wine—New Mexico, by the way, produces some damn good wine; we can certainly thank the Franciscans for that, if nothing else—and open your heart to him. Since both of you speak French and you're a Catholic, you already will have something in common. Take advantage of it and build on it. Believe me, it will pay big dividends in the future."

Lang stood and brushed off his trousers. "I've talked enough. Tomorrow starts early. Just because it's Sunday doesn't mean we can take a holiday. Drop by my office before you leave. I have a packet that needs to be delivered to General Barksdale."

Smiling, he extended his hand. "Good luck, Jean. You're going to need it. If you have a problem you can't get resolved in Santa Fe and you feel comfortable talking about it, my door's always open. So come back when you can. If nothing else, I want to hear some more of those ghost stories. I'm a real zealot for tales about the supernatural. In fact, make sure to ask Don José about some of the miracles that have been recorded in New Mexico. This place is almost as spooky as New Orleans."

8

Benoit lay on the hard bed, staring at the ceiling, his hands locked behind his head. It felt wonderful, he thought, not to have to be anywhere in particular for the next twenty-four hours. General Barksdale was at Fort Union for a meeting with a group of civilian suppliers, so he had been given the day off. "Explore Santa Fe," Barksdale had told him. "Begin to learn the city." And that, Benoit had decided, was precisely what he planned to do.

In the two weeks since he'd first reported for duty, he had been so busy he had hardly left Barksdale's office, which was located in the old Spanish *presidio* renamed the "Post of Santa Fe" by the Americans, except for two quick trips to Fort Marcy itself. An imposing star-shaped fortification built on a hill overlooking Santa Fe proper, Fort Marcy was encircled by nine-foot-tall walls built of two-foot-thick adobe bricks. In addition, an eight-foot-deep trench had been dug around the outside, making it seventeen feet from the top of the walls to the ground, a formidable height for any potential attacker to scale, although the likelihood that was going to happened seemed to be diminishing daily. While the original plans for the fort had included a garrison to house 280 men, it had never, not since it was built in 1846, quartered any large number of troops. Instead, the soldiers, Benoit included, lived and worked out of the facility off the central plaza, the administrative heart of the military operation in the territory.

For fourteen days Benoit had been tied up from dawn to dusk in a confusing whirl of meetings, briefings, and planning sessions, although he was still not sure exactly what was being briefed or planned. It had taken him no more than two days to confirm what Lang had been trying to tell him that night at Fort Union, that virtually nothing was being accomplished at Fort Marcy because of a bitter, ongoing feud between Barksdale, who was commanding officer of the Ninth Military Department—essentially all the military installations in the territory, eleven of them, to be precise, ranging in size from a 37-man detachment in Alburquerque to 227 men at Fort Defiance, far to the West—and McNamara, the commanding officer at Fort Marcy.

The command situation, Benoit acknowledged, was a sensitive one. There was an analogous situation in the navy, where there might be two commanders on a single ship if it was a flag vessel: the commander of the ship itself and the commander of the fleet. In this case, the two commanders, Barksdale and McNamara, were based at the same post and were constantly at each other's throats.

McNamara, an ambitious artillery officer in his mid-forties, thought that he, as ranking officer in the entire department before Barksdale arrived, should have been given the job when the previous commander,

Brigadier General John Garland, was recalled to Washington to take a staff job in the War Department. McNamara's expectations, Benoit recognized at once, were totally unrealistic. It had been stretching the limits of army policy when he was jumped in rank from second lieutenant to brevet captain, and that came about only because a senator and a former secretary of war had involved themselves in the process. For McNamara to envision that he would be promoted from major to brigadier general, leapfrogging over lieutenant colonels and colonels, was too farfetched for anyone but the egotistical McNamara even to consider.

Barksdale, on the other hand, felt he had been slighted by being posted to New Mexico. As commander of Fort Sumpter, a strategically important facility near Charleston, he had expected his next posting to be one of authority in Washington. The last thing he'd anticipated was being exiled to the frontier. Charleston was one of the South's great cities; Santa Fe was a collection of mud huts in the middle of the desert. As a Southerner, Barksdale had felt at home in South Carolina; his wife and three children adored the place. When he'd gotten his orders to report to Fort Marcy, his wife, the oldest daughter of a very influential banker in Richmond, had stomped her foot and refused to budge from the gracious, columned house they had bought on one of the city's oak-lined streets. "*You* go to New Mexico," she had told her husband, "Neither I nor the children ever intend to set foot in that wretched land."

Since he was fifty-eight years old and looked every day of it, Barksdale also felt that the New Mexico posting would be his last, and he was bitter that he was being forced to end a moderately distinguished career in a territory that nine out of ten people east of the Mississippi would not be able to point to on a map. As a result, he was less than enthusiastic about the command. The fact that he was forced into a war with the local post commander only added to his dissatisfaction. Frustrated and angry, Barksdale took refuge in the bottle. In the bottom left-hand drawer of his desk he kept a fresh quart of the fiery local whiskey called Taos lightning, a concoction strong enough to burn a man's tongue if it was not swallowed immediately. What it did to one's stomach, Benoit could only imagine.

Barksdale traditionally began the day by doctoring his coffee with a modicum of the Taos whiskey. By lunch he was chugging it straight from a water tumbler. After a two-hour siesta, he returned to the office moderately sober, only to be soused again by the end of the working day.

Just how much official business penetrated Barksdale's alcoholic fog, Benoit was unsure. After he had been there several days, he probed gently to see if the general knew about his connection to the office of the secretary of war, Senator Clement Couvillion, and his unwelcome assignment as an unwilling spy for the Confederacy. The result of Benoit's carefully put inquiries was completely inconclusive. Either Barksdale was totally ignorant of the purpose behind his new aide's posting or he was much cleverer than Benoit gave him credit for.

Regardless of Barksdale's awareness of his purpose, Benoit was not overly worried about carrying out Cle's directive. In the time he had been at Fort Marcy, Benoit had yet to see or hear anything he imagined could be of possible use to the Confederacy in the event of war. His duties so far consisted mainly of listening to Barksdale's alcohol-induced ramblings and shuffling papers, none of which had any strategic significance. New Mexico was so isolated, Benoit had come to conclude, that there was nothing he could learn about military developments within the territory that would make any difference to Jefferson Davis or any other Confederate planner. There was, he had further decided, no reason to pass on this information to Cle. Sooner or later Cle would come to him and ask for a report, and Benoit could tell him then that there was nothing to narrate; that New Mexico was a backwater unworthy of consideration. Nothing could happen in Santa Fe, Benoit reckoned, that could have the slightest influence on a war between the North and the South, a conflict that undoubtedly would be fought within the established boundaries of the United States, that nebulous entity Westerners always referred to as "back east."

In the meantime, since he was in New Mexico and there was nothing he could do to change it, he might as well learn to make the best of the situation. Becoming fluent in the local language was on the top of his list. In the last two weeks, just from listening to the natives who came and went through Fort Marcy, Benoit had noted the strong similarities between Spanish and French, both of which were based on Latin, which had been drummed into his head by the Jesuits when he was a youth. The pronunciation of French and Spanish was different, but the sentence structure was almost identical and, in many cases, the vocabulary was amazingly alike. In French, for example, the word for captain was *capitaine*; in Spanish it was *capitán*.

However, despite these semblances, Benoit knew

from trying to use his New Orleans French in conversation with French Canadians that the difficulties would come in learning to master the local idioms. In a place that has been isolated far from its linguistic home for 250 years, a distinctive dialect naturally had evolved. Attempting to grasp formal Spanish—the language spoken in Spain—would be about as useful in New Mexico as an umbrella. The only way he was going to become fluent in New Mexican Spanish, Benoit acknowledged, was to speak and listen to the locals. And today he planned to take the first step in that direction.

Two days after he had arrived, Barksdale had sent him to the office of Bishop Lamy to introduce himself. It had been a very formal meeting, Benoit recalled. He had not spoken directly to Lamy, only to his chief aide, Vicar General Joseph Machebeuf, the man Lang had referred to familiarly as Don José. He had spent less than ten minutes with Machebeuf, who had appeared harried and preoccupied. However, recognizing a French name when he saw one, Machebeuf had immediately been curious. When Benoit told him that his home was New Orleans, the vicar general's eyes had lit up. "I have a niece there," he had said excitedly. "She's in the Ursuline convent."

"I know it well," Benoit had said. "My sister was educated at the Ursuline Academy. My father contributed financially to the institution until his death three years ago."

On such fragile threads, Benoit marveled, lasting relationships are sometimes built. When he'd heard of his family's ties to the Ursuline sisters, Machebeuf had immediately issued an invitation to Benoit to have dinner at the bishop's residence. "I see by his calendar that Bishop Lamy has to be in Alburquerque the previous day—an important conference with a local priest and some city leaders—and he may or may not be back. If he is not, we can have dinner alone, a friendly tête-à-tête. It is not very often that I get the opportunity to speak French to anyone except the bishop or a fellow cleric."

"It would be my pleasure," Benoit had said graciously.

"Good," Machebeuf had replied, beaming. "Let's say nine o'clock, then."

"I very much look forward to it." And with that, Benoit had backed diplomatically out of the cramped office.

That was two nights away. Today, Benoit could do whatever he wanted.

As anxious as he was to begin his exploration, he took the time to reread the short letter from Inge that had arrived the day before. He had been surprised how quickly mail had been received when it traveled eastward from Fort Laramie to Independence, Missouri, via the Oregon Trail, then southwestward down the Santa Fe Trail to Fort Marcy. The letter, actually little more than a hastily scribbled note, had been written two days after he'd left. In it, Inge mostly told him how much she missed him. There was, however, a brief summary of Erich's condition. There had been no improvement, she said, but his spirits remained high. The real change she had noticed was in the behavior of her stepfather, Ashby. Apparently riddled with guilt about what had happened to Erich, irrationally convinced that if he had been with him the situation would have been different, he had begun to drink more than usual. Although it had not yet gotten out of hand, she was worried that it was going to get worse before it got better.

Benoit himself had felt more than a twinge of guilt when he read his wife's words. If he were there rather than here, he reckoned, he might be able to convince Ashby that he was in no way to blame for what had happened to his stepson. But it was a notion that he quickly put out of mind, realizing that even by allowing it to enter his head, he was falling into the same trap as Ashby. He was *not* at Fort Laramie; he was at Fort Marcy, and there was nothing he could do about it. What had happened to Erich had been tragic, but it was something beyond any human's control. By the same token, whether Ashby ended up a day-long drinker like Barksdale was beyond Benoit's ability to manage. Even the fact that Inge was hundreds of miles away, and pregnant at that, was a situation he could only mourn. The decision to stay there until the baby was born had been hers. He could concur in it or not. What he could *not* do was tie her up, load her on a travois, and drag her to New Mexico. Life was frustrating. He agreed, but that was life.

Sighing, he rose from the rock hard cot in the cell-like room he had been allotted and shrugged into the least dusty uniform in his wardrobe. One of the first things he planned to do was arrange for some civilian clothes. It had been four years since he had worn anything except army blue, and the color was beginning to grate on his nerves. It might be just the thing to lift my spirits, he thought: find a tailor and splurge on some new clothing. Whistling happily with that thought in mind, Benoit closed his door behind him and set off on foot for the central plaza, a three-minute walk away.

Benoit stopped at the edge of the plaza, both to survey
the scene and to gather his bearings. He had
approached from the northwest, so he was looking
southeast across a space large enough to serve as a
military parade ground. To the north and east were
the cedar- and pine-covered slopes of the Sangre de
Cristo Mountains, the tail of the mighty Rocky
Mountain chain. To the south, some sixty miles away
but looking much closer because of the thin, clear air,
was another mountain range that Benoit knew from
the maps he had studied were the Sandias and
Manzanos. To the southeast, although he could not see
them from where he stood, were the Jemez Mountains.
It was the foreground, however, and not the mountains that Benoit was interested in.

The plaza was as flat as a billiard table, carved out
of the rolling terrain by the Spanish two and a half
centuries earlier, almost 125 years before his native
New Orleans had been founded by the Sieur de
Bienville. But, Benoit thought, gazing around, New
Orleans looked like a proper city; Santa Fe looked like
a brickyard. The buildings all had flat roofs and were
of a uniform height—one story. They all were made of
adobe, baked mud, so they were of an identical color,
brown, which was the same as that of the mud streets.
The plaza itself, Benoit reckoned, was attractive
enough, a broad open space bordered by irrigation
ditches that were needed to nourish the scrawny cottonwoods that had been planted several years before.
With their bright new spring leaves, which sometimes
were slow to emerge at Santa Fe's 7,500-foot elevation,
the cottonwoods provided the only splotches of color

in an otherwise drab panorama. For attractiveness, Benoit reflected, the plaza could not compare to the parks in his home city, which were grassy and shaded by towering oaks. In comparison, the only shade to be found around the plaza, except for the minuscule amount created by the cottonwoods, was under the *portales* that jutted out from the buildings on three sides of the plaza, covering the uneven plank sidewalks.

For an instant Benoit felt terribly sad. Looking at the brown that surrounded him on all sides, he wanted so much to see the trees and flowers of his home, sit once again on the bank of the swift-flowing Mississippi River, that he was afraid he would cry. With a huge mental effort he banished thoughts of Louisiana from his mind and forced himself to concentrate on his present surroundings.

Turning slightly to his right, he studied a long, low building he knew had to be the Palace of the Governors, the original and still current seat of provincial power. On his left, also facing the plaza, were other structures so undistinguished that he knew they also had to be governmental structures. It was the buildings opposite that caught his attention. Several, he assumed, were private residences, since the front of each contained two small windows with wooden bars and thick shutters, which were closed. Interspersed with these, however, were several that Benoit could readily see were shops. It was in that direction that he was headed when half a dozen small boys, followed by a pack of noisy dogs, each as brown as the buildings' mud walls, came running into the plaza.

"¡Los carros!" shouted one of the youths. "¡Los Americanos! ¡La entrada de la caravana!"

Benoit did not need to be fluent in Spanish to understand that they were cheering the approach of a trade caravan from the United States. Excited by the prospect, he returned to the shade of the portal to see what developed.

In a matter of minutes the plaza began filling with eager townspeople and off-duty soldiers, all anxious to see what wares the traders would exhibit.

As the crowd began to form, the first of the wagons appeared from around one of the residences on the south side of the plaza. Pulled by a six-mule team, the animals arranged carefully in ascending order from small to large, a monstrous-looking Conestoga, its sideboards painted bright blue and red, nosed around the corner. Atop the largest mule, the one at the left rear of the team, sat the driver, a burly, bearded American. Cracking his long whip and cursing at the mules, who wore expressions proclaiming they had seen it all before, the teamster guided the wagon so it made a slow circuit around the plaza, heading toward a spot it had occupied many times before.

While the crowd shouted lustily and the teamsters bellowed, more wagons arrived, until the entire space, which only a few minutes before had seemed so vast, was filled. While the owners, their hair slicked back and wearing their best clothing in anticipation of the grand entrance, hurried to one of the buildings that Benoit assumed was the customs house, assistants began unloading, stacking their goods in neat piles for examination and sale.

Circulating through the crowd, as exhilarated as any of the Santa Feans, Benoit was amazed at the variety of material that had made its way down the trail.

Accustomed to the "people" caravans that passed through Fort Laramie—trains composed not of traders, but of settlers bound for the West with nothing to sell but excess baggage—he gaped at the shiny new merchandise like a country boy on his first visit to town. Amid cheers and exhortations from the bystanders to hurry, the traders spread blankets in the dust, then began loading them down with an astounding assortment of commodities ranging from watches and combs, axes and shovels, to scissors, needles, thread, buttons, and trays of jewelry. One wagon, Benoit noted in surprise, contained nothing but alcoholic beverages: neatly stacked cases of whiskey, claret, sherry, and Champagne. The collection of dry goods alone shocked him. There was not only plain cotton, both bleached and unbleached, but muslin, broadcloth, drills, prints, flannels, linen, calico, nankeen, pongee, taffeta, velveteen, cashmere, alpaca, merino, and bolt upon bolt of delicate and expensive silk. One wiry mer-chant with a huge handlebar mustache and different-colored eyes—one was blue and one was brown—set up makeshift racks on which he hung a conglomeration of ready-made clothing. Enthusiastically joining the scramble in front of the man's wagon, Benoit grabbed two pairs of trousers, three shirts, and four pairs of gray woolen stockings, congratulating himself for his foresight in having brought along a pocketful of currency.

Remembering that he also might need something dressier to wear on special occasions, Benoit paid a hugely inflated price for several yards of linen to be fashioned into shirts and a suitable length of dark broadcloth that could be used for a proper suit.

Clutching his purchases, he began to look for someone who might be able to steer him to a tailor. It was no sense asking the traders, he knew, because they were not familiar with the city. Looking around, he spotted a distinguished-looking man who was examining a display of fine writing paper, an indication to Benoit that he probably was literate and might speak at least a little English.

"Can you tell me where I might be able to find a tailor?" he asked, speaking slowly and distinctly.

The man looked at him blankly.

"Tailor?" Benoit asked, hoping the single word would have significance.

The man shook his head.

"*Tailleur?*" Benoit ventured, deciding to try French on the chance that the Spanish word might be similar.

The man shook his head and sighed.

"Shirt," Benoit said desperately, holding up the length of linen and pulling on his blouse. "Suit," he added, displaying the broadcloth and touching the man's frock coat.

The man beamed. "¡*Ah—Sastre!*"

Damn, Benoit thought. That sure doesn't sound like either English or French. "*Sastre,*" he repeated, nodding vigorously.

The man, laughing, pointed toward the north and said something in Spanish. Noting the uncomprehending expression on Benoit's face, he knelt and began making lines in the dust with a long, thin finger, carefully drawing in streets and buildings.

Thanking him profusely, Benoit set off in the direction the man had pointed.

Why in hell didn't I get him to put that map on paper? Benoit asked himself fifteen minutes later, staring

agitatedly at the row of identical-looking brown buildings, each seemingly on the verge of collapse. He was
forced to admit that he was hopelessly lost. So far he
said seen nothing resembling a tailor shop, although
he was certain he had followed the old man's directions.

Stepping carefully to avoid a fat-bellied pig that
was dozing contentedly in a water-filled hole in the
center of the street, Benoit found himself eye to eye
with an angry-looking goat, seemingly ready to charge.
A large, reddish brown dog glared at him from a patch
of shade, growling deep in its throat. Hot and frustrated, he was about to knock on a door and plead for
help when he caught a movement out of the corner of
his eye. Thankful for someone who might come to his
rescue, Benoit turned expectantly, a smile on his lips.

Instead of the friendly face he was hoping for,
however, he found himself in front of a slightly built
youth with long, unwashed hair, dressed in patched,
worn trousers and a stained shirt with baggy sleeves.
Staring into the youth's large brown eyes, Benoit saw
not compassion for a confused stranger, but bubbling,
burning hatred.

"¡Americano!" the youth spat, making it sound like
the worst curse Benoit had ever heard.

Benoit jerked as if he had been slapped.
Involuntarily, like a wolf faced with unexpected danger, he felt the hair rise on the back of his neck. His
heart rate jumped, and there was a sudden, cold feeling in the pit of his stomach. Dropping his packages on
the dirt, he leaned forward, hunching his shoulders,
readying himself for an attack, cursing the fact that he
had not worn his sidearm. As he waited for the youth
to make a move, he swiveled his eyes, surveying the

scene to see what his options were. Immediately he wished he hadn't.

To his right another youth suddenly appeared, looking just as ragged and just as angry. Behind him there was still another. The last one, Benoit noticed, had his arms filled with smooth, dark river stones, none smaller than a man's fist, which he dumped on the ground.

"*¡Pendejo!*" called the third youth, grabbing one of the stones. He hurled it at Benoit, and it missed his head by three inches, slamming into the mud wall behind him with a solid thud.

Jesus! Benoit thought. This is just what I was warned about. They're going to stone me to death and leave my body lying in pig shit.

Benoit sensed movement to his left. He turned just in time to see the first youth grab a clod of dried mud, which he threw with all his might. It struck Benoit on the left thigh, hitting with the force of a mule kick. "Goddamn!" Benoit cursed as his leg crumpled beneath him, sending him to his knee. Don't go down, he told himself sternly. If they get you down, they'll kick you to death.

"*¡Desgraciado!*" yelled the first attacker, throwing another rock at Benoit's head. It also missed, but it came closer.

The third youth, who so far had neither spoken nor thrown a stone, stared unsympathetically at Benoit. "*¡Maten el carajo!*" he said, picking up one of the rocks.

What a hell of a way to die, Benoit thought, watching the youth draw back his arm.

He closed his eyes, waiting for the blow. Halfway through a hurried Our Father, he was jolted by a voice from behind him.

"*¡Entonces morirás tú primero!*"

Spinning to see if he was going to be facing yet another attacker, Benoit was astounded by the sudden appearance of a well-dressed man in a floppy hat, standing with his legs spread and both arms raised in front of him. Clutched in his fist was a pistol, its barrel pointed straight at the youth with the raised arm.

Benoit was baffled. Had this newcomer joined the fray? Using a pistol to claim him as his victim, in effect stealing his life from the poorly dressed youths?

There followed several exchanges in Spanish, none of which Benoit could remotely comprehend. Then, much to his relief, the youth lowered his arm, staring malevolently at the man with the pistol.

The stranger said something else, making a waving motion with his revolver.

After tossing the rock on the ground in disgust, the attacker turned and walked away, followed by his two companions, cursing as they went.

"Are you all right?" the stranger asked in perfect English, lowering his pistol and rushing to Benoit's side. "Were you hit before I arrived?"

"Yes," Benoit replied in a squeaky voice. "But it was a mud clod, not a stone. I think I'll live."

He tried to stand, only to sink again when he put weight on his injured leg.

"Let me help you," the man said, grabbing Benoit's elbow and hauling him to his feet.

Benoit was surprised at his strength. The man was several inches shorter than he and looked rather slim in an expertly cut suit and a snow white silk shirt; but his forearm, when Benoit grabbed it for support, felt as solid and as large as a wagon tree. Because of the exceptionally wide brim of his hat, most of his face was in shadow, so Benoit could not accurately determine his age or nationality, although he spoke English like an American.

"I don't know how to thank you," Benoit said. "You don't know how grateful I am that you happened by."

"I didn't just *happen by*," the man said, leaning forward and brushing the dirt from Benoit's trousers. "I was in the plaza when I saw you walk off into the *Barrio de Analco*."

"The what?"

"This place," he said, sweeping his arm around him. "This garden spot. This asshole of our fine city."

"I don't understand."

The man chuckled. "Of course you don't. Why should you? The *Barrio de Analco* is a neighborhood populated exclusively by Mexican Indians. They are rough people, and they live in a rough place. They don't like Americans, especially American soldiers."

"What did we ever do to them?" Benoit asked naively.

"You won the war. You invaded their land. You are rich and they are poor. Therefore, you are the enemy."

"As simple as that, huh?"

"Not really. They hate everybody, so don't take it personally."

Benoit laughed despite himself. "A rescuer with a sense of humor. But tell me, why did you say you did not exactly 'happen by'?"

"I saw the old man drawing you a map in the dust, then I saw you leave in the direction you thought he had indicated."

"What do you mean, I 'thought' he had indicated?"

"You must have misunderstood. I know Señor Salazar. I know he would not send you into the *barrio* on purpose. What did you ask him?"

"I asked if he could direct me to a tailor."

The man guffawed. "A tailor! I know where you intended to go. Actually, you were two streets off. It's a good thing I followed you. I feared you were headed for trouble. I guess I was right, huh?" he asked, grinning. Benoit could see his teeth gleaming brightly under the heavy shade of his hat brim.

"Whatever possessed you to go wandering around like that?" the man asked harshly, as an angry father might talk to a wayward son. "Didn't anyone warn you that there are neighborhoods in the city where a white man just does not go?"

"I was warned," Benoit said meekly. "I forgot. I thought it would be safe in the daylight."

"There are a dozen or more soldiers buried at the fort who thought the same thing," the man said.

"Okay," Benoit said, his cheeks flaming. "You don't have to belabor the point. I made a mistake."

"Almost a fatal one."

"Look, I said I was wrong. What else can I say? But how about you? Do you follow every stranger who seems to be going astray?"

"Good question," the mean replied, his voice suddenly turned friendly. "I was in the plaza on business when I saw you approach Señor Salazar. I thought I knew all the officers at Fort Marcy, so I figured you must be new."

"But that still doesn't explain why you risked your own life to help a complete stranger."

"Let's just say I feel some obligation to American soldiers. I didn't want to see one killed unnecessarily."

"I don't know why you feel that way, but I'm grateful nevertheless. Can I buy you a drink or something? I feel I should do something to show my appreciation."

The man paused and reached inside his coat, withdrawing a gold watch with a beautiful carved case. "It's lunchtime," he said. "Why don't we go over to La Fonda and get something to eat? Then you can prove to me that you're not as dumb as I thought you were. Can you walk?"

"Of course I can walk," Benoit said, trying not to limp. "Tell me something else?"

The man nodded. "Sure."

"What did that guy say to me? The ugly one who was about ready to crush my skull just when you showed up."

"Oh, him!" The man chuckled. "He said you were a scoundrel and he was going to kill you."

"And what did you tell him to make him stop?"

"I told him that he would be the first to die. Apparently he believed me."

"Hell, *I* would have believed you, too. A pistol speaks a lot more forcefully than a rock. You know," Benoit said, stopping, "I don't even know your name. You saved my life, and I don't even know what to call you."

Again the man laughed. "My American friends call me Alex."

"I'm glad to know you, Alex. My name is Jean Benoit. If you see it written, it looks like Ben-oight, but it's pronounced Ben-wah."

"Well, my surname is Ortiz. If you see it written, it looks like Ortiz."

"More humor," Benoit said dryly. "How come you

have a Hispano surname and an English Christian name?"

"I said my American friends called me 'Alex.' I didn't say my *name* was Alex."

"Are you playing games with me?"

"No. My name is Alejandro. Alejandro Federico Valentin Valencia Ortiz, to be exact. In Spanish, the nickname for Alejandro is Alejo. The English version of that is Alex. That's why I said my American friends call me Alex."

"You're a man of mystery," Benoit said, studying his companion, still unable to distinguish his features clearly because of the shadow cast by his hat brim. "You're a Hispano, but you speak flawless English. Why is that?"

"Why don't we wait until we've eaten. You *do* like *carne de carnero*, don't you?"

"I don't even know what it is."

"It's mutton cooked with chili peppers. Very tasty."

"Sounds great!" Benoit said enthusiastically.

I wonder, he asked himself as he limped hurriedly after his rescuer, why my conversations always seem to be about sheep?

Ortiz stood on his toes, gazing across the crowded dining room. "If you ever need to find someone, come to La Fonda. Sooner or later, everybody shows up here. Look! Over there, in the corner. An empty table. Let's go get it."

Benoit, tying not to limp, followed Ortiz as he weaved among the tables, stopping occasionally to shake a hand or exchange a quick greeting.

"Looks like you're pretty well-known around here," Benoit commented, sliding into the empty chair.

"In a city of only five thousand, it's hard not be known," Ortiz said, sitting on the opposite side of the table. Reaching up, he removed his hat and then hung it over the back of an empty chair.

Benoit, who had been looking around the room, turned back to face his companion. "Oh!" he gasped involuntarily.

"Quite a shock, huh?" Ortiz asked pleasantly.

"N-no," Benoit stammered. "I mean, yes. Er, sort of . . ."

"Don't be embarrassed. It happens all the time."

Benoit stared. Ortiz's face, which had been hidden

in shadow, was red and peeling from just above his jawline to the top of his head. At first Benoit thought he had suffered a bad sunburn. But that would not account for the lack of hair on the top of his head, which looked like a ripening radish and was even redder than his face, a mass of bumps and scar tissue.

"Burns," Ortiz said matter-of-factly. "I'll be this way for the rest of my life."

"W-wh . . . what happened?" Benoit asked softly, trying not to stare.

"Let's order first," he said, waving to a harried-looking waiter. Holding up two fingers, he signaled for a beer for each of them.

"What do you think of Santa Fe so far?" he asked while they waited for their food and refreshment.

"Honestly?"

"Of course."

"It's not quite what I expected. A little, uh, *coarse*."

"Very tactfully put." Ortiz laughed. "Personally, I like to compare it to Valladolid when it was the capital of Spain in the sixteenth century. A tourist visiting the city at the time described it as a place filled with—and I quote, *'pícaros, putas, pleytos, polvos, peidras, puercos, perros, piojos, y pulgas.'*"

"And that means?"

"Rogues, whores, fights, dust, stones, swine, dogs, lice, and fleas. For Santa Fe I'd like to add mud and muck, but *lodo* and *estiércol* ruin the alliteration."

"I'm impressed." Benoit smiled. "Obviously you're very well educated."

"You mean for a Hispano?"

"No, I mean for *anyone*. There's only one other person I know personally who has such an apparent command of such diverse information. And he's a surgeon. Are *you* a surgeon or a professor?"

"God forbid. Ah, here comes the food. Let's eat. I'd suggest you be careful with the peppers. They can be fiery for someone not accustomed to New Mexico fare."

"You didn't answer my question," Benoit said stubbornly. "By the way, what kind of bread is this?"

"It's called a *tortilla*. You can tear it and dip it in the stew. Do you really want to know my life story?"

"By God, that is spicy," Benoit said, reaching for his beer. "Yes, I do."

"Water works better than beer," Ortiz said, pointing toward a jug sitting on the edge of the table. "Let me see, where's a good place to start?"

"How did you get such an extensive education? Santa Fe doesn't strike me as an intellectual capital."

"Now *that* is less tactful," Ortiz said, chuckling. "Do you know where the Mora Valley is?"

Benoit shook his head.

"Have you ever heard the term '*rico*'?"

Benoit looked blank.

"My home," Ortiz continued, "is in the Mora Valley, which is north of here. You passed fairly close to it when you came down from Fort Union. It was off to the west, between Las Vegas and Taos, on the east side of the Sangre de Cristos. The soil there is very rich; it's wonderful farmland. About a quarter of a century ago there were very few people living there because the valley was so isolated. Also, it was a favorite hunting and trapping area for *los bárbaros*."

"Who?" Benoit interjected.

"The savages. The Comanches, the Apaches, the Navajos . . ."

"Okay. I understand."

"For people who wanted to settle the area, there was no protection from Indian raids. *Unless* they came in fairly large numbers. Then they could protect each other."

"The government didn't protect them?"

"Don't make me laugh," Ortiz said caustically. "But a man named José Tapia went to the governor, I forget who it was at the time, and asked for a grant so he and others could come settle the area."

"Were these grants common?"

"Oh, yes. There was no one living on the land, so the governor was free to give it to whomever he chose. Who was going to contest it?"

"Sorry I interrupted."

"No matter. The Tapias and seventy-five other families were granted parcels of land. All they had to do was settle it and hold on to it. My parents, Epimeño and Virjinia, were among the grantees. I was barely a year old at the time. My father built a small adobe and began to grow wheat, oats, and barley. He was, and he still is, a very good farmer. Every year he managed to end up with a surplus of crops, which he'd bring to Santa Fe to sell at the market. He took the money he made from the sales and invested it in more land so he could grow more wheat, oats, and barley. Then he began to expand beyond farming. He, his brother, Maclovio, and another man bought a wagon and began running freight along the Santa Fe Trail. Within only a few years they had become very wealthy, with a whole fleet of wagons making the trip from Missouri to New Mexico. Then they expanded and began running freight on the Chihuahua Trail as well."

"The what?"

Ortiz smiled. "I forget you're practically a *turista*. The Chihuahua Trail is a three-hundred-year-old route between Santa Fe and the Mexican cities of El Paso del Norte, Chihuahua, Durango, and Zacatecas. It follows the old Royal Road, the El Camino Real de Tierra Adentro. Although it has been used since the time of the *Conquistadores*, it didn't begin to flourish as a trade route until after Mexican independence and the opening of the Santa Fe Trail. In 1822, the year after independence, there was only about fifteen thousand dollars' worth of merchandise traveling southward from here. In 1843, when my father sent his first wagon to Mexico, there were more than two hundred wagons using the route, carrying merchandise worth almost a half million dollars. By investing his money judiciously and making good, instinctive decisions about what type of merchandise to buy, my father became a *rico*, a wealthy man. Our family was included among the *gente fina*, the elite. Although my father cannot read and write, he nevertheless realized the value of an education for his children. In 1845, the year I celebrated my eleventh birthday, he enrolled me in a Jesuit school in St. Louis. After I went as far as I could in that school, he insisted I go on to the university, which I did."

"Ah," Benoit said. "That explains your command of English. It also explains why you said your 'American friends' call you Alex."

Ortiz nodded, sipping his beer. "I'm the oldest child; I have a brother and four sisters. Early on, I showed an aptitude for business, so it was decided that I would take over the freight business. My brother, Narciso, who is six years younger, has no interest along those lines. My father sent him to St.

Louis to school, too, but he didn't like it. He ran away three times before my father finally gave up and let him stay at home. Narciso will take over the farming operation."

"And your sisters?"

"My sisters?" Ortiz frowned. "They are just women. They have nothing to do with business."

"How about your father's partners?"

"One died, leaving my uncle. Poor *Tío* Maclovio," Ortiz sighed. "His wife gave him only daughters, so when he dies he has no one to inherit his share. That leaves only me. I guess I, too, will one day be a *rico*."

"You don't sound very happy about it," Benoit observed.

"I would rather be a normal-looking person. Children cry and bury their faces in their mother's skirts when they see me. Women turn their heads in disgust. Behind my back, I am called *El Desfiguraro*. The Disfigured One."

"What happened?" Benoit asked. "Were you the victim of an accident of some sort? A house fire?"

"No," Ortiz said bitterly, "what happened to me was no accident. Three years ago, after I graduated from the university, I was returning to New Mexico to begin the process of taking over my father's business. I was with a small caravan that included two of my father's wagons. The wagonmaster was in a hurry to get to Santa Fe, so we took the Cimarron Cutoff, which at time was a little more risky route than it is today. We had just forded the North Canadian River when a party of Comanches under a son of a bitch named Buffalo Hump attacked. They killed just about everybody in the first rush. I was wounded; had an arrow through my thigh. It may have been because of the loss of blood or perhaps shock. But I passed out. The next thing I knew, I was hanging upside-down from a cottonwood limb and the Comanches were piling some brush under me. Buffalo Hump was enjoying himself immensely. There was another survivor, one of the teamsters; I can't even remember his name. Buffalo Hump had disemboweled him and was forcing him to eat his own intestines."

"And you?" Benoit asked quietly, grimacing.

"When the teamster ruined Buffalo Hump's sport by dying too quickly, he turned his attention to me. I'll never forget the evil grin on his face when he lit the pile of brush. The idea was to get the blood in my head boiling so my skull would split like an overripe tomato."

Benoit looked at his plate of mutton and shoved it aside, discovering his appetite had disappeared.

Ortiz noticed the gesture and smiled. "But before that could happen, an army patrol showed up. They had been only a couple of miles away and they heard the shooting. When they came charging in, Buffalo Hump and his followers couldn't get out of there fast enough. That's why I said I felt obligated to the soldiers. They didn't arrive in time to stop me from suffering some pretty bad burns, but they sure as hell saved my life. It's something I won't quickly forget."

"But you seem to have recovered very well."

Ortiz nodded. "It took about a year for the wounds to heal. I damn near died from infection, but an old *curandera* my father knew treated me with some sort of salve she probably made in a big cauldron, like Shakespeare's witches, and that took care of that."

"And you left the family farm—"

"*Hacienda.*"

"Okay, you left the family *hacienda* to come live in Santa Fe and run the family business?"

"*Más o menos.*"

"Come again?" Benoit said.

"More or less. I *could* be doing the same thing from Mora, but my father thought it would be more efficient to do it from here. He's right, in a way. But there's more to it than that."

"I don't understand."

"Well, I believe my father wanted me out of his sight. Every time he looks at my scarred face, he feels guilty. I think," he said with a smile, nodding at Benoit's still unfinished bowl of stew, "my presence also affects his appetite. He couldn't stand to look at me across the table from him every night."

"That's terrible," Benoit blustered.

"Maybe, but it's true. I've learned to live with it. I am what I am. Besides, I think it gives me an edge in business. Those bleeding hearts from back east look at me and they say, 'Oh, that poor bastard,' so they cut me a better deal. I don't feel sorry for myself. I'd rather be disfigured than dead, which I surely would have been in another three minutes if those soldiers hadn't arrived. Are you going to finish that stew?"

"You bet I am." Benoit laughed and reached for his spoon. "Are you in a hurry?"

"No, but there's someplace I want to introduce you to. And the afternoon is a good time, because that's the slow period. Leave your packages at the front desk. You can pick them up later."

"Okay." Benoit raised his spoon. "But let me finish first. This is good," he said, slurping noisily. "What do you call it again?"

"*Carne de carnero.* You really need to learn Spanish, you know."

"I know," Benoit said. "My lessons are starting now. By the way, what shall I call you?"

Ortiz shrugged. "As I said, my American friends—"

"No, I'm in New Mexico now. When in Rome and all that. What was your nickname in Spanish?"

"Alejo." Ortiz grinned.

"If you don't mind, I'll call you Alejo."

"That's fine with me. Unless," he added impishly, "you want to call me El Desfiguraro."

"Jesus!" Benoit said snappishly. "You have a strange sense of humor."

"Sure I do. It's part of my charm."

"I think I'll stick to Alejo. You're beginning to make me wonder if maybe your brain *didn't* boil just a little bit."

Ortiz roared. "That's very good! I'll have to remember that."

Santa Fe's premier gambling establishment was not at all what Benoit had expected. When O'Hara had told him it was a gambling house, Benoit had immediately thought of the places he had visited in New Orleans. Without exception they had been elegant casinos located in the city's best neighborhoods: expensively furnished salons with shiny oak floors, plush velveteen drapes, and elaborately carved mahogany tables shipped over from Europe. The customers were dressed in expertly tailored suits, and the hostesses who circulated among them, offering French Champagne or smooth Kentucky bourbon, wore

gowns that cost as much as Benoit made in a month.
The dealers uniformly were clean shaven, freshly bar-
bered young men who had their nails manicured daily
so they would not appear unclean when they passed
out the cards. Overall there was a feeling of gentility.
Conversations were conducted in low, polite tones,
and a raised voice was rarely heard. If there were dis-
agreements, they were settled quietly, in gentlemanly
fashion, under the oaks—pistols at thirty paces or, better yet, with the traditional *rapière*. Hard currency was
never in evidence. Customers purchased chips from a
cashier, then turned them in for dollars when they left.
The featured games had been baccarat, chemin de fer,
and roulette. A few tables were set aside for blackjack,
poker, and *bourré*, which were tolerated but regarded
as somewhat déclassé, especially the latter, which was
a game invented in Louisiana's Acadia country and
had little standing among the sophisticated New
Orleans Francophiles.

When Ortiz led him down a narrow path filled
with puddles, carefully sidestepping a grizzled sow
dining on a dead cat, Benoit began to wonder if his
trustworthy guide had somehow become lost in the
maze of alleys that passed for streets in the capital.
Stopping in front of a traditional one-story adobe,
larger than most but otherwise undistinguished, Ortiz
smiled at Benoit. "Welcome to La Estrella," he said,
swinging open the rough plank door.

Inside, both men had to wait while their eyes
adjusted to the dim light. There were no windows in
the building, and the only illumination came from
wall sconces and chandeliers that dangled from the
slightly higher than normal ceiling. The packed-earth
floor, Benoit noted, was covered with sawdust, which

was heavily stained by tobacco juice. Smoke hung so thickly in the air that it reminded him of a foggy morning along the Mississippi River, except the air was not heavy and moist: it was as dry as a desert cave and redolent of cheap cigars, unwashed bodies, and raw liquor. The gambling tables, which as far as Benoit could tell were devoted exclusively to cards, were carefully lined along the side walls, with the dealers facing out into the rooms.

Through the haze, Benoit could see two doorways at the back, obviously leading off to other rooms. In between them was a raised platform. Remembering what O'Hara had told him about entertainment, he assumed it was a stage. Behind them, running about sixty feet from just behind the door to the east wall, was a bar fashioned from roughly trimmed Ponderosa pine.

"Drink?" Ortiz offered, leading the way to the end, where there were several empty spots. "Local whiskey?"

Benoit, recalling the potent Taos lightning that General Barksdale kept in his bottom drawer, shook his head. "Beer," he said firmly.

"¡Cobarde!" Ortiz laughed. "Cowardly, but smart. I'll have the same."

While waiting for the bartender to finish with another customer, Benoit studied the clientele. Ninety-eight percent of the customers, he figured, were men. But there were several women among the crowd, mysterious looking in the dark *rebozos* they wore over their heads, nearly covering their faces. Scampering unscolded among the crowd were a half dozen children.

"Do many women come in here?" he asked Ortiz, surprised because the gambling houses in New Orleans admitted only men.

"A few." Ortiz shrugged. "Mostly, though, they like to play *chuza*, a complicated card game that is as popular in New Mexico as bridge is with American women. But there's nothing to keep them out. For a woman, being seen in a gambling house attaches no stigma."

"There!" Benoit said excitedly, pointing to a figure in the far corner. "That man! He looks like he's wearing a cassock. Could that be a priest?"

Ortiz squinted to see through the gloom. "Oh, yes," he said, smiling slightly. "That's Padre Trujillo. I understand he's in here *a lot*, much to the consternation of Bishop Lamy. He and the bishop have been feuding for years, ever since the bishop arrived. Padre Trujillo was vicar general of the territory under Bishop Zubiría, and he took it as a personal insult when Bishop Lamy came in with his own chief aide. In retaliation, Padre Trujillo tried to evict Bishop Lamy from the house in which he was living, claiming he had bought it from Bishop Zubiría years ago for three hundred sheep. Bishop Lamy offered to buy it from Padre Trujillo, but he demanded too much money. In the end, Bishop Lamy moved into another house. I'm kind of surprised the *padre*'s here, though. I heard he had been in ill health lately."

Benoit shook his head, still perplexed by the gossip involving the clergy in New Mexico. In New Orleans one never heard such talk. Some Louisiana priests might be just as corrupt as the New Mexican priests apparently were, but their antics were never discussed publicly. Here, it seemed, everyone knew what was happening in church politics.

After waving at the bartender to remind him they were still waiting, Benoit turned his attention back to the room. Most of the men, as far as he could see, were locals, since they dressed in the style that he had come to think of as New Mexico peasant: serviceable but crudely made trousers made of goatskin and home-woven woolen shirts topped by the poncholike garment Benoit had learned was called a *sarape*. Most were barefoot, but a few wore simple sandals fashioned from ox hide. They ranged in age, Benoit guessed, from their mid- or late teens to middle age and beyond. All had smooth dark skin, and large, sad-looking eyes. Their teeth, when they smiled, looked unnaturally white, which made Benoit wonder if they polished them with some sort of pumice. The younger ones sported slim mustaches, while those of the older ones appeared thicker and bushier.

Scattered among the Hispanos were a few Americans, teamsters from the newly arrived caravan, Benoit presumed. They were not difficult to pick out. Although their trousers and shirts were not much different from those of the Hispanos, they all wore distinctive weatherbeaten slouch hats pulled low over their eyes, as if they were expecting a rainstorm at any minute. They also tended to be larger, with broader, well-muscled shoulders, thicker arms, coarser facial features, and wild-looking beards. When they spoke, their voices were loud and their vocabulary was heavily salted with curses.

All in all, Benoit told himself, it was a rough-looking crowd.

"Good," said Ortiz, breaking him out of his reverie. "Here's the beer."

Benoit looked at what had been placed before him: a pottery tankard filled with a thick, dark liquid that smelled strongly of hops.

"A toast," Ortiz said. "Another Spanish lesson for you. Colorful, but not one to use in mixed company. *Salud y pesetas*," he said with mock solemnity, "*y señoritas con buenas tetas.*"

Benoit laughed heartily. "I don't need a translation of *that*. I get the idea." Sipping his beer, he found he was pleasantly surprised. "Hey, that's not bad," he said approvingly. "A little stronger than what I'm used to, but pretty good."

"I'll pass your compliments along to the brewmaster," Ortiz joked.

"Tell me," Benoit said, nodding toward the closest table. "What are they playing?"

"In this room, all the tables are reserved for monte. One of the back rooms is for poker, the other for billiards. They put them out of sight because they're not as popular here as in the United States."

"A fellow officer was telling me about monte. I've never seen it played."

"In that case, don't start by playing for money," Ortiz cautioned. "You can lose everything in your pocket in a very short time."

"Is it like poker?"

"Not at all. Come on, let's go watch a few hands. But take my advice and leave your purse in your pocket. Later, if you feel like living dangerously, you can risk losing your pay. Over there," he said, pointing at a table on the left. "Let's go watch Doña Rosalia. She's probably the best monte dealer in the territory."

As they approached the table, mugs in hand, Benoit studied the woman he had come to believe was a living legend. O'Hara, he recalled, had described her as old and unattractive. But that, Benoit realized as they drew closer, had been youth speaking. In actuality,

Doña Rosalia was what his father would have called a *femme de certain âge*, meaning that while she might have been a little past her prime, as far as years went, she still retained much more than a trace of her youthful beauty.

A plump, cheerful-looking woman with tiny hands that moved with hummingbird swiftness, Doña Rosalia watched them approach with quick, alert eyes as black, Benoit noted, as Colonel Kemp's.

"Hello, Doña Rosalia," Ortiz greeted her robustly, lifting her hand and brushing his lips across it gently. Benoit noticed she had a ring on every finger, including her thumb.

"Ah, Señor Ortiz," she replied, saying something in rapid Spanish that Benoit assumed was a friendly greeting.

"I've brought someone I would like you to meet," he said in English. "Doña Rosalia, this is my new friend, Captain Benoit," he added, stressing the *wah*. "He's a Frenchman, so he's sensitive about the pronunciation of his name," he added with a wink.

"It's my pleasure," Benoit said with a slight bow. "I'm delighted that you speak English."

"Oh, she doesn't *speak* English." Ortiz laughed. "She understands it well enough, but she refuses to speak it."

Benoit smiled. "Nevertheless, it is a pleasure to meet you."

He studied her more carefully. Up close, he realized that she probably was a little older than he had first thought, but uncommonly handsome nonetheless. Her thick dark hair, showing only a few strands of telltale gray, was piled on top of her head and held in place by exquisite silver combs that Benoit

figured were imported from Spain. Her dress was of
fine dark silk, cut in what he assumed was the latest
fashion. Over her shoulders was a large scarf, also
made of expensive silk, and around her neck were
half a dozen gold chains, one of which held a crucifix as large as his fist. There was a spot of rouge on
each cheek, and her lips had been darkened with
some sort of dark red stain. In her other hand, the
one that Ortiz had not kissed, was a long, thick
cigar.

"What does that say?" he asked, pointing to a sign
nailed to the wall behind her.

Ortiz chuckled. "'*Pleitos con todos menos con la
cocinera.*' 'Fight everyone except the cook.' That's her
way of saying to the gamblers at her table that if their
cards are not winners, it's not her fault. Once you
learn Spanish, you'll find out that Doña Rosalia is
obsessed with proverbs and adages. She uses them the
way you and I use verbs."

"She talks in proverbs?" Benoit asked, amused.

"Almost always." Ortiz grinned. "Tell her you
had a lucky night with the cards and she'll reply, '*A
caballo regalado no se le mira el colmillo.*' 'Never look a
gift horse in the mouth.' Or if you mention, for example, that you are considering asking a friend for a loan,
she'll likely tell you, '*No le busques cinco patas al gato.*'"

"Which means?"

"Literally, 'Don't be looking for five paws on the
cat.' In other words, don't go seeking trouble."

While Ortiz was talking, a slight, elderly man with
a patched *sarape* thrown over his shoulders sidled up
to the table. He reached beneath his blanket and, with
a gnarled hand, produced a single silver coin that he
thumped on the table.

"I've never seen one of those," Benoit said, staring at the small piece of silver.

"It's a *real*," Ortiz explained. "A Mexican coin worth an eighth of a dollar, or about twelve and a half cents. It's by far the most common currency you'll see in New Mexico, where virtually all the people are poor. Also there's the *peso*, which is equivalent to a dollar but highly preferred over the American coin because it contains more silver. Just one more thing the Hispanos don't like about the Americanos. Occasionally you'll see an *onza de oro*, a coin containing exactly one ounce of gold. It's worth sixteen *pesos*. But those are fairly rare in here."

The slap of cards on the table drew Benoit's attention. Doña Rosalia had dealt four cards face up: a seven of clubs, a three of swords, a knave of cups, and a horse of clubs.

"Ignore the face value of the cards," Ortiz explained. "The important thing is the suit."

The old man reached out and pulled two of the cards to his side of the table: the swords and the cups. He pointed at the swords.

"He's betting that Doña Rosalia will deal another swords before she deals a cups," Ortiz explained.

Doña Rosalia peeled a card off the deck. It was an ace of clubs.

The man grunted, and Doña Rosalia dealt another card, an eight of suns.

The man smiled slightly and nodded at the table. Doña Rosalia flipped over another card, the three of cups.

"¡*Maldito!*" the man muttered. Dammit. Without another word he shuffled off.

"*Mal no venga que por bien no sea*," Doña Rosalia called after him.

"She told him that something good comes often out of something bad," Ortiz translated. "In other words, don't lose faith. Do you play billiards?"

"Not in a long time," said Benoit, "but I'm willing to try."

His lack of practice was quickly apparent. Ortiz ran the table on him in the first match, then soundly defeated him twice more.

"You must spend all your spare time down here," Benoit said after knocking the cue ball off the table when he overstruck a simple straight-ahead knock-in. He was retrieving the ball from the corner when he stopped and straightened up. "What's all the racket?" he asked, frowning.

From the other room came the sound of shouts and curses.

"*¡Ay, mierda!*" Ortiz cursed. "Sounds to me like a brawl is in the making."

At the door, they looked out on a scene of mass confusion. Half a dozen teamsters had formed a crude ring in the center of the room, standing back-to-back and taunting the surrounding crowd of Hispanos. "Come on, you sonsabitches," one of the Americans roared, waving a huge fist in the air like a hammer.

"*¡Gringo salado!*" yelled a young Hispano half his size. "You insipid white man." Ducking his head and swinging his arms as if he were trying to swim the Río del Norte, he let out another scream and ran straight at the imposing teamster.

"You stupid bastard," the American grunted, stepping neatly aside and booting the man in the rear as he went by, sending him flying through the other side of the ring.

Laughing, the American turned back to the crowd. "Any other dumb son of a bitch out there?" he roared.

In reply, a slim Hispano ran forward, brandishing a chair he had taken from behind one of the tables. With what seemed a huge effort, he lifted it as high as he could and brought it crashing down onto the American's head. The American bellowed and threw up his arms. Blood was spurting from his forehead in a bright fountain. Groaning, the mule driver staggered backward for three steps and collapsed in a heap, making a faint mewing sound as his eyes rolled upward.

That broke the impasse. With a roar, the Hispanos attacked in a wave, overwhelming the Americans by sheer numbers.

Ortiz looked at Benoit. "Should we join in?"

Benoit looked at him as if he had asked for a million dollars. "Hell, no. I may not be too smart, but I'm not crazy."

"My sentiments exactly." Ortiz laughed and turned to watch the carnage.

Suddenly, over the rumble, they could hear a woman's voice. Doña Rosalia, anxious to bring the fracas to an immediate end before her establishment was destroyed, had climbed onto the stage to use the only tool at her command. In as clear and beautiful a contralto voice as Benoit had ever heard, she was singing.

Ave Maria, gratia plena, dominus tecum.
Benedicta tu in mulieribus,
Et benedictus fructus ventris tui Jesu. . . .

"I'll be damned," Benoit said, turning to Ortiz. "That's the first time I've heard Latin in years."

"Maybe you ought to go to Mass more often."

"Sure. There's a Catholic church just down the road in Fort Laramie."

"No excuse here. Santa Fe has four churches. Listen!"

"Listen to what?" Benoit asked. "All I hear is Doña Rosalia singing the Hail Mary."

"That's what I mean. Look. The fighting's stopped."

Benoit leaned out the door and glanced around the room. The Hispanos had withdrawn from the fight and were standing as still as if they were before the altar. Several of them, Benoit noticed, were making the sign of the cross. A few at first, then almost all, joined Doña Rosalia in the prayer.

"*Sancta Maria, mater dei*," their voices rang out.

Ora pro nobis pecatoribus,
Nunc et in hora mortis nostrae.

Before the final "*amen*" reverberated around the room, the battered teamsters had pulled themselves off the floor. Dripping blood and dragging their unconscious comrades behind them, they made for the exit, thankful for the reprieve.

"That was some show," Benoit muttered.

"You mean the fight?"

"No, the power of prayer among the Hispanos."

Ortiz chuckled. "You haven't seen anything yet, friend. One day I'll tell you about *Los Hermanos*."

"The what?"

"The Brotherhood. The *Penitentes*."

"What is that? Some type of fraternal organization?"

Ortiz laughed. "Sort of."

"Is it religious?"

"Oh, yes. Very religious."

"Well, why won't you tell me about it?"

Ortiz shook his head. "Not yet, Jean. Be patient."

"Ortiz . . . ," Benoit began.

"No, Jean. No sense pestering me. That's all I'm going to say about the subject right now."

Benoit paused. "Fair enough. Whenever you're ready. In the meantime, tell me what you know about Doña Rosalia."

"That's easy." Ortiz smiled. "No one knows much about her. She just showed up one day about five years ago with enough gold in her purse to buy this place. From the day La Estrella opened, it's been a tremendous success. *Everyone* in New Mexico knows Doña Rosalia, but no one knows her surname."

"There're not so many people in the territory that you haven't heard something about where she came from or how she ended up here?"

"You asked me what I knew, not what I'd heard."

"Okay." Benoit smiled. "What have you *heard*?"

Ortiz put down his cue stick. "Rumors. That's all. It is said that she was either born into or married into a wealthy family from a mountain village called *Nuestra Señora del Rosario, San Fernando y Santiago del Río de las Truchas*."

"That's a real mouthful."

"Most people just call it Truchas. In any case, her husband, an alleged *rico*, is now dead, either of natural causes or a victim of a deed most foul."

"You mean murdered?"

"That or a suicide. Perhaps killed in a duel. No one knows. The reports vary. One says her late husband was much older than Doña Rosalia and died while performing his conjugal privileges. Another says he was killed in a political squabble. Still another says he died in a fight over a woman other than Doña Rosalia."

"Which do you believe?"

Ortiz shrugged. "None of them. All of them. Who knows? Anything is possible in the mountains of Río Arriba."

"The Río Arriba? I've never heard of it. Is that a local name for the Río del Norte?"

"It's not an actual river," Ortiz explained. "'*Arriba*' means 'upriver'—that is, the upper stretches of the land drained by the Río del Norte. It refers to the territory north of La Bajada Mesa, which is just south of here. Santa Fe is in the Río Arriba. Alburquerque, on the other hand, is south of the mesa and is in the area called Río Abajo—'*abajo*' means 'downriver.' Almost everything in New Mexico, you'll discover, revolves around the church and the Río del Norte. "

"And that's all anyone knows about her?"

"What does anyone *need* to know?" Ortiz asked, irritated. "Her tables are honest. Her whiskey is not watered. She sings every Sunday at the St. Francis *parroquia*. As she herself would say, if someone proves too nosy, *En todo esta menos en misma*. That means, 'He minds everyone's business but his own.' Now," he said, gesturing with his cue stick, "are you going to rack them, or do you want to admit total defeat?"

10

Benoit sighed contentedly and leaned back in his chair, smothering a polite belch. Waving off a proffered black cigar, he sipped his coffee tentatively, smiling in delight when it met his expectations. "You don't know how good it is to have some real French coffee that I didn't have to make myself," he told a beaming Joseph Machebeuf. "In fact," he added fervently, "it was a wonderful meal. It reminded me of holidays at home, where roast duck was a real treat."

"It's kind of you to say so," Machebeuf replied, "but I can't take the credit. Bishop Lamy and I share a *cuisinière* who comes in to prepare special dinners. Señora Dominguez has learned well the art of French cooking, don't you agree?"

"She would be welcome to cook for me at any time," Benoit said, smiling. "But tell me, how on earth did you manage to get oysters in the middle of this godforsaken desert?"

"It's a desert true enough," Vicar General Machebeuf replied with a smile, "but it certainly hasn't been forsaken by God."

Benoit blushed. "Bad choice of words. What I meant to say was—"

"I know what you meant." Machebeuf laughed. "I just couldn't resist. Not for nothing do my friends say I have a twisted sense of humor. But to answer your question, you'd be surprised what travels up the Chihuahua Trail, and what you can get if you know the right people. They came, I am told, from the Gulf of California."

"They must have cost a fortune."

Machebeuf shook his head. "A benefit of the Roman collar, especially when you're dealing with Catholic tradesmen."

Benoit chuckled appreciatively. "And this?" he asked, lifting his wineglass. "Did this come via the Chihuahua Trail? France to Mexico to Santa Fe?"

Machebeuf laughed. "It *is* a good wine, isn't it? But it isn't French. It was made right here in New Mexico from grapes imported from Spain. That is one thing we certainly have to thank the Franciscans for. That and planting the seed of Catholicism."

"And they planted it very deeply, didn't they?" Benoit said. "I think," he added earnestly, "the thing that has impressed me the most so far about New Mexico is the religiosity of the people. No," he said quickly, shaking his head. "That's not right. I mean, I am impressed by the role religion plays in everybody's life. I was amazed, for example, when I saw how everything, all commerce, even horsemen on the streets, pause three times a day for the Angelus. They don't even do that in New Orleans anymore, although I understand it was common not many years ago."

"You can't compare Santa Fe and New Orleans," Machebeuf said. "New Orleans is an international city.

Santa Fe is an isolated village in the middle"—he paused and winked—"of a godforsaken desert."

"Touché," Benoit said, wincing. "But I'm still fascinated by the devoutness of the people."

"Giving lip service to ritual doesn't make you a good Catholic," Machebeuf pointed out.

"I understand what you're saying, but to me it apparently goes much deeper than that. From what I have seen, it seems that New Mexicans have an unshakable personal belief in the *power* of religion. As we were talking earlier this evening, miracles seem almost a matter of routine here."

"Many of these so-called miracles have to be taken with a grain of salt. As you know, before the church will certify a miracle, it has to be put to a severe test."

"From my point of view," Benoit said slowly, "whether an incident merits certification is almost beside the point. To me, it seems like the important thing is that the *people* believe in it."

"That's true enough as far as it goes, but there are many deeper issues involved," Machebeuf said, rising. "Excuse me for a moment. I'll get us some brandy."

"Oh, no," Benoit said, shaking his head. "Thank you very much, but I think I'll stick with my wine. I'm a little out of practice with my alcohol consumption."

"I'll get the bottle anyway." Machebeuf smiled. "Maybe you'll change your mind."

As his host rummaged through a cabinet, searching for the brandy, Benoit studied him covertly. A small man, probably no more than five-four or five-five, Machebeuf looked to be in his early or mid-forties, Benoit calculated, not quite old enough to be his father. He had eyebrows so light, they could hardly be seen, and sparse blond hair that he wore long and brushed back, exposing a wide brow. His eyes were brown, magnified by silver-rimmed spectacles. Despite the fact that he was a Frenchman, Machebeuf reminded him of an Irish leprechaun: a tiny, mischievous bundle of energy capable of surprising feats, like finding oysters in landlocked New Mexico.

"Here we are," Machebeuf said, plopping a nearly full bottle on the table. "This is made locally as well, and it's quite good. Are you sure you won't have a taste?"

"Well," Benoit said hesitantly. "Maybe just a drop."

"Good," Machebeuf said, smiling. He poured two fingers of golden brown liquid into one of the two clean glasses he had brought with the bottle. "Now where were we?"

"I think, Vicar General . . ."

Machebeuf waved his hand. "Don't be so formal, Jean. The New Mexicans usually call me Don José, but in some circles I'm also known as *El Vicario Andando*, the Traveling Vicar, because of my insatiable desire to get around and about the territory. Among the clerics the bishop and I brought over from France I'm known as Père Joseph. So take your choice; I'm a man of many names."

"And," Benoit added with a slight bow, "many talents. We were discussing how deeply committed New Mexicans seem to be to Catholicism."

"Oh, yes, of course. But you have to understand, Jean, that Catholicism in New Mexico is not as seamless as it appears at first glance."

"I don't understand," Benoit said, frowning.

"The faith has gone through two distinct phases in

the territory," Machebeuf said patiently, "and we're now in the third. The first was what I think of as the explorer phase. That's when the Franciscans who accompanied the very first *Conquistadores* began spreading the faith among the Indians. They were fortunate to have found a number of tribes, they called them Pueblos, that were sedentary. It is always easier for a missionary to deal with a sedentary people, as opposed to roving bands like the Apaches and the Comanches. In fairly short order, the Franciscans converted the majority of the Pueblo Indians. The early settlers were either Spanish or Mexican Catholics, so that meant that practically everyone, excluding the nomads, of course, in New Mexico was Catholic, at least in name."

"And the second phase?"

"I call that the Mexican phase," Machebeuf said. "It began when Mexico won its independence and the Franciscans withdrew to Spain. To serve the substantial Catholic population, the bishop in Durango, the diocesan seat, began recruiting priests in New Mexico, training them in Durango, then sending them back here."

"And you represent the third phase?" Benoit asked.

"Yes. Bishop Lamy, me, and the priests we have brought over from France to replace the ones trained in Durango."

"Are they being replaced because of the corruption I have heard about?" Benoit asked. "Charging exorbitant fees for religious services, for example."

"That's part of it." Machebeuf nodded. "But not all. There also are doctrinal differences that Bishop Lamy feels he cannot tolerate."

"Oh?" Benoit asked, raising an eyebrow. "I haven't heard of those."

"No, you probably would not have. But believe me, they are just as significant as the other issues."

"Can you give me an example?" Benoit asked.

"Easily," Machebeuf replied solemnly. "Right now one of our major concerns is the *Penitentes*."

Benoit's eyes flew open wide. "How ironic! I just heard that name for the first time two nights ago. They are also called *Los Her . . . Her . . .*"

"*Hermanos*," Machebeuf said. "The Brotherhood. Or *Los Penitentes*, the Penitent Ones. In the villages, they also are known as *el unión*, *el fraternidad*, *el hermandad*, and *el sociedad*. Formally, they call themselves the *Cofradía de Nuestro Padre Jesús Nazareno*, the Confraternity of Our Father, Jesus of Nazareth. More commonly, though, it is just the Brothers. I'm curious. What did you hear?"

"Only the name. I got the impression it was some sort of fraternal organization."

Machebeuf sighed. "If only it were that simple."

"I take it, then, it isn't. Simple, I mean."

"Far from it. Would you like to hear about it? I think it is probably something you should be aware of."

"Very much. Please go on."

"Then have a little more brandy," he said, tipping another dollop into Benoit's glass. "This may take a while."

"I'm going to regret this tomorrow." Benoit smiled and lifted his glass. "But tell me about the Brothers."

Machebeuf took a large swallow of brandy. "Very well," he said, somewhat sadly, Benoit thought. "Earlier, we were talking about the Franciscans planting the seeds of Catholicism in New Mexico. Remember?"

Benoit nodded silently.

"Well, Bishop Lamy and I fear they may have planted those seeds too deeply."

Benoit was surprised. "How can that possibly be?"

"The Franciscans, like good missionaries are supposed to do, converted the natives to an amazing degree. But then they made a big mistake. They erred in not realizing the necessity of providing an adequate number of priests to sufficiently administer to the needs of the faithful."

"I'm not sure I understand."

"In almost all New Mexico villages and towns every resident is a Catholic. . . ."

"From your point of view, that's good, isn't it?" Benoit interrupted.

"To a degree, yes. But, particularly in the northern villages, the people are so isolated that even today they hardly ever see a priest. Part of the reason for this is geographical. Many of the villages are snowed in from late October until mid-May, so they are accessible only for . . . what? Four or five months a year? But they also are widely spread; it may take several days to a week to get from one village to another even if the paths aren't blocked by snow."

"I don't get your point."

"What I'm trying to say is that these villagers, left to themselves without a resident priest to guide them in proper doctrine, have developed their own forms of Catholicism, a sort of local dialect, if you will. A religious one, though, not a linguistic one. Have you seen any of the local holy figures?"

"As a matter of fact, yes. When I was en route here

there was a man who traveled with us whose profession was carving figures that he could bring to Santa Fe to sell. He called himself . . . what was it?"

"A *santero.*"

"That's it!" Benoit said, snapping his fingers. "Is that a bad thing to do?"

"You mean, is it a sin?"

"Yes, I guess that's what I mean."

"Definitely not. But did you see any of his works?"

"Yes," Benoit said. "In fact, I bought a small statue from him for my wife."

"Did you notice anything about the features of the figures?"

"Come to think of it . . ."

"They all looked Hispano, didn't they?"

Benoit nodded. "Yes."

"That's one of the things I mean about isolation," Machebeuf said. "Recall the holy images in the churches and homes of New Orleans. Christ and the saints all looked very Caucasian, didn't they? As if they came from northern Europe."

Benoit smiled. "Yes. God is represented as an old man with a flowing white beard."

"Have you ever seen a Hispano with a long white beard?" Machebeuf asked, his eyes twinkling.

"No, but—"

"That's a minor thing. I brought it up only to underline the fact that thousands of New Mexicans have begun practicing a form of Catholicism that is different from that endorsed by Rome. In some cases—and this is what the bishop and I find most troubling—there is a serious conflict. We don't care if their holy figures look like their neighbors. In

Guatemala there is a village named Esquípulas that is famous for its *Cristo Negro,* a black Christ."

"A black Christ?" Benoit said, almost choking on his brandy. "How can that be?"

"When the Spaniards were in control," Machebeuf explained, "they were not known for their gentility. They ruled the natives with an iron fist. In fact, they were so cruel that the natives, although converted, had trouble accepting the representation of Christ as a white man. In order to alleviate this fear, the bishop, a very wise man indeed, commissioned a famed local carver to create an image of Christ on the cross out of mahogany wood, reasoning that since the color of the wood closely resembled the natives' skin color, the representation would be more acceptable. The decision was a good one. The natives readily accepted the brown-toned figure and hung it on the altar. However, over the years, smoke from incense and candles turned the brown wood a deep black. *Voilà!*— a black Christ."

"That's amazing," Benoit said, shaking his head. "I've never heard that story before."

Machebeuf wagged a finger. "Maybe you need to be more in touch with the church," he teased. "*El Nuestro Señor de Esquípulas* is famous for His miracles. There is even a connection between the Guatemalan Christ and New Mexico. But," he added hurriedly to close off Benoit's question, "that's a story for another night. Back to the *Penitentes.*"

Benoit lifted the bottle and gestured toward Machebeuf's glass. "More brandy?"

The vicar general nodded. "A tad. But we were talking about the seeds of Catholicism. Continuing with that analogy, the bishop feels it is our duty to rip

out the wild roots that have sprung from the original
Franciscan planting. In some areas of New Mexico,
notably the northern mountains, a hybrid form of
Catholicism has sprouted and become embedded. I
think of it as a deviation, an unholy tendril, if you will.
Because it developed from the Catholic tree, it still
carries the mark of Catholicism. But because it has ger-
minated so far from the tree, it has taken on character-
istics of paganism. In essence, what the people who
practice this . . . this . . . I'm not sure what to call it.
Perversion, perhaps? Deviancy? Yes," he said, almost
to himself, "I like 'deviancy.' In any case, what these
people have done is distort some of our basic tenets
and turn them into something, uh, deviant."

"And that *deviancy*," Benoit said, brightening, "is
the Brotherhood."

"Exactly!"

"But I don't see the significance."

"No. Perhaps I've been moving too quickly. Let
me go back a little. You'll remember from your catechism that we Catholics recognize seven sacraments:
baptism, confirmation, the Eucharist, which is the
Mass, penance, extreme unction, holy orders, and mat-
rimony."

"Naturally, I remember that. Père Eusèbe—"

Machebeuf held up his hand. "Patience, my young
friend. I'm not testing your devotion. I'm only filling
in some of the background."

"My apologies," Benoit said. "I imagine that did
sound defensive."

"What these *deviants*, the Brothers, have done is
outrageously misinterpret the mechanisms of some of
the sacraments, especially penance."

"Penance?" Benoit asked, puzzled. "You mean

like after confession you have to say five Hail Marys, four Our Fathers . . ."

Machebeuf smiled. "In its most simple form, yes, that's what I mean. But these reprobates, these miscreants, have made a virtual *religion* out of penance. They have garbled our doctrines so thoroughly that all the other sacraments revolve around penance. In other words, they have raised personal suffering to the highest order, all in violation of what Pope Pius and his predecessors have determined is contrary to the meaning of Catholicism."

"I'm afraid you've lost me again," Benoit said. "How can penance—"

"Very well, let me start again. I realize that this concept may not be too easily grasped by someone who does not devote his entire life to the intricacies of the faith, but I'll try to make it brief. As far back as the Middle Ages it was believed by many European Catholics that the only way to counter worldly evil was through extreme self-sacrifice. The most popular way of doing this was through flagellation. A believer, in repentance for a sin, either real or imagined, was to take a whip and literally beat himself almost to death. This proposition was later rejected by Rome, and the practice of self-flagellation was condemned. The pope declared such beliefs heresy. However, the practice continued in Spain and probably was brought here, in one form or another, by the Franciscans and the *Conquistadores*. In his journal, Don Juan Oñate writes that self-flagellation was committed by himself and his soldiers while on their way to New Mexico more than two hundred and fifty years ago. Let me read you what he says."

Machebeuf bounded into the other room and

returned five minutes later with a thick volume, which he opened to a previously marked page.

"Here," he told Benoit, "Oñate is writing about a scene in an expeditionary camp near what is now El Paso del Norte on Holy Thursday in 1598. His men, he said, were eager to seek redemption through pain. I quote: 'The soldiers, with cruel scourges, beat their backs unmercifully until the camp ran crimson with their blood. The humbler Franciscan friars, barefoot and clothed in cruel, thorny girdles, devoutly chanted their doleful hymns, praying forgiveness for their sins. . . .'"

He slammed the book closed and laid it on the table. "There have been many, many other reports of self-flagellation and processions of flagellants throughout New Mexico ever since."

"You mean," Benoit asked earnestly, "that to be a Catholic in New Mexico—"

"Oh, no!" Machebeuf said emphatically. "Not all Catholics subscribe to this perversion. Not by any means. But there are a sizable number who do. Most of them reside in the mountains, isolated for years from mainstream Catholicism."

"And you yourself have seen this?"

Don José nodded grimly. "Last year, during Holy Week, I got permission from Bishop Lamy to travel to the north so I could see for myself what had been reported to us."

"And what did you witness?" Benoit asked, leaning forward, his face flushed with excitement.

"I was traveling incognito, you understand. Disguised as a peasant."

"Yes, yes. Go on," Benoit said anxiously.

"It was near a village known as Chimayó, on

Good Friday morning. The people, most of them women and children, had lined themselves along the road in anticipation of the display that was to come."

"They knew what was about to happen?"

"Oh, yes. They've been doing this for generations. After waiting for quite a while, just when I was certain I would be discovered, men from the village began emerging from this windowless hut in which they traditionally gathered and began walking in our direction. They were chanting in a mixture of Latin and Spanish, and from the glazed look in their eyes, I could see that they were entranced."

"Do you think they had been drinking too much wine?" Benoit asked.

Machebeuf shook his head emphatically. "Oh, no. This was mental drunkenness, not physical."

"So what happened?"

"Many of them were wrapped in chains, and they carried whips made of leather studded with cactus branches. As they walked, they began beating themselves, wailing and begging for forgiveness. Blood flowed like water down their backs. Among the group were several carrying huge wooden crosses, one of whom was called 'Christ.' Behind them followed other Brothers, some of whom were brandishing whips that they used on their fellow travelers. One man was reading from a missal, and one was playing a mournful tune on a flute. All were barefoot although the path was lined with sharp rocks. And despite the fact that it was a very cold day with a bitter wind and occasional snow, they were clad only in white trunks with black hoods over their heads to preserve their identities. At the very rear was a *carreta*, a small cart, carrying a wooden skeleton representing Death and armed with

a drawn bow and an arrow. The sight made the hair
on the back of my neck rise, and I thought I was going
to be sick. When they got to the place where the
women were waiting, a few females, who I later
learned were called Veronicas, ran forward with cloths
and wiped their bleeding forms. One woman was supposed to be the Holy Mother, and she attended to the
man who represented her son."

"Where were they going?" Benoit asked. "Were
they just parading around the village?"

Machebeuf shook his head. "No, they had a definite route. They were moving up a hill they called
Calvario. Three times on the journey up the hill, the
man called Christ fell, and each time he rose again.
When they got to the crest, 'Christ' laid his cross on
the ground and then stretched out on top of it. Other
Brothers rushed forward and bound him to the boards
with white cloth, then they raised the cross and left
him to dangle there."

"Did he die?" Benoit asked, spellbound by the
tale.

"Not that day," Machebeuf replied, "but I understand that sometimes happens. The Brothers watched
him carefully, and when they judged he was close to
death, they hurriedly brought him down and spirited
him away to their private building, which they call a
morada, and treated him."

"And if he died?"

"In such a circumstance, I understand, the hapless
villager is buried secretly by the Brothers and his family is informed of his passing when they find his shoes
on their doorstep the next morning."

"How gruesome." Benoit shuddered.

"It is much worse than that," Machebeuf said

heatedly. "It is barbaric. It is a terrible sacrilege that mocks the sacrifice of Our Lord Jesus."

"If this has been going on for so long, why is it just now becoming an issue?" Benoit asked.

"Oh, this isn't new by any means," Machebeuf replied. "Bishop Zubiría, despite the differences we have had with *him*, denounced the Brotherhood a quarter of a century ago. Still, we find it paradoxical that the *Penitentes* underwent their most rapid growth under Bishop Zubiría—that is, after the Franciscans left and before Bishop Lamy arrived. We believe this has to do with the general deterioration of the official church under the Mexicans. The growth period coincides with the time that Bishop Zubiría was installing his own priests throughout the territory. Remember I talked about phase two? So you see, the problem we have been facing with the priests trained in Durango and ordained by Bishop Zubiría extends beyond civilian corruption."

"This may seem like an impertinent question, but what is Bishop Lamy trying to do to resolve the problem?"

"It is not impertinent at all. I'm grateful for your interest and your desire to understand the difficulties with which we're trying to cope. Both Bishop Lamy and myself have made trips to France to recruit young priests to come to New Mexico. Slowly we are trying to replace the Bishop Zubiría priests with our own. But we have run into difficulty because those priests installed by Bishop Zubiría are New Mexicans, and they have strong followings. In other words, we are meeting with severe local resistance. Regarding the *Penitentes*, Bishop Lamy has issued an order to the parish priests, instructing them to have anyone desiring to receive the sacraments swear that he is not *Penitentes*. But it has been largely ignored, particularly by those priests not named by him."

"It sounds like you have a problem, sure enough," said Benoit. "But I don't see how this affects the army. You know the American Constitution prohibits the mixing of church and state."

"Indeed it does," Machebeuf agreed, nodding. "That is the way we want it as well. But the church and the state have been one for so long in New Mexico that it is not a concept that is going to be erased very quickly. We—that is, Bishop Lamy and myself—do not expect General Barksdale or you or any officer to do anything *about* the *Penitentes*. I only wanted to explain the situation to you so you could better understand the people of the territory. Mainly, we feel it is not to the benefit of the church or the army for us to work at cross-purposes. That does not mean we have to be . . . what is the term among the Indians? Blood brothers? But we can agreeably coexist."

"Very well put," Benoit said. "I don't think you'll have any difficulty on that score from General Barksdale, and certainly not from me, although I'm only a lowly subordinate."

Machebeuf laughed and slapped Benoit on the shoulder. "Maybe that is true today, but who knows about the future? The church has not prevailed for almost two centuries by acting for the moment."

11

Benoit sat half-reclined on his cot, his portfolio spread on his lap. Outside, the summer sun was setting, casting a rosy glow on the whitewashed wall of his cramped quarters. The evening air had a cool, brisk feel, which was welcome after an especially hot afternoon. The climatic differences in the places he had lived held a certain fascination for Benoit, making him wonder occasionally if he should not have been a scientist rather than a soldier.

During his childhood he had accepted heat, humidity, and dampness as three of life's givens, never really aware that every place was not as sticky, moist, and sultry as New Orleans. Then, as a student at the academy in upstate New York, he had experienced his first snowfall. He still remembered how surprised he had been to learn that the white powder about which he had heard and seen only in book illustrations actually was *cold*. But it was not until he got to Fort Laramie that he learned what the word "winter" really meant. As a youth in southern Louisiana, swimming in Lake Pontchartrain on Christmas Day, it had been impossible to imagine the numbing cold of a Great

Plains winter. Trying to comprehend what January in
the Nebraska Territory was like from New Orleans
was as frustrating a mental exercise as trying to grasp
the meaning of eternity.

In New Mexico Benoit had discovered still
another climatic shift. Before arriving at Fort Marcy,
he had heard that Santa Fe was in the desert, so he'd
had visions of sand dunes and Sahara-like heat. To his
relief, it had not been that way at all. Soon after his
arrival, a fellow officer fresh from the Calabasas
Presidio in the southwestern corner of the territory had
explained that there were two kinds of desert. One
was the kind from which he had only recently
escaped, and the other was the *high* desert that characterized the Río Arriba country. Calabasas, near the
Mexican border, was incredibly hot from May through
October, with temperatures above 100 degrees routine.
In fact, he had been told, it was not unusual for the
thermometer to hit 120. Santa Fe, on the other hand, at
seven thousand feet elevation, rarely had afternoon
temperatures over 95. After sunset it was a rarity if the
thermometer did not plunge by thirty degrees as the
land's heat fled rapidly into the cloudless sky. June,
Benoit had learned, was the hottest month on the high
desert because the wet season arrived in mid-July.
From then until mid-September there were almost
always afternoon showers. And in the Río Arriba
country the storms were actually cooling, unlike New
Orleans, where late afternoon rain only increased the
heat, turning the entire city into a giant steambath.

Smiling to himself, Benoit forced his mind back on
track. Without Inge to keep him company in the
evenings, he found he spent too much time daydream-
ing and not enough doing something constructive, like

practicing his Spanish. Although he was amazed at how quickly the language was coming to him, he still had not reached the point where he considered himself fluent. The hard part was the vocabulary. And the only way he could overcome that obstacle was through practice.

Work, whether it was in General Barksdale's office or in perfecting his Spanish, was a way to keep his mind occupied. Otherwise, his longing to hold Inge or argue with Jace became nearly unbearable. At those times, homesickness swept over him like a wall of water surging down an arroyo after a thunderstorm. For the first time, Benoit was beginning to comprehend precisely how lonely a soldier's life could be.

In one respect, though, he considered himself lucky. Although he was several hundred miles distant from his wife, he at least had access to an efficient and speedy mail system. Inge might be at Fort Laramie, but a letter from here to there took only a week. Mail was a poor substitute for actual contact, but at least it presented an alternative. Newly resolved to take advantage of the opportunity the postal service offered him, Benoit dipped his pen in the inkwell at his elbow and began to write.

Fort Marcy, Territory of New Mexico
23 August 1858

My Dearest Inge,

Needless to say, I am delighted to learn via your latest correspondence that you continue in excellent health. It is a matter of great concern to me, being so far away. Thank God your mother and

Jace are there or I would be too nervous to eat or sleep.

I was disturbed, though, at the news about Erich and his lack of progress. It's been some three months now since the accident. Does Jace offer no hope at all? It is important, nevertheless, that his spirits remain high. To date, that does not seem to be a problem, but I dread the day, if it ever comes, that you report that Erich has plunged into despair. Knowing Erich as I do, however, I can't see that as a possibility. I think I am more worried about Jim and his drinking. As I've mentioned before, General Barksdale also has a problem along those lines. So far, he continues to perform his duties in a very competent fashion, but I know he must suffer from dreadful headaches. Following my usual curious nature, I sneaked a sip from the bottle he keeps always at hand in a lower desk drawer. I have to confess that I don't see how he drinks it. It reminded me of nothing less than horse liniment, and I spat it out immediately. Or at least as soon as I could reach the window.

Compared to Fort Laramie, my duties here are remarkably tame. I remember how upset you used to get when I was out on patrol or when I was attached to Colonel Sumner on the Cheyenne expedition. You can rest easy that nothing like that is occupying my days here. For the most part the work so far has proved exceedingly dull. I get up early, report to General Barksdale, and spend the rest of the day shuffling papers or running errands. So far I have not been out of Santa Fe except for a rapid trip last week to a nearby village called Abiqui to pick up some documents for the general. It hardly proved to be a sight-seer's Mecca, composed as it is of a mere collection of adobe huts even more miserable than the commonest *barrios* in Santa Fe.

There has been a change, nevertheless, in the way I have come to view the city. At first, I was appalled at the sameness of everything—the mud adobes, the mud streets—but lately I have learned to see things in a new light, thanks to guidance from my new friend Alejo. He provides a perspective on life in New Mexico that I would not otherwise see, and for this I am very grateful. One advantage of our friendship is that it gives me additional exposure to the Hispanos, therefore the opportunity to improve upon my Spanish. Jace was right about one thing: The language is coming to me very swiftly, thanks no doubt to my background with French. When I go for an evening with Alejo I find I can understand almost all of what is being said around me, but so far I can't speak it very well. One of his favorite places is a gambling house called La Estrella. Don't worry, I'm not losing all my pay: we go to play billiards.

Last week there was a special treat. One of Alejo's cousins was getting married, and he invited me to attend the ceremony as his guest. It was quite a thrill. The ceremony took place in the interior courtyard of the house of the cousin, who was the bride. It was my first visit to the home of a *rico*. The courtyard was decorated for the occasion with pine boughs, which were fastened to the posts of the *portal* that runs around the interior area. A New Mexican priest named Padre Trujillo was the celebrant. Although it was in the house, the couple will go at some future date to Padre Trujillo's church, San Miguel, to repeat the vows during a nuptial Mass so they can receive the formal blessing.

After the ceremony, which was very brief, kegs of local wine and brandy were tapped. The feast itself was something to behold. There were roasted chickens basted in spiced wine and stuffed with meat, *piñon* nuts, and raisins; baked hams; ribs of beef; bowls of hot chili with platters of *tortillas*; cakes, sweets, and beakers of chocolate. Once the tables were demolished, the musicians were called in: two men with violins, one with a guitar, and one with a distinctive bass guitar called a *guitarrón*. Servants spread fresh wheat straw over the bare earth to keep down the dust that ordinarily would be raised by the dancing. The music ranged from quadrilles and minuets to a dance called *la cuña*, which is a sort of waltz. There was another that featured much heel stomping called *la raspa*. The dancing went on until past midnight, but Alejo and I left fairly early because of the long ride back into the city.

The wedding also gave me a good opportunity to practice my Spanish, since I was the only Anglo there and the only one who spoke English. In actuality, there is no excuse for me not to work even harder to perfect my ability with the language. Since the General and I start work early, we usually finish early as well. And that leaves me with my evenings free. With the long summer days I have sufficient time in the evenings to explore and begin searching for a suitable place to live for you and our son. So far, everything I have seen has been quite dreary, but I have to confess I have not yet made a determined effort since your arrival seems so far away. I try not to let my thoughts dwell on that. It just makes me miss you all the more.

An advantage of being at Fort Marcy is that there are so many interesting things to see in Santa Fe. This is going to surprise you because I know you have never thought of me as a religious person, but there are a number of intriguing churches. Right here in Santa Fe, for example, there is one known in Spanish as *La Castrense*, which signifies it was originally a military chapel, since it was built almost a hundred years ago to serve the Spanish troops. Among the Anglos, it is referred to as the Chapel of Our Lady of Light. I am told that it fell into terrible disrepair during the Mexican period. The roof had been allowed to collapse, and across the earthen floor were scattered the bones of those who had been buried there in previous years. After Bishop Lamy arrived, however, it was quickly repaired and is now under his personal attention. Within its walls are a number of screens, called *reredos*, dating to the time of its construction, as well as an impressive panel of paintings of the saints, and a beautiful bas-relief of the Virgin Mary, who is, of course, Our Lady of Light.

What sounds even more interesting, however, is a church in the northern village of Chimayó. Called simply *El Sanctuario,* it is

reputed to have been the site of a whole host of
miracles, especially those in which the lame have
regained the use of their limbs. Unfortunately,
Chimayó is a day's ride from here, and I have
not yet—

There was a loud rap on the door, causing Benoit
to look up in irritation. "Yes," he called loudly. "Who
is it?"

"It's Private McGowan, sir," replied a squeaky
voice.

"Oh!" Benoit replied sharply, wondering what
General Barksdale's personal attendant was doing
pounding on his door this time of the evening.
"Come in."

"Sorry to interrupt you, sir," McGowan said,
sticking his head around the door.

"I was just writing a letter to my wife, Private.
What is it?"

"It's the general, sir. He wants you to come to his
office immediately."

"Now?" Benoit said shocked. "This is highly
unusual."

"I realize that, sir. But something has come up,
and the general sent me to fetch you right away."

"Very good," Benoit grunted. "Let me slip into my
shirt. Tell General Barksdale I'll be right there."

"Yes, sir," McGowan replied, closing the door
firmly behind him.

Benoit looked at the letter and sighed. I'll finish it
later, he told himself, setting aside his portfolio. After
shrugging into his uniform shirt, he tucked it in his
trousers and hurried across the compound to
Barksdale's office.

"Enter!" Barksdale barked after Benoit knocked and announced his arrival.

Inside, Benoit was surprised to see Vicar General Machebeuf sitting in front of the general's desk, a tumbler containing a dark brown liquid in his hand. Barksdale's ever-present bottle of local whiskey was sitting on his desk. A half-full glass sat to the general's right.

"Grab a seat, Benoit," Barksdale commanded, nodding to a second chair, "and join us. We have a matter of extreme delicacy to discuss."

Frowning, Benoit did as he was told. He was not, he noticed, offered a drink. He sat stiffly, saying nothing, waiting instead to be told what the unusual summons was about.

"Don José is asking for our help," Barksdale began.

Benoit, nodding silently, noticed that the general's eyes were as red as the cliffs of the Sangre de Cristos at sunset, but his voice was firm and steady.

"A priest has been murdered," Barksdale said, getting immediately to the point.

"A priest!" Benoit gasped involuntarily. "Murdered? You mean killed in an Indian attack?"

"No, I do *not* mean killed in an Indian attack," Barksdale said brusquely. "I mean murdered. Killed at the altar."

"*Sacré merde!*" Benoit exclaimed. Looking quickly at Machebeuf, he blushed. "Excuse me, Don José."

Machebeuf waved his hand in dismissal. "I felt the same way when I heard the terrible news."

"Don José," Barksdale said, turning to the vicar

general, "would you mind explaining what happened one more time? I think you can do it better than I."

"Certainly." Machebeuf swiveled to face Benoit. "The crime occurred in the village of Mora. The victim was Padre Rabalais, one of the priests Bishop Lamy recruited from France. He had been here only six or seven months."

"What happened?" Benoit asked.

Don José paused, taking a sip from his glass. "Very briefly, he was saying Mass two days ago and he was poisoned."

Benoit stared in disbelief. "Poisoned? How could he be poisoned during the Mass?"

"Someone doctored the sacred wine."

"No!" Benoit said, shocked almost beyond words.

"Yes," Don José replied, nodding.

"F-forgive me," Benoit stammered. "I have a little trouble adjusting to this. I've never heard of such a dastardly crime. Can you please tell me all the details?"

"I don't know much," Don José said. "The reports I have received indicate that everything appeared normal. Padre Rabalais heard a few confessions, then went into the sacristy to don his vestments. When he came to the point in the service where he was required to sip the wine, he must have known something was amiss because he whispered to his acolyte, a young man named Pol Sena, that it was sour."

"Did he ask for fresh wine?" Benoit broke in.

"No. Sena offered to go get some, and Antoine— that is, Padre Rabalais—said no, that he didn't want to interrupt the service."

"So he continued?"

"Yes. He completed the Mass. But, almost as soon

as he had finished, he returned to the church and knelt in front of the altar to pray. At that point, he knew what was happening to him."

"How do you know that?"

"He turned to the church and spoke to the few people who were still there. According to Sena, he whispered, 'Pray for me, for I am dying. I have been struck down with poisoned wine.' Saying that, he collapsed and went into convulsions. Within a half hour he was dead."

Benoit waited for him to go on, but Don José apparently was finished. He took another sip from his glass and stared solemnly into space.

"Is that it?" Benoit asked.

Don José appeared not to have heard him.

Benoit looked at Barksdale, who coughed loudly but politely.

Don José shook himself, looking like a man who had just been awakened from a sound sleep. "I'm sorry," he said softly. "Did you say something?"

"I just asked if that was all," Benoit said.

"Well, that's how Antoine met his death," Don José said. "But it isn't the entire story."

"If you please," Barksdale said, "tell Captain Benoit what else you told me."

"You mean the background and my suspicions?"

Barksdale nodded. "Yes. Give him all the details."

"Very well," Don José said. "Jean"—he looked earnestly at Benoit—"do you remember the conversation we had the night you joined me for dinner? The part about how Bishop Lamy has been trying to replace the priests appointed by Bishop Zubiría with those of his own choosing?"

"Oh, yes," Benoit said, bobbing his head. "I remember very well."

"And do you also recall my telling you about the *Penitentes*—"

"Vividly, Don José."

"—and how Bishop Lamy had issued an order stating that a person desiring to receive any of the sacraments would first have to renounce *Los Hermanos*?"

"I remember."

"Good. And do you also remember how I explained that the Zubiría priests were ignoring the order?"

"Yes," Benoit said slowly. "Do you think this murder had something to do with the *Penitentes*?"

"I think," Don José said firmly, "that it had *everything* to do with the Brotherhood."

Benoit turned to Barksdale. "General, I don't understand. As terrible as this crime is, I don't see how it has to do with us."

Barksdale looked down at his desk. "Officially, Benoit, it doesn't. Unofficially, Vicar General Machebeuf has asked for our help in finding the murderer. I intend to grant that request."

"Certainly this is a matter that should be left to the civil authorities," Benoit argued.

"There *aren't* any civil authorities in that part of the territory," Don José interjected. "Certainly not one we could trust. Virtually every male above seventeen in Mora is a *Penitente*. They would never do anything to see one of their brothers punished."

"So we *are* going to be involved?" Benoit asked Barksdale, appealing for a change of mind.

"Not *we*, Benoit. Just you. Since this is not an army affair, I can't order you to help the vicar general. However, I'm going to free you up from your duties for the next three weeks. Put you on leave, as it were. I'm *hoping*," he said, locking eyes with Benoit, "that you might take that time to see some of the countryside. *Maybe* wander up toward Mora and sort of introduce yourself around. You know, just be friendly. Quietly ask a few questions."

"You can't go as an army officer," Don José said quickly. "The Moreños have no love of the army for reasons that are too complicated to go into at this time. They don't think much of Americhans, either. But you seem so open and aboveboard that they might open themselves up to you."

Benoit thought quickly. "My Spanish!" he said in desperation. "It isn't that good yet. And they probably speak a different dialect in Mora. I'd never be understood."

"We thought about that," said Don José. "The general agreed that you couldn't take the post interpreter. He's a *genízaro* and he wouldn't be accepted at all in Mora."

Benoit looked puzzled. "What's a *genízaro*? I've never heard that term."

"A *genízaro* is a nomadic Indian who has been raised as a Christian. In Joaquin Guerra's case, he's an Apache who was taken captive as a child and brought up in a Hispano home. The Moreños hate Apaches even more than they hate Americhans and army officers."

"So what am I supposed to do?" Benoit asked, puzzled.

Barksdale paused. "I believe you have a Hispano friend, a fellow named Ortiz. . . ."

"Alejo."

"That's the one. I think you also said he was from Mora."

"I couldn't ask Alejo to do *that*," Benoit said quickly.

"Why not?" Benoit asked.

"Because those are his people," Benoit said. "He couldn't betray them."

"Don't look at it as betrayal," Don José said. "Certainly he will agree that the murder of a priest is an obnoxious deed. We're not talking about someone who killed his neighbor in a fight over a sow or a man who murdered in a drunken rage. This is a cold-blooded murder of a cleric. A *cleric*," he repeated for emphasis.

Benoit was silent, considering his options. "Okay," he said after several moments. "I'll go. I don't think I really have a choice. Not," he said, glancing at Barksdale, "if it's an, uh, *request* from my general—"

"Consider it asked," Barksdale said firmly.

"—but I can't answer for Alejo. I'll explain the situation to him and *ask* him if he'd be willing to accompany me. If he says no, which he probably will, then that's that. I'll either take Guerra or we'll find someone else. Agreed?"

"Agreed," Don José said, smiling.

"It's your show," said Barksdale. "You handle it however you want. I'm not involved in any way. Do you understand?"

Benoit nodded. "Understood. Now," he added, turning to Don José, "perhaps you'd better tell me why you think Padre Rabalais was killed by the *Penitentes*."

Ortiz, Benoit could see, was just as astounded as he had been when he'd learned about the murder of Padre Rabalais.

"Incredible! Inconceivable! Somebody murder a priest? Pour poison in his chalice so he would die in the very act of saying Mass! It's outrageous. It's unbelievable. Whoever would do that would have to be totally without principle. Who could possibly stoop so low?"

Benoit paused, studying his friend. "Vicar General Machebeuf thinks it may have been part of a conspiracy by the local *Penitentes*."

"What!" Ortiz exclaimed, shocked. "One of the Brothers? No! Impossible! Never! That's absurd. Why would an *Hermano* do something like that? What would be the gain?"

"Removal of pressure," Benoit suggested. "Maybe a warning to Bishop Lamy himself."

Ortiz shook his head rapidly. "I don't understand what you're trying to say."

Carefully Benoit explained the politics of the situation, how Padre Rabalais had been sent in to replace the longtime pastor in Mora, the much beloved Padre Adan Romero, who was one of Bishop Zubiría's appointees.

"I didn't know the Frenchman was sent as a *replacement*," Ortiz said. "I know that Padre Romero is getting on in years, and I thought the new priest was simply an assistant."

"Apparently it was more than that," said Benoit. "For reasons that I have not been made privy to, Bishop Lamy seems to have been convinced that Padre Romero was too closely aligned to that priest in Taos who has been causing trouble for years."

"Padre Martinez?"

"I believe that's his name."

"I know who he is. It's rumored that he was one of

the instigators in the 1847 revolt, the one in which Governor Bent was killed."

"I'm sure that's who Don José was talking about."

"You knew about the Taos uprising, then?"

"A lieutenant at Fort Union told me."

"Did he tell you also that at the same time there was an incident in Mora?"

Benoit looked at him in surprise. "No!"

"It's true," said Ortiz. "I was away at school in St. Louis, but my family told me about it. A half dozen Americhanos were killed by a mob under the direction of a man named Porcopio Sandoval. The opinion in Mora was that Sandoval was not bright enough to organize such a plot on his own, so someone else must have been pulling his strings. It had never occurred to me before now—and I still think it's farfetched—but if what you've told me is correct, Sandoval could have been acting under the direction of Padre Romero. Within days, troops were sent in from Fort Marcy to arrest those who took part in the murders, especially Sandoval. But the Moreños tried to fight them off. At first they were successful, but then the soldiers brought in cannon and pretty much destroyed the village. A number of people were killed, including several women and children."

"So that's what Don José meant when he said soldiers were not very welcome in Mora. Did they get Sandoval?"

"No. His men were either captured or killed, but Sandoval somehow escaped. He simply disappeared. My guess would be he's hiding in Mexico, although his wife and son still live in Mora. But what evidence does the vicar general have to connect the murder of Padre Rabalais to the Brotherhood?"

"Not so much evidence as suspicion," said Benoit, who then explained how Bishop Lamy viewed the *Penitentes* as a heretical sect and was determined to eradicate them throughout the territory. "You know about his order to the priests to refuse sacraments to anyone who does not denounce the Brotherhood?"

Ortiz laughed bitterly. "An exercise in futility. That is just the new bishop trying to exert his authority. When he has been here long enough he will learn that it is *impossible* to get the people to renounce the *Penitentes*. The Brotherhood has been a powerful force in New Mexico for two hundred and fifty years, and it will continue to be for two hundred and fifty more. You have no conception how deeply it is entrenched. In actuality, the *Penitentes* are not just religious fanatics, you know. They do many other things."

"No, I didn't know that," Benoit said. "What do you mean?"

"They perform all kinds of good works. If a member—or anyone, for that matter—needs help, they are the first to provide it. Maybe it means supporting a woman whose husband has been killed by the Indians or who died in an accident on his farm. Somehow they find the money. Every year they spend long hours working in the *acequias*, dirty, backbreaking labor to make sure the irrigation water flows smoothly to all the farms. We have no law enforcement officers, so members of the Brotherhood keep the peace and, if necessary, act as a court to make sure the guilty are punished. . . ."

"But they will not punish the killer of Padre Rabalais, will they? Not if he's a Brother."

Ortiz was quiet. "That's a good point. Are there any *good* reasons to suspect the *Penitentes*?"

"Padre Rabalais was young and perhaps over-anxious to do what his bishop commanded. While Padre Romero may have been comfortable with ignoring the order to refuse the sacraments, Padre Rabalais almost certainly was trying to enforce it. Also," Benoit added hurriedly, "there had been several threats against him."

"Threats?" Ortiz said in surprise. "Against Padre Rabalais?"

Benoit nodded. "That's what Don José says. His residence was stoned once or twice, but he was never able to catch the culprits. Also, there were whispers in the confessional, warning him to be careful. He reported to Don José that he had withheld the sacrament of penance from several men after they refused to denounce the *Penitentes*, and they were not happy about it."

"I'm sure they were not. But tell me . . . what's your role in this? Why are you becoming so involved?"

Benoit sighed. "As a favor to Bishop Lamy, my general has *requested* that I go to Mora to see if I can find out who killed Padre Rabalais."

"A request, eh? Is that like an order?"

Benoit nodded. "The same thing. Except I can't travel in an official capacity. I plan to wear civilian clothes and not voluntarily disclose that I'm an army captain."

"That's wise," Ortiz agreed. "But how do you expect to communicate? Your Spanish isn't good enough yet. You'd never be able to pick up on the subtleties."

"The general has offered the post interpreter, Joaquin Guerra."

"The *genízaro!*" Ortiz chuckled. "Forget that. No Moreaño would give him the time of day."

"Then I'll find someone in town. There's bound to be someone."

"And what's going to be your story? That you're just a couple of innocent travelers who happen to have a lot of questions about the murder of a priest? Don't make me laugh. They'd see through that in about five minutes. Then you'd be in real danger. They might find your body along the road. Or, like Sandoval, you'd just disappear. You might never be heard from again."

"I'll think of something plausible."

"No, that's not likely," Ortiz said. "*Extranjeros* just don't wander into that area. Not ones who ask a lot of questions about very sensitive subjects."

He was quiet for several moments, chewing his lip. "I could go with you," he said quietly.

Benoit pretended to be surprised. "Thanks, Alejo, but I couldn't ask you to do that. That's too much."

"I'm your friend. Besides, I feel sort of responsible for you. I can't just let you wander off to Mora with some interpreter you found at Doña Rosalia's bar. That would be like signing your death warrant."

"Well, suppose you *did* go with me. How that's going to change the situation? Even though your family is well respected there, they can't let *you* put a noose around the neck of one of the Brothers, either."

"That wouldn't be my reason for being there," said Ortiz. "From the beginning, we'd have to be honest about it. You don't have to tell them you're an army officer, but admit that you're a representative of Vicar General Machebeuf, who is well liked and admired among the Hispanos, by the way. Tell them right out that he has asked you to help find Padre Rabalais's murderer. Also say that the vicar general suspects the killer may have been a *Penitentes* acting in an official capacity."

"But what about you?"

"Ah-ha!" Ortiz grinned. "I'm the devil's advocate. I will say that I don't think a Brother could possibly commit such a terrible crime, and I am along to prove it. The only way that can be done is to find the killer and show that he acted independently."

Benoit rubbed his jaw, thinking about what Ortiz had said. "You think that will work?"

Ortiz smiled. "I guess it will have to. I don't think there's any choice."

12

The four men sat in a rough circle on the patio of Epimeño Ortiz's *hacienda*, sipping strong black coffee from imported china cups. Sunlight filtered downward through the towering cottonwoods from a bright blue sky, casting shadows that danced like spirits performing some wild supernatural jig. Although it was still summer the morning was cool, thanks to a breeze blowing steadily off nearby Truchas Peak.

Before gathering for the conference with Alejo's father, Epimeño, and his uncle, Maclovio, Benoit had been given a brief tour of the Ortiz homestead. Although he had been brought up with access to some of the finer homes in New Orleans and himself lived in a grand two-story house along St. Charles Avenue, Benoit nevertheless had been impressed by the simple grandeur of the Ortiz domicile, with its three-foot-thick walls built of fireproof adobe and its flat roof surrounded by a two-foot-tall parapet that served as a barrier behind which defenders could seek protection while fighting off a band of hostiles.

Much thought, Alejo explained, had been given to the design of residences, since the primary concern of

the settlers was how best to protect themselves against
los indios bárbaros, the savage nomadic tribes prone to
raiding without warning. Even the patio, which now
was used mainly as a family area since the Indian
threat had lessened considerably in recent years, had
been constructed with defense in mind. It was large
enough, Alejo pointed out, to accommodate the family
livestock, which would be driven inside in case of an
attack. Entry to the patio from outside was gained
through a narrow twenty-foot-long covered passage-
way blocked at both ends by stout wooden gates. The
passage was wide enough to admit only a single
horseman at a time. That way, if the Indians somehow
managed to break through the gates, they could easily
be picked off by the defenders, who would be firing at
them from the roof. Also with defense in mind, the
house had been constructed without exterior windows. Instead all the rooms had openings onto the
patio.

Although the house was built like a fort, it certainly did not, as far as Benoit could determine, lack
for luxury. The most lavish room of all was the great
room, or *sala*, which was large enough for *bailes*, the
much loved formal dances, and spontaneous
fandangos, both of which, Benoit deduced, were
favorite forms of entertainment among the Hispanos.
Also within the walls were five spacious bedrooms,
the largest of which contained its own fireplace and
compact sitting area; a well-appointed kitchen large
enough to seat the entire family at informal meals; a
customary formal dining room jammed with massive,
dark furniture imported from Spain; a private chapel;
and two large storage rooms, one for meat and game
and another for dried fruits, bags of *piñon* nuts, and

large jars of wheat and corn. There also were three small, dark rooms at the rear that were set aside as servants' quarters, although only two were currently occupied. Living in one was a male Comanche of about sixteen years of age whom Epimeño had christened Alberto. In the other was a frail-looking Navajo girl of about fourteen called Rafelita. Both had been purchased several years previously at the salve market in Santa Fe. The two *genízaros* were treated as members of the family, which meant that they were given catechism lessons and basic instruction in reading, writing, and ciphering. When they were deemed old enough, Alejo said, they would be freed. After that, they could marry and all their children also would be free. Also part of the *hacienda* but set a little distance from the house was a fully equipped blacksmith shop, a carpentry shop, and a large stable that adjoined a shed for milk cows and a row of cages for hens and rabbits.

As they sat drinking the dark coffee that Benoit discovered was not much different from that of the French, Benoit covertly studied his hosts. While he knew the two older men were brothers, he thought they looked enough alike to be twins. And if Alejo had not been so horribly scarred by Buffalo Hump, they could have been triplets. Each had a large, square head crowned with thick, dark hair. It might eventually turn gray, Benoit thought, but none of the Ortiz men, with the exception of Alejo, would ever have to worry about becoming bald. Each was clean shaven, although Benoit could tell by looking closely at their jowls that each would need another pass with a razor before the end of the day. The eyes of all three were penetrating and shrewd, as black as a starless night.

And while all three dressed in fine clothes that
undoubtedly were quite expensive, their peasant heritage was betrayed by their hands. Although smooth
and well manicured, the fingers were short and
stubby, topped with thick nails.

During the long ride from Santa Fe, Alejo had
briefed Benoit on the history of both the Ortiz family
and the Mora Valley. His grandfather, named
Cresencio, hailed from a small village near Cádiz, on
Spain's southern coast. At fourteen he had run away
from home and signed on as a soldier-recruit in a military unit headed for service in Mexico. From there he
had come north with the army, eventually finding
himself in Santa Fe. When his long enlistment was
completed, he decided to remain there, opening a
small shop where he practiced the trade he had
learned in the army—gun making. His son and Alejo's
father, Epimeño, had preferred working with the soil,
so he'd eagerly signed on with José Tapia when he'd
learned he was seeking people to go with him to settle
an isolated area on the eastern side of the Sangre de
Cristos. His younger brother, Maclovio, followed soon
afterward. Therefore, Alejo said proudly, they were
among the first permanent residents of the beautiful
vale.

It was still somewhat unclear exactly how Mora got
its name, Alejo had said. There were some who said it
derived from *demora*, the Spanish word for camp-
ground, since the valley was beloved by trappers and
migrating tribesmen. This belief was given credence by
the fact that the area was often referred to as Lo de
Mora, or "stopping place." There were a few who said
the name came from a well-known trapper whose surname was Mora. Fewer still said the appellation was a

shortening of the Spanish noun *moras*, which meant "mulberries." However, since there were few mulberry trees in the valley, only a few stubborn Moreños held this view. An even more fanciful version of where the name came from held that the famous French trapper and adventurer, Ceran St. Vrain, had christened the place after he found human bones along the tiny river that flowed through the area, the Río la Casa. Upon finding the remains, St. Vrain was supposed to have identified it by the phrase *L'eau de Mort*, the "water of the dead."

Wherever the name came from, Alejo said, it had come to include two separate sections of the fertile plain known as the Mora Valley. One of the sections was upstream on the Río La Casa and it was called El Valle de San Antonio or El Valle de Arriba. The other section, the one where the Ortiz *hacienda* was located, was known as El Valle de Santa Gertrudis. This area also contained the only village of any size. It was called Mora.

Although he occasionally had to ask about a particular word or phrase, Benoit, much to his delight, found he could follow the discussion, which was held entirely in Spanish, as long as the men spoke slowly and used a rudimentary vocabulary. Helping himself to more coffee from a fresh pot hurriedly deposited by Rafelita, Benoit listened carefully as the two men stoutly defended the *Penitentes*. This did not surprise him, since he also had learned from Alejo that his father and uncle, as well as his brother, Narciso, all were absorbed in the Brotherhood.

The two older men, as longtime members, belonged to the division of *Penitente* veterans known as *Los Hermanos de Luz*, the Brothers of Light. That signified they had gone through the preliminary, bloodier period during which its members were identified as *Los Hermanos de Sangre*, or Brothers of Blood. The Brothers of Blood were the ones who participated most actively in the gruesome Lenten penitential exercises that included, but were not restricted to, the sanguinary ceremonies on Good Friday. Alejo had told him that his brother, Narciso, barely eighteen, had only been admitted to the Brotherhood a year earlier and was still regarded as a *novicio*. Epimeño and Maclovio, on the other hand, had not only passed on to the "cleansed" stage, but were officers in the local chapter. Epimeño was the *mandatorio*, the one in charge of notifying others of meetings and collecting dues, while Maclovio was the second highest ranking member of the chapter, the holder of an office known as *el Hermano segundo*. As such, he answered only to the chapter head, *el Hermano mayor*. The present *Hermano mayor*—a position that Benoit learned was an elected one—was currently held by a man who owned a nearby farm named Melquiares Nuñez.

Benoit, since he was an *extranjero*, kept a respectful silence while the older men discussed Don José's suspicions.

"I was always very fond of the vicar general," said Maclovio. "I thought he was a fair man, and despite being a Frenchman, he seemed to have a real empathy for *los hispanos*."

"We, too, have to be fair about this," said Epimeño, who in addition to being the *mandatorio* also served on the *Penitentes* court that administered justice throughout the valley. "Before we condemn him too thoroughly, we have to try to see his side of the argument."

"And what is that?" said Maclovio in a confrontational tone.

"You and I, because of our positions with the organization, know Padre Rabalais's murder was not arranged by the *Penitentes*, that no Brother was ordered to commit this cowardly act. But Don José, on the other hand, not only does not know the *Penitentes* and has no conception of how the Brotherhood operates, but cannot comprehend the respect we feel for *all* priests. Therefore we have to excuse his ignorance. Given the circumstances, we can't blame him for thinking that the murder of Padre Rabalais may be related to the Brotherhood."

"I disagree with that," Maclovio said heatedly. "Don José may not know the *Penitentes*, but he knows *us*. He knows we are honorable men who would rather suffer eternal damnation than murder a priest in cold blood, no matter what that priest has done. I take it as a personal affront that he even harbors such suspicions."

"Let's be reasonable about this," Epimeño said calmly. "First, do you agree that Padre Rabalais was murdered? That is, that he did not die of natural causes or, God forbid, take his own life?"

"Of course. That much is obvious."

"All right, then, do you also agree that the murderer was a man?"

Maclovio paused. "There, I think, we are getting on a little shakier ground. Poison is a woman's way of committing murder. A man usually finds a more violent method."

"That is true." Epimeño nodded. "But we also have to consider that poison was chosen because the murderer wanted to conceal his identity. If he had simply gone up to the father and stabbed him or shot him, he would have been caught immediately. Also, we know with some certainty that Padre Rabalais led a chaste life. Otherwise we would have heard. There are not many secrets in the valley. If he was killed by woman, what was her motive? I think we are safe in believing it was a man."

"For argument's sake, I'm willing to concede that," Maclovio said grudgingly.

"Very good. Now we have to make another assumption."

"And that is?"

"That the killer lives here in the valley. An outsider would not be able to move unseen among us, and most certainly he would not have been able to walk into the church and poison the wine without being noticed."

"That I definitely agree with."

Epimeño sighed. "Therefore," he said, "we can assume three things." Lifting his hand, he ticked them off with his squat fingers. "One, Padre Rabalais was murdered. Two, his killer was a man. Three, the killer was a Moreño."

Maclovio bobbed his head but said nothing.

"Now," Epimeño said, his voice growing sad, "we have to carry this process another step forward. If Padre Rabalais was killed by a man from the valley, the chances are very, very good that the killer was a Brother since there are very few males in Santa Gertrudis who are *not* members of the organization.

"Do you agree with that?" he asked when Maclovio did not respond immediately.

"I think that's a good possibility," Maclovio replied.

"In that case, Don José is only half-wrong in his assumption. He is very likely correct in his belief that the killer is a Brother—"

"But he is very likely wrong," Maclovio interrupted, "in his belief that the murder was part of a *plot* by the *Penitentes*."

"And I agree with *that*," Epimeño said. "So what do we have? We have a Brother who killed a priest in a way that defies imagination. Now what would make a man do that?"

Maclovio rubbed his chin. "Maybe it was over money," he said tentatively.

"That's a thought," agreed Epimeño, "but except for the two of us and a handful of others, there is no one with enough money to kill over. Someone would have to be insane to kill a priest over a few pesos."

"Then perhaps what we are dealing with is a crazy man."

Epimeño thought about that. "In that case it would have to be someone who appears sane, but in reality is not. That's a possibility, I agree. But I tend to believe it is for another reason."

"And what would that be?"

"Politics! To me, it seems that it has to be politics."

Benoit leaned forward. "Is there any type of political campaign going on right now?"

Both men shook their heads. "No, nothing," said Epimeño. "This is an off year."

"Maybe something to do with the *Penitentes*?" Benoit asked hopefully. "I mean, with the election of officers?"

"No," said Maclovio. "Elections were held in April. There were no disputes, no hard feelings."

For several moments no one said anything. At last

Benoit broke the silence. "Since there seems to be no obvious suspect or even a readily apparent motive, I guess the only thing I can do is start talking to everyone involved to see what I can find. Will you gentlemen help me? Or at least not hinder me?"

Epimeño looked at his brother, who nodded briefly. "You can say you have our support," he said. "After all, it is to our benefit to find this person as well. Obviously it is someone who is somewhat deranged, and that person could only be a danger to other Moreños. Also, we would like to be able to show that Don José is wrong about Padre Rabalais's death having anything to do with the *Penitentes*."

"Then, Father, you have no objection if I help my friend in his search?" Alejo asked.

"No. None. And you can tell that to the people you talk to." Turning to Benoit, he asked, "Where do you plan to start?"

"I think," Benoit said quickly, "with the last person who had any meaningful contact with Padre Rabalais. The acolyte. What was his name?"

"Pol Sena," said Maclovio. "Adolfo's son. You know where the farm is, don't you?" he asked Alejo.

Alejo nodded. "We had better get started," he said to Benoit. "It will take us a while to get there."

For the last hour Benoit and Alejo had been riding across the fertile valley, passing through fields of waving grain, skirting herds of sheep and cattle. "Moreños are becoming quite prosperous these days," Alejo said. "There are now five gristmills in the valley. The farmers have discovered they can make a fairly decent living by selling grain to the soldiers at Fort Union. There is a sawmill, too, owned by the Frenchman St. Vrain. You wouldn't know it by looking at the condition of the buildings there, but Moreños also sell the soldiers a considerable amount of lumber."

As they rode along the borders of the bright green fields, Benoit noticed that in each one, while many workers were busying themselves among the crops or the herds, there was always a single man standing off to the side, a musket thrown over his shoulder.

"That's the guard," Alejo explained when Benoit asked. "It's a well-ingrained habit. A few years ago, when Indian raids were more common, it was wise to have one man always on the alert, ready to sound the alarm at the first sight of approaching hostiles. Now that most of the nomads have moved off to the east and north, where the picking is easier, the guard is almost superfluous. Still, it doesn't hurt to be prepared. Look," he said as they topped a small rise. "There"—he pointed to the west—"there's the village where Pol Sena lives. Wait here while I go ask one of the farmers where I might find him."

Marking the village's northern flank, Benoit could see, was a thick grove of cottonwoods. Among the trees, he assumed, was the Río la Casa. Alejo rode off in that direction since most of the workers were toiling at that end of the field. Fifteen minutes later he was back. Although his face, as usual, was in heavy shadow because of the exceptionally wide brim on his hat, Benoit could sense his friend was worried.

"Is there a problem?" he asked.

"No, not really," Alejo replied. "I talked to Pol's father, and he said his son was home sick. He said he had not been feeling well ever since Padre Rabalais was murdered. The boy seems to think he is somehow responsible for what happened to the priest."

"That's absurd," Benoit said. "We have no reason to believe he was anything other than an innocent bystander."

"I know that," said Alejo. "And you know that. But these peasants are very superstitious. Poor Pol probably believes that Padre Rabalais's murder had something to do with a message from God telling him to mend his own ways."

"Well," Benoit said, remembering how the Plains Indians also were unswerving believers in omens and portents, "let's go see what he can tell us."

Except for the fact that adobe was used in its construction, just as it was with the Ortiz *hacienda*, the Sena house bore almost no resemblance to the grand dwelling Alejo and Benoit had left not long before. A squat, dismal-looking place, it sat on the end of a square of houses clustered around a courtyard. Constructed on the same principle as the Ortiz patio, the village plaza was large enough to hold their *burros* and sheep in a time of emergency.

Reining his horse to a stop, Alejo called loudly, "Pol! Pol Sena! It's Alejo Ortiz and an Americhano from Santa Fe. We would like to talk to you, if you would please show yourself."

The Senas were so poor, Benoit noticed, that they could not afford even a door on their dwelling. Instead the entrance was covered with a mud-splattered blanket that had holes in it the size of his fist.

"Yes," Pol said, pulling the blanket back about a foot and sticking his head outside. "What is it that you want?" His voice was reedy, weak.

Benoit guessed that Pol was no more than sixteen

and, from the looks of him, probably would not live to be seventeen if he did not pull himself together. His face was as pale as if it had been powdered, and his cheeks were sunken. His eyes were puffy, as if he had been crying, and surrounded by deep, dark half circles. The whites were streaked with red.

In a friendly tone Alejo explained who they were and outlined the purpose of their visit. "We'd like to talk to you if you feel up to it," he added. "Mainly we just want you to tell us what happened the morning that Padre Rabalais was killed."

For a moment Benoit was not sure that the youth understood, so uncomprehending was his stare. Then a faint smile crossed his face. "Please come in," he said, pulling aside the blanket.

Walking through the doorway, Benoit noticed that the walls of the peasant's house were just as thick as those of the Ortiz *hacienda*, at least three feet and constructed of adobe blocks. No bullet will ever go through those, he thought. And, like the Ortiz house, there were no exterior widows. What little light there was filtered in through thin slits that faced the courtyard, barely wide enough to stick a rifle barrel through. Inside, it was not as dark as Benoit had expected it to be. The walls were freshly whitewashed to make the interior look brighter, and several pieces of highly polished metal were hung in crude frames at strategic intervals. They served as mirrors to reflect light from the window slits. The low ceiling was supported by wooden beams that Benoit knew were called *vigas*. These, in turn, were crosshatched with small branches called *latillas*. They not only helped support the roof, but kept mud from dropping inside. They also cut down on the number of spiders and other insects that might work their way in from outside.

The floor, like the roof, was bare earth, but the dust was kept to a minimum by inexpensive blankets that served as rugs. There was no furniture, Benoit noticed, not even a table or a wardrobe. The few clothes the family owned dangled from pegs in the wall, each garment carefully turned inside-out to help keep it clean. There were no beds, either, Benoit observed, their place being taken by the adobe benches called *bancos*, which were built into the wall and extended out about three feet. A blanket tossed haphazardly over one told Benoit that Pol had been lying under it when they arrived. Although they could not afford even a chair, there was, in one corner, a small shrine with a locally carved *santo* as its central figure. Benoit was unable to tell which saint it was supposed to represent because its features were so generichally Hispano. On the wall, over a built-in fireplace so narrow that logs had to be stood on end rather than lain horizontal, there was a large crucifix with a wooden Christ. A wooden-beaded rosary dangled from each cross-arm.

Pol took a candle that had been sitting on the *banco* near the fireplace and lit it from a small votive that was already burning in front of the shrine. Although the candle added more light, it also threw the youth's face into deep shadow, giving him a cadaverich look.

"Would you like some water?" Pol asked in a soft voice, reaching for a heavily beaded clay jug. Next to it sat a single mug.

"No, thank you," Alejo said politely. "We won't be long."

"How can I help you?" the youth asked, knotting his thin hands together and squeezing them tightly.

Pol, Benoit discovered, was harder to understand than Epimeño and Maclovio had been. The two men had sensed his lack of facility with the language and, out of politeness, spoken slowly and deliberately. Pol, on the other hand, had a heavy local accent and a slight lisp. The difficulty with the language seemed to run both ways, since twice Pol had to ask Benoit to repeat himself.

"I think it would be better if you talked to him," Benoit said at last, turning to Alejo.

"Can you tell us precisely what happened the morning that Padre Rabalais was killed?" Alejo asked.

"I've told it so many times, it's starting to sound confusing," Pol said, giving Alejo a pathetic look

"Please. Try one more time," Alejo said kindly. "It's very important because we have been asked to find the murderer and see that he is brought to justice."

"Very well." Pol sighed and lifted the water mug to drink deeply. "Are you sure you won't have some?" he asked as an afterthought.

When Benoit and Alejo shook their heads, Pol began his story.

As usual, he said, he had gone to the church early that day because it was his duty as acolyte to make the preparations for Mass. Also, he'd wanted to go to confession.

"Were there any people in the church when you arrived?"

"Just a handful," Pol replied. "They also came to confess. But when it was time for Mass to begin, the church was almost full. There were almost fifty people there."

"Do you remember those who were there early?" Alejo asked.

Pol scratched his head and stared at the far wall. "Let's see," he said, screwing up his face. "Señora Dominguez was there, with her young daughter, Oricilla. The widow Cordova was there, too. Señora—"

"Who were the *men* who were there?" Alejo interrupted.

"Domingo Gallegos was very close to the front, I remember. Also Casimiro Ramirez. And Panfilo Lucero." He paused. "I think that was it."

"Was—"

"Oh, I almost forgot," said Pol, interrupting Alejo. "Melquiares Nuñez was there, too. He was standing in the back, looking very solemn."

Benoit turned quickly to Alejo. "Isn't he—"

"Yes," Alejo replied quickly, cutting him off. "So what is the first thing you did when you got to the church?"

"I laid out the vestments for the father, then put on my cassock and surplice and lit the candles."

"And then . . ." Alejo prompted.

"I filled the cruets."

"Ah," Alejo said, exhaling softly. "Where did you get the wine?"

"From the usual place. The jug that the priests keep in the sacristy cupboard."

"Do you know where the wine comes from?"

"Oh, yes. It arrives once a month in a shipment from Santa Fe, a gallon at a time. I think it comes from a local winery or maybe up the Chihuahua Trail from El Paso del Norte."

"Was there much wine left in the jug?"

"No. It was almost empty. A new shipment is

expected any day. In the meantime, if it did not come in soon, Padre Rabalais said we would have to start watering it to make it last."

"All right," Alejo said gently. "After you filled the cruets, what did you do?"

"I went to confession."

"After that?"

"I returned to the sacristy and said my penance. Two rosaries."

Alejo smiled. "Two rosaries, eh? You must have been naughty."

Pol shot him a frightened look. "Don't tell my father."

"I won't," Alejo agreed. "So while you were saying your penance someone from inside the church could have poured the poison in the wine cruet?"

"No," Pol said slowly. "If that were true, then everyone else in the church would have witnessed it."

"But he could have been the first to arrive?"

"That's true," Pol said. "But I don't think it happened *after* I got there."

In response to more questions from Alejo, Pol told them how the service itself had been routine up until the point that Padre Rabalais took a sip of the wine. "He made such a face that I knew immediately something was wrong. I asked him if he wanted me to go get him some fresh wine from the jug."

"And what did he say?"

"He said no, that it had been consecrated and he would go ahead and finish the Mass with what was in the chalice."

"And then what happened?"

Padre Rabalais finished the Mass, Pol said, and hurried back to the sacristy, where he took off the vestments.

"By that time he was starting to have stomach cramps and I could tell there was something seriously wrong. I volunteered to run fetch my aunt, who is a *curandera*, but he wouldn't let me. He said whatever happened was God's will. After he said that, he went back into the church and knelt at the altar to pray. A few—"

"Did you go back in the church as well?" Alejo asked.

"Yes." Pol nodded vigorously. "I was worried about him."

"Was the church empty by then?"

"No, there were still a few people there, continuing to pray."

"Do you remember who?"

Pol shook his head. "No. I was too worried about Padre Rabalais to pay much attention."

"So he just collapsed?"

"Yes, he gave a big groan, grabbed his stomach, and toppled forward, face first."

"Think very carefully now," Alejo said. "What happened then?"

Pol's face turned crimson. "I wasn't very much help. That's why God is punishing me by making me sick."

"What do you mean, you weren't much help?"

"I mean, I was scared to death. I couldn't do anything. I just stood there, as if I were made of wood."

"For how long did you stand there?"

"Oh, I don't know. It seemed like a very long time, but it probably wasn't. I was standing there when Señor Lucero—"

"Who?" Alejo interrupted.

"Señor Lucero. Panfilo. Remember, I said I saw him in church before Mass."

"And he was still there afterward?"

"Maybe he had a lot of sins to repent for." Pol shrugged. "In any case, he ran forward and tried to help Padre Rabalais. He was very upset."

"How about Señor Nuñez?"

Pol shook his head. "I didn't see him after Mass."

"What did Señor Lucero do?"

"He tried to get Padre Rabalais to vomit, but nothing would come up. He stuck his finger down the Father's throat, but all Padre Rabalais did was gag."

"Did Padre Rabalais speak anymore?"

"Yes," Pol said, blinking back tears that had started to form in his large brown eyes. "He asked for God's help in enduring the pain."

"Is that all?"

"No," Pol choked. "He asked God to please forgive the person who had poisoned him. It was a prayer, really. He said that the person did not know what he had done and that God, if He was just, would forgive him."

Pol paused, tears running down his cheeks. "And then he died. His whole body shook three times, and he was dead."

Alejo and Benoit said nothing, waiting for the boy to cry himself out.

"Just a few more minutes and we'll be through," Alejo said, placing his hand on Pol's shoulder.

"It's all right. There's not anything else to tell, anyway."

Benoit leaned forward and spoke to Alejo in English. "Ask him about the jug."

Alejo nodded. "The wine jug," he said in Spanish. "Is it still there?"

"The jug is, but it's empty now."

"What do you mean, it's empty?" Alejo asked, surprised. "What happened to the wine?"

"Padre Romero instructed me to pour it out. So I did."

Benoit and Alejo looked at each other.

"Padre Romero." Alejo nodded. "I'd forgotten all about him. Where was he when all this occurred?"

"He was in the rectory. In bed. He had a gout attack and couldn't be there to say Mass."

Alejo spoke very slowly, making sure that Pol understood. "What do you mean, he couldn't be there?"

"He was the one who was scheduled to say Mass that day," Pol replied. "But because of his gout, he couldn't stand on his feet. Padre Rabalais was a last-minute replacement."

13

After slipping Pol an *onza* gold piece in appreciation for his help, Benoit was swinging into his saddle when a rifle shot reverberated across the courtyard. The shot was followed immediately by shouts and, minutes later, the pounding of running feet.

"*Indios!*" a man yelled, dashing into the square. "The Apaches are attacking. Quickly! To the roof!"

Alejo and Benoit scrambled up a rickety ladder that stood against the wall nearby. Pol was close on their heels, brandishing a musket with a rusty barrel that must have been hidden somewhere in the house.

After throwing himself on his stomach behind the parapet, Benoit lifted his rifle to his shoulder and looked down the sight. A hundred yards away, a dozen mounted Indians were charging madly across the wheat field. Barely thirty yards in front of them were the villagers who could not move quite so rapidly: three women that Benoit took to be middle-aged, two young boys who looked about six, and an old man brandishing a musket. He must have been the one who had fired the warning shot, Benoit reckoned, because he was trying to reload and run at the same time.

Two of the Indians, in an act that seemed rehearsed, urged their horses forward, one on each side of the two young boys. Without even slowing their mounts, they leaned over and scooped up the terrified, screaming youngsters. Tucking them under their arms, they loosed loud whoops, then wheeled their horses around and headed for the trees. The other Indians continued straight ahead.

The old man, giving up the effort to reload his rifle, threw it to the ground and turned to face the Indians, fists raised. The closest Apache, without breaking stride, plunged his lance in the old man's chest, leaving him to flop on the ground like a speared fish, while he continued straight ahead.

Benoit leveled his sights on the Indian. Squeezing the trigger slowly, he nodded in satisfaction as he saw the Apache fly backward just he was reaching for one of the women. The force of the bullet carried him completely clear of his horse's back and dumped him, like an overturned scarecrow, in the wheat, where he lay sprawled on his back, completely still.

Out of the corner of his eye, Benoit saw Alejo training his rifle on another Indian. There was a loud report and the Apache's horse went down, its feet kicking wildly. The Apache squirmed from under the wounded animal and struggled to his feet, dragging a shattered leg behind him. Benoit was aiming at him, intending to finish him off, when another Apache appeared, putting himself between Benoit and the wounded warrior. As easily as the others had plucked the children off the ground, the mounted *bárbaro* lifted his wounded comrade. Benoit, distracted, fired too quickly, cursing under his breath when his shot missed and kicked up dirt ten yards to the pair's right. Before he could pump another round into the chamber and re-aim, the two had reached the safety of the trees.

To his left, Benoit saw Pol aiming carefully at an Apache who had ridden far in front of the others, looking as if he planned to gallop into the courtyard. Pol jerked the trigger, then looked surprised when the firing pin clicked harmlessly. He forgot to load the damn thing, Benoit thought, bringing his Sharps to bear. After squeezing off another round, he saw the Indian's head explode in a blur of red.

To Benoit's surprise, Pol leaped suddenly to his feet, grabbing his useless rifle like a club. An Apache, unseen by Benoit, had ridden up close to the house. He loosed an arrow, which whistled harmlessly into the air, before turning abruptly and riding parallel to the building for several yards.

Pol, seeing an opportunity, intended to club the Indian with his rifle. Benoit opened his mouth to yell a warning, but before he could get out the words, Pol leaned forward and swung with all his might. If he had hit the Indian, Benoit thought later, everything might have been all right. But when he missed, and the rifle swished unchecked through the air, Pol lost his balance. "Help!" he screamed, teetering forward. Benoit's arm shot out, but all he grasped was air, missing Pol's ankle by a quarter of an inch. He watched helplessly as the boy tumbled over the parapet, plunging headfirst toward the ground. Despite the noise all around him, Benoit was sure he could hear Pol's neck snap when he hit the hard-packed earth.

With a roar of anger and frustration, Benoit leaped to his feet, raising his rifle. But he was too late. The

Apaches were gone, leaving only a cloud of dust and a crowd of wailing Hispanos in their wake.

News of the Apache attack reached the *hacienda* before they did. After turning their horses over to one of the servants, Benoit and Alejo went inside to find the family in the chapel, praying for Pol and the others killed or captured during the raid.

It was a small, plain room, Benoit noticed, freshly whitewashed, its pine floors highly polished. Against the far wall was a candle-bedecked altar draped with a spotless white cloth embroidered with roses and lilies. In the center was a four-foot-tall wooden crucifix. Although the figure of Christ exhibited decidedly Hispano features, it had been painted a stark white, which was even more conspicuous because of the bright scarlet slashes representing the Savior's wounds. Representations of saints, none of whom looked familiar to Benoit, hung on the walls. In the corner to the left of the altar, standing atop a waist-high pedestal, was a figure of a tonsured man with outstretched arms. In each hand was a sparrow and a squirrel snuggled comfortably on his shoulder. St. Francis, Benoit said to himself, happy to have recognized at least one figure.

Lined up in front of the altar were four ornately carved prie-dieus. Kneeling on the benches, praying the rosary aloud, were four women: Señora Ortiz and three of her daughters.

Epimeño, who had been standing at the rear, his lips moving along with the women's prayers, looked up when Benoit and Alejo entered. Gesturing with his head for them to meet him outside, he led the way to the kitchen. "Coffee!" he told the servant girl, Rafelita, who bustled off to get fresh water.

"It is sad, what happened today," he said, looking at Benoit with large, moist eyes. "Just when we think we are free from raids, *los gentiles* appear out of nowhere. *¡Qué vajesa!*" he said, a tear forming in the corner of his eye. "How awful!"

Shaking his head, he produced a silk handkerchief from the inside pocket of his coat and dabbed at his eyes.

"I guess this seems very emotional to you, doesn't it?" he asked Benoit.

"I understand. I've lost friends to the Indians as well."

"Our community is not so large that we don't all mourn the death of a single member, especially when it's unnecessary deaths like this."

"What will become of the children?" Benoit asked.

"It depends," said Epimeño. "The boys they may try to sell at the fair in Taos, which is a favorite gathering spot for *los indios bárbaros*. Or they may keep them and raise them as members of the tribe. If they are malleable, this is what they usually do. But if they prove too troublesome, they will kill them without a second thought, bashing their heads against a boulder so as not to waste the bullets. As for the women, they will keep them if they find them comely enough or if they think they will make good slaves."

"Will you not try to form a group to try to track them down?"

"No," Epimeño said sadly. "We don't have the manpower for that. We've already sent a rider to Fort Union to ask for help from the army, but by now there is no telling where the Apaches are. This is a big territory, and much of it is rugged mountains. About all we can do is bury our dead and continue on. But tell me," he added, brightening somewhat. "Did you get the chance to talk to the Sena boy? What did he tell you?"

"We talked to him," Alejo said. "In fact, we had just finished when the Indians attacked. Most of what he said we already knew. But he did reveal one thing that we were not aware of."

"Oh, yes?" Epimeño said, raising an eyebrow. "And what was that?"

"He told us that Padre Romero was supposed to celebrate the Mass, that Padre Rabalais was only filling in because Romero was incapacitated with the gout."

Epimeño pondered what his son had said. "So you think there is a possibility that Padre Romero was the intended victim, not Padre Rabalais? That's interesting indeed."

"It's something we have to consider," said Benoit. "If that were the case, it would almost certainly wreck the theory that the *Penitentes* were behind the murder."

"Padre Romero has been here a long time," Epimeño pointed out. "Almost as long as I. As far as I know he has no enemies. The *Penitentes* hold no grudges against him."

"In that case, we had best talk to him as soon as possible," said Alejo.

"Then you had better get an early start. For the next few days, he will be very involved with funerals."

The sun was barely creeping over the horizon, bathing the tree-covered Truchas Peak in bright, unfiltered light, when Benoit and Alejo set off for the village church, a good two dozen miles from the *hacienda*.

"He's not going to appreciate us dragging him out of bed so early," Alejo said. "Especially if he's been ill for the last few days."

"Unfortunately, we don't have any choice," Benoit said. "You heard what your father said about the funerals. You know," he added as they clomped along the path, their horses' hooves throwing up small clouds of dust in the still morning air, "if he were the target rather than Padre Rabalais, that would put everything in a whole new light. What do you know about the good father?"

"Not a lot," Alejo replied. "I left the valley when I was still a child, and I had very few dealings with him. He and my father seemed to get along. I know he was a regular dinner guest at the *hacienda*, but that may have been just because he was a priest and my father felt obligated. He's a very religious man."

"What was Padre Romero's relationship with the *Penitentes*? Do you know?"

"If it had been bad, I think my father would have said so. I imagine Padre Romero had adopted a live-and-let-live attitude. I'd be surprised if he thinks of the Brotherhood the same way Bishop Lamy does."

"What about his politics? If he had been active in organizing that revolt in 1847, could that have anything to do with why someone might want him dead?"

Alejo was quiet for several minutes, thinking about Benoit's question. "I can't see how it could. That's ancient history now. Just about everyone who was involved is dead."

"Padre Romero isn't."

"That's true," Alejo conceded. "But no one knows how deeply he was involved, if at all. That was eleven years ago. Nobody talks about it anymore."

"How about that Taos priest?"

"Padre Martinez?"

"Yes. Isn't he still alive, too?"

"Very much so." Alejo chuckled. "Alive and causing many problems for Bishop Lamy and Don José."

"And the man who lived here in the valley . . . the instigator?"

"Porcopio Sandoval? Surely he must be dead. No one has heard anything about him for years."

Benoit rode in silence, trying to work out the possibilities. "It's very confusing, isn't it?" he said, glancing at Alejo. "I wonder if we'll ever be able to figure it out."

Padre Romero was, indeed, still in bed when Alejo and Benoit arrived at the rectory. When he shuffled to the door after five minutes of knocking, he was clad in a long nightgown, the front of which was dotted with old coffee stains and the remains of breakfasts long forgotten. His hair, which was totally white and growing thin, stuck out at all angles from his head. Tall and thin, with a long, pointed nose and pale lips, the priest studied them suspiciously with beady, dark eyes.

"What do you want?" he asked crossly. "Don't you realize it's the middle of the night?"

"Not hardly," said Alejo, disliking the man instantly. "The sun's been up for twenty minutes."

"Aren't you Señor Ortiz's son?" Padre Romero asked, squinting. "Didn't the Comanches teach you any civility?"

"We apologize for getting you up," Benoit said hurriedly.

The priest stared at him, the corner of his mouth twitching. "Who is this *gringo*?" he asked Alejo.

"He's a friend of mine," Alejo replied, carefully not mentioning the Don José connection.

"I'm not going to talk to him," Padre Romero said petulantly. "I don't like *gringos*."

"Then talk to me only," said Alejo. "I'm sure it would make my father happy."

The priest gave Alejo a shrewd look, calculating if he could afford to offend the older son of the richest man in the valley. After a moment of thought, he decided he could not.

"Come in," he said brusquely, opening the door. "But don't expect me to make you any coffee. And I don't have much time. I have to go bury some people who were killed by the Indians." He led the way into a small kitchen, limping on a bandaged foot that Benoit assumed was a result of the gout attack.

"We know about the raid," Benoit said, ignoring Alejo's warning glance. "We were there."

Padre Romero grunted, ignoring him. "What do you want?" he asked Alejo.

"The other day, when Padre Rabalais was killed . . ."

"You expect me to get all sorrowful about that?" Padre Romero replied. "He was an *extranjero, un francés*. He had no business here. What does he know about the Spanish people or our customs? He was a *lambioso* as well. A real ass licker. He'd do anything to keep those *pendejos* in Santa Fe happy."

Benoit, struggling to keep his temper, turned and pretended to look out the window.

"That day," Alejo repeated doggedly. "Wasn't it you who was supposed to say the Mass?"

"So what if it was? That's why we have two priests here. If one is absent, for one reason or another, the other takes over. I've done the same for Rabalais. Just a week before, when he was out of town, I had to go visit that dying woman, that *puta* . . ."

"But it *was* you who was supposed to celebrate the Mass," Alejo asked, his voice sharp.

"My gout made it impossible."

Alejo sighed. "Why did you order Pol Sena to pour out the wine?"

"Why?" asked Padre Romero, his voice rising. "That's one of the most stupid questions I've ever heard. Because it was poisoned. It had the devil in it."

"Do you have any enemies? Anyone who might want you dead?"

"What are you talking about? Have you been drinking or are you just naturally stupid?"

"Think about it," Alejo said, gritting his teeth. "The wine is poisoned. Someone wanted to kill the priest. You were supposed to be the one who said Mass. Therefore, it seems logical that the poison was intended for you, not Padre Rabalais."

Padre Romero stared silently at Alejo. Benoit could tell that the thought that he could have been the one someone wanted dead had not occurred to him.

"Well?" Alejo asked. "You didn't answer my question. Who hates you enough to want to kill you?"

Padre Romero looked frightened. "I've been here almost thirty-five years. A man makes a lot of enemies in that time."

"But is has to be a *real* enemy if he hates you enough to want to kill you."

The old priest shook his head, refusing to meet Alejo's eyes. "I can't think of anyone," he said unconvincingly

"Try hard," Alejo said. "It may have been a long time ago. Maybe at the time of the revolt?"

Padre Romero paled and his hands began to tremble. "Why do you mention that?" he asked in a shaky voice, staring at his hands as if he could will them to be still.

Alejo and Benoit exchanged a quick look. "What was your connection with Padre Martinez? The priest in Taos."

"We went to the seminary together. In Durango."

"Were you friends?"

Padre Romero nodded.

"Did you have anything to do with the uprising here in Mora?"

The priest paused. "I introduced Padre Martinez to Porcopio Sandoval. And that is all I'm going to say."

"Ah," Alejo exhaled. "Finally we're getting somewhere. Do you know where Sandoval went after he left here?"

Padre Romero nodded. "Mexico."

"Have you kept up with him?"

"From time to time," the priest said, his shoulders slumping.

"Is he dead? Do you know where he is now?"

Padre Romero looked at Alejo, his eyes wide with fright. "I know."

"Then he's alive!"

The priest's lips began to tremble. "I saw him two weeks ago."

"You saw him!" Alejo said excitedly. "Here?"

"He's been back seven or eight months. Living

secretly in a cabin halfway up Truchas Peak. He sent word for me to come see him. He wanted my help in organizing another revolt. He thought the time was ripe to make another attempt to get rid of the Americhanos. I told him he'd been out in the Chihuahua Desert too long; that the Americhanos were stronger than they had ever been. He disagreed. 'Look,' he said, 'they're even getting ready to start killing each other. *Everybody* knows that. When they go to war, that will be the time for us to make our move. The whole country will be in disarray.'"

"What did you tell him?"

"I told him to go back to Mexico."

"And how did he take that?"

"He got very angry. He said if I refused to help him, he would tell the Americhanos about my role in the 1847 uprising. I told him to go ahead. No one cared about that anymore." He paused. "We did not part as friends," he added.

"Then he had reason to want you dead?"

"Reason, yes. But not the opportunity. He could not have come into the village to poison the wine because someone would have seen him and recognized him. Then, if anything had happened to me, they would surely have gone looking for him."

Alejo turned to Benoit. "What do you think?"

"I think we should go see Señor Sandoval."

"I agree. *Padre*," he said to Romero, "you will tell us how to find him."

The old priest stood immobile for several moments, then turned and walked to a nearby cabinet. After pulling out a sheet of paper, he sketched a map with a hand that shook so badly, he could hardly hold the pen.

Benoit and Alejo stopped at the edge of the small clearing in front of Sandoval's cabin. Instinctively Benoit nudged his horse several paces to the left. "If he decides to start shooting," he whispered, "let's make it difficult for him to get both of us."

Alejo waited until Benoit got into place, then called loudly, "Señor Sandoval! This is Alejandro Ortiz, son of Epimeño. My friend and I wish to talk to you. Please come out."

Only the bluejays answered.

"Señor Sandoval," he tried again, "can you hear us?"

Again there was no reply.

Benoit motioned to Alejo, indicating that he was going to approach the cabin. He dismounted and drew his pistol, then began to walk forward cautiously. When he got to the door, he lifted his arm to knock, but as his fist met wood, the door swung open. Lifting his pistol, he jumped backward, but there was no movement inside the hut.

"I'm going inside," he called to Alejo, plunging through the doorway.

Alejo hurried to join him.

"Looks like there's been a hell of a fight in here," Benoit said, glancing around the small interior. A small table lay broken against the far wall, and the blankets that Sandoval apparently used as a bedroll were bunched in a corner. A coffeepot had been hurled against a wall, its contents making a dark stain in the bare earth floor. A tin cup was squashed into an unrecognizable shape.

"Look," Alejo said, stooping and pointing at a dark spot about five inches in diameter. It was surrounded by a number of other smaller spots. Gingerly he dabbed at the earth, which was as hard as tile. He lifted his finger, studied it, then showed it to Benoit. "Blood."

"Here, too," said Benoit, pointing to another large stain. "And here. What the hell happened?"

Alejo was examining a dark object on the floor on the other side of the room. "I think this is our answer," he said, handing the object to Benoit.

"Jesus!" Benoit said, almost dropping it. "What is it?"

"If I'm not mistaken, it's a strip of leather."

"A strip of leather?" Benoit said, uncomprehending.

"I'd say part of a thong from a whip."

"Oh!" Benoit said, understanding. "The *Penitentes*."

"That would be my guess," Alejo confirmed. "I think it's time to talk to someone from the Brotherhood."

Melquiares Nuñez was not in his field. Neither, Benoit and Alejo soon learned, was he at his house.

"That leaves only one place to look," said Alejo. "The *morada*."

The *Penitentes* chapter house was a long narrow building totally without windows, set deep in a stand of pine and mountain juniper. It was a forbidding place, even in the daylight. Studying the building, Benoit felt a chill run down his spine. "I certainly wouldn't want to be here on a moonless night," he said to Alejo.

For several minutes they sat quietly on their

horses, waiting to see if anyone had heard them approaching and would come out to see what they wanted.

"Listen," Alejo whispered, cocking his head. "Do you hear that?"

Benoit leaned forward. "Yes," he said, his reply barely audible.

Over the chirping of the birds, the men could hear a rhythmic slapping sound, like someone establishing a beat by smacking his palm against his thigh. Except there was an added effect: after each slap they could hear what resembled a muffled groan.

"Someone's being whipped," Benoit said, putting the sounds together.

After tying their horses to a tree, they hurried forward and pounded on the door. There was no response. Alejo tried again, louder. "It's Alejo Ortiz," he called. "Please open the door."

After a moment of silence, a strained-sounding voice replied, "Go away!"

"I can't do that," Alejo said. "I'm not here to cause trouble. I just want to talk to you."

There was a pause, then the noise of shuffling feet. The door opened about two inches and a bloodshot eye peeked out at them.

"Señor Nuñez?" Alejo asked.

The eye blinked. "What do you want?"

"We would like to talk to you."

"I have nothing to say. Please leave me alone."

"Señor Nuñez, please let us in. We need to see Porcopio Sandoval."

"He's not here," Nuñez said. "There's no one here. I'm alone. Now please go away. I'm in the middle of my prayers."

"It doesn't sound like you're praying," Benoit said. "It sounds as if someone is being thrashed."

Nuñez's eye swung toward Benoit. "Who is this?"

"A friend of mine," said Alejo.

"We have no use for *gringos* here," Nuñez said, starting to close the door.

"Wait!" Alejo said, stopping it with his palm. "All we want to do is talk to Señor Sandoval."

"I told you, he isn't here."

"Then let us see for ourselves. One quick look. After that, I promise we'll go away."

Nuñez looked at him closely. "Then look," he said, opening the door and stepping back.

Benoit studied the *Penitente*. He was short and compact, with dark skin and hair the color of coal. He had a high forehead, which was beaded with sweat, and he was breathing heavily, as if from exertion. Nuñez, the chapter's *Hermano mayor*, glared at him, challenging him with his eyes. Benoit glanced at his lip, which was raw and bleeding where he had been chewing it. Blood ran in a small rivulet down his chin.

Benoit let his eyes go lower. Nuñez, he saw, had a thick neck, broad, muscled shoulders, and a deep, hairless chest that was speckled with spots of blood that had dripped off his chin. In his right hand was a whip made from a dozen strands of leather studded with cactus thorns.

As comprehension dawned, Benoit felt the bile rise in his throat. "You've been flogging yourself!" he cried.

Nuñez stared at him, then dismissed him with a slight flick of his head. "As you can see," he said to Alejo, "there's no one here."

When Nuñez turned to Alejo, Benoit could see

that his back was striped with raw welts. Forcing himself to look away, he let his eyes roam around the room. Along one wall was an altar, but unlike the one in the Ortiz *hacienda*, this was crudely made from rough pine boards and bare except for several candles. Leaning against the other wall was a cross large enough for a man. Made of unfinished cottonwood, it was weathered and splintered. Toward the end of the cross-arms and about three feet from the bottom, the wood was darkly stained. Pulling his eyes away, he looked around the room. Hanging from pegs on two of the walls were several lengths of chain and eight or ten whips, all of which appeared to have been well used.

"Look there," Alejo said, pointing behind Benoit.

Turning, Benoit saw what Alejo was pointing at. It was a rough wooden cart, a type known throughout the territory as a *carreta*. In typical fashion, it was long and narrow and very simply built, essentially an uneven platform with sides of rough logs fastened to end posts. The wheels were of solid wood, perhaps a cross section of a sizable tree trunk, and irregular, so that when pulled by a *burro*, it bounced and jerked along more than it rolled. Benoit had seen entire families riding in such carts, everyone standing to make more room, the children with their hands clasped against their ears to shut out the penetrating shriek of an ungreased axle. But this *carreta* was not designed to carry a happy family to the village market. Its sole occupant was a wooden skeleton, its death head carved into a hideous rictus, propped on a rough bench. On the platform, at the skeleton's feet, was a crude wooden bow and a single, amateurishly fletched arrow.

"Have you satisfied your curiosity?" Nuñez asked angrily, breaking Benoit out of his gape-mouthed scrutiny.

"Why are you flagellating yourself?" Alejo asked. "What sin are you doing penance for?"

"That's none of your business," Nuñez said belligerently. "You said you wanted to see. Now that you have seen, get out."

"There's no need to be so truculent," Alejo said consolingly. "We have an interest in the murder of Padre Rabalais. We're trying to find the killer."

"That's none of your business either. The *Penitentes* administer justice in the valley. We will take care of it. You had best stay out of it. It could be dangerous for you to interfere."

Alejo looked at Benoit and shrugged. "Very well," he said quietly, "we'll leave."

Nuñez followed them to the door and slammed it behind them. They had barely untied their horses and pulled themselves into the saddle before the repulsive noise renewed itself.

Slap . . . groan. Slap . . . groan . . .

"It makes my stomach turn over," Benoit said as they rode away.

"I just don't understand it," Benoit said as they headed toward the *hacienda*.

"Nor do I," admitted Alejo.

"It appears that Porcopio Sandoval played some part in the murder of Padre Rabalais. At least the *Penitentes* think he did."

Alejo nodded. "Yes."

"But how did he do it? Padre Romero had a good

point when he said that Sandoval would not have been able to go into the village unseen."

"Maybe he tried and he *was* seen. By one of the *Penitentes*."

"That's possible," said Benoit. "But if that's the case, why has it taken them so long to act? That blood we found in Sandoval's cabin was fresh. I'd say no more than a few hours old."

"Maybe he had an accomplice," Alejo said. "Maybe it took them a while, but they found the accomplice first. Then he led them to Sandoval."

Benoit was silent, digesting what Alejo had said. "That sounds plausible," he said after several moments. "It would make the events as we know them more rational. But who could it be? What are we over-looking?"

"Whoever it was, he was able to enter and leave the church without arousing suspicion. It would have been someone who seemed to belong there; someone everyone knew."

"That could have been anyone in the congregation."

"Put yourself in this fellow's shoes," said Alejo. "If you were going to try to poison someone in a public place, wouldn't you want to be there yourself? To make sure everything went right?"

"That's ghoulish," said Benoit.

"Well, we're not talking about someone who's entirely sane. Someone would have to be unbalanced to kill a priest, anyway. Remember when we were talking to Pol and we asked him who had been in the church before Mass began?"

"Of course!" Benoit said enthusiastically. "Do you remember their names?"

"I definitely remember that Melquiares Nuñez was one of them."

Benoit snapped his fingers. "That's it! He could have seen something at the time that he did not understand until later. That led him to someone who led him to Sandoval. Who else did Pol say was there? God, I wish Pol was still alive so we could go ask him again."

Alejo searched his memory. "I recall Domingo Rodriguez and one of the Ramirez clan, I'm not sure which one. Then there was Panfilo Lucero—"

"Lucero!" Benoit said excitedly. "Didn't Pol say he was also there after Mass?"

"Yes," Alejo agreed. "He was the one who rushed to the priest's aid. Tried to get him to vomit out the poison."

"So Lucero was there both before and after. I'm not sure about you, but I think we should go talk to Lucero. At the very least, he may have seen something that will help us some more. Do you know where he lives?"

"I think so," Alejo said, turning his horse. "It isn't far."

"It's strange that you should ask about Panfilo," Felipe León said, glancing shyly at the ground, running his bare toes through the dust. "No one seems to have seen him for the last two days. He hasn't been home, and he hasn't been in the field."

"What about his wife? What does she say?" Benoit asked.

"His wife died three years ago," León said. "He has not remarried. In fact, poor Panfilo has had very bad luck with women."

"What do you mean by that?" Alejo asked.

"After his wife died, he began living with a young widow, Reina Luján. But she died, too. About a month ago. That really seemed to upset Panfilo. After that, he just didn't seem quite right in the head anymore."

"Oh?" Benoit replied with a quizzical frown. "How's that?"

"I would be talking to him, asking him if he was going to the cockfight on Saturday night or if he thought it was going to rain, and he wouldn't hear me. Everything I said to him, I had to say twice. I was worried that he might suddenly have gone deaf. But others noticed it, too. Ciriaco Guerra asked me why Panfilo looked mad all the time, and why he was always cursing and mumbling under his breath. Until Reina died, Panfilo had always been a very religious man. He was aware of his responsibilities to the community, too. You may not know this, but he was a *mayordomo* in the Brotherhood. *Un Hermano de Luz.* But after Reina died, he lost his faith. He had nothing good at all to say about the church, and he seemed particularly angry at Padre Romero."

Benoit looked at Alejo, then turned to León. "Did he say why he was perturbed at Padre Romero?"

León shook his head. "Not to me. Why don't you find him and ask him yourself?"

"We would like nothing better," Benoit said. "Do you have any idea where we should be looking?"

León shook his head. "Before she came to live with Panfilo, Reina lived over there, about five miles," he said, pointing to the west. "In El Alto. I think she still has a sister there."

"Does Panfilo have no family?" asked Alejo.

"I don't know. He came here many years ago from

El Valle de Arriba. So maybe he has brothers and sisters there."

After thanking León, Ortiz and Benoit held a quick conference.

"I think we're getting close," said Benoit. "That's very interesting, don't you think? What he said about Panfilo being angry at Padre Romero."

"Extremely interesting," Alejo agreed. "I have a feeling, though, that time is running out for us. Sandoval's abduction disturbs me. I think the quicker we act, the better."

"I agree," said Benoit. "What do you say we split up? We can cover twice as much ground, and the day is getting short."

"Do you think you can handle the language?"

"My confidence is growing by the hour." Benoit smiled. "I've been able to understand just about everything being said for the last two days. If I really have trouble communicating, you can come back later and help me."

"Okay," said Alejo. "I'll take Panfilo's family because that's farther and I know the way. El Alto is just down the road."

"I'll meet you back at the *hacienda*," Benoit said, riding off.

"Be careful," warned Alejo.

"Don't worry," Benoit said, laughing. "Caution is my middle name."

14

Benoit had no trouble finding the village or locating Reina's sister. But after talking to her for half an hour, he knew little more than when he arrived.

Yes, said Vitoriana, Reina had died of a fever only a little more than a month previously. Yes, up until that time, for the last year or so, she had been cohabiting with Panfilo Lucero. One day, maybe not too far off, they planned to wed. But both had spouses who died, and they were afraid of taking that big step. "Reina was silly," Vitoriana said. "She believed the marriage vows were some type of death warrant."

Had Panfilo been good to her? Benoit asked.

Oh, yes, Vitoriana replied. He brought home what little money he had instead of wasting it on drink and on the *perdidas* in the *ramerías* in Las Vegas, as some of the other men in the village did when they went to the city to buy supplies. When it was apparent she was dying, Vitoriana added, it had been Panfilo who had gone for the priest to administer the last rites.

"Oh," Benoit asked, his interest quickening. "And who had that been?"

"Padre Romero. Reina liked Padre Rabalais much

better, but unfortunately he had not been available that day. So Padre Romero came instead. Isn't it odd?" she asked Benoit, "that she and Padre Rabalais died so very close together?"

"Yes, that is very coincidental. . . ."

"And the fact that they are buried in the same *camposanto* as well."

"What?" Benoit said, jerking his head up. "Would you please say that again, speaking more slowly?"

"I said," Vitoriana repeated, talking to Benoit as if he were a three-year-old, "that Reina and Padre Rabalais are both buried in the graveyard in Mora. She was born there, and that's where she said she wanted to return."

Benoit thanked her profusely and rode away, trying to sort out what she had told him.

Maybe it was all just happenstance, he told himself. Reina's fatal illness. The appearance of Padre Romero to administer the last rites. Her death. Panfilo Lucero's sudden hatred for the church, especially Padre Romero. Then Padre Rabalais's murder with poisoned wine that without doubt had been intended for Padre Romero. Panfilo's disappearance. The fact that both Reina and Padre Rabalais were buried in the same cemetery. Of course, he argued with himself, there was no explanation for Porcopio Sandoval's possible involvement and abduction. What was his connection with Lucero? And what about the *Penitentes*?

It was getting more complicated all the time, Benoit thought, rubbing the back of his neck. It's beginning to give me a terrible headache. "Still," he murmured, "I can't get over the coincidence of the burials. Both in the same ground. How strange fate is."

Benoit looked at the sky. About two hours of

sunlight left, he reckoned. Plenty of time to make the short detour to Mora and visit the cemetery. It wasn't far out of his way. But what could he possibly learn from looking at two relatively fresh graves? On the other hand, what harm would it do? At least he'd be able to describe the scene to Alejo, who surely would be as shocked as he had been to learn about the twists of destiny.

The sun was just dipping behind Truchas Peak when Benoit, after three times asking directions, found the Mora *camposanto*. Although they were usually located adjacent to the church, this cemetery was off the old road, in a grove of cottonwoods that grew along the Río la Casa. In New Mexico a tree-filled area along a river was known as *el bosque* since it was the closest thing in the territory to a real forest. The *original* church had been there, he was told, but it had been leveled by army artillery during the 1847 revolt after a group of rebels sought refuge there. Because the ground had been bloodied, it was decided to build a new church a mile or so away. The cemetery remained where it was, though.

As he rode into the *camposanto*, Benoit was impressed by the peacefulness of the scene. In the soft, golden light that characterized dusk in New Mexico, the cemetery looked as though it could have appeared in a Currier and Ives print. Weathered wooden grave markers, some tilting at crazy angles, were scattered seemingly haphazardly around the plot, their shadows forming long, dark rectangles that only highlighted the brilliant yellow of the sunflowers that traditionally bloomed in late August. If there was any organization to the location of graves, Benoit thought, it eluded him. Impatient now to find the graves, Benoit rode deeper into the burial ground.

There was a light breeze blowing off the Sangre de Cristos, and as it swept through the *bosque*, it rustled the cottonwood leaves, creating a soothing sound that perfectly complemented the burble of the river as it flowed against its rock-lined banks. It had taken many hours of hand labor, probably by the *Penitentes*, Benoit reflected, to gather and lay the rounded river stones so they would form a protective barrier preventing the spring-enlarged river from flooding the *camposanto* and washing away the graves.

Benoit looked around him, searching for mounds that had not yet subsided. Over in one corner, near the edge of the trees, he spotted a mound of fresh-turned earth. Nudging his horse forward, he reverently approached the site, which he could see as he got closer was marked only by a crude, newly painted wooden cross. He dismounted and squatted to read the words scribbled in black paint on the cross arms. In flowing old world script, there was a simple tribute: "Reina Luján, 1832–1858." So young, Benoit thought, studying the handful of wildflowers that had been placed there in a crude clay vase. Already, he observed, they were starting to wilt.

Standing over the grave, Benoit felt himself enveloped by a wave of sadness. Suddenly impatient to leave, he swung into his saddle, chastising himself for making the trip in the first place. It was a stupid gesture, he told himself. What could you possibly have hoped to gain by coming here? Deciding that he did not need to see the priest's grave as well, Benoit turned his horse back in the direction he had come, toward the setting sun.

He had gone no more than a few yards, however, when he heard the sound of another animal. A horse from the village, he reckoned. It must have slipped out of its corral and wandered down to the river. The right thing to do, he told himself, was to collect it and return it to its owner. Trying to determine where it might be, he was peering into the cottonwoods, where dusk was much more advanced than in the open field where he stood, when he saw a faint movement. There it is, he thought, urging his own horse forward.

Moving from the sunlight into the shade of the huge trees was like moving from a lighted room into a closet. Although it was not yet dark, he had to pause to let his eyes adjust to the sudden change. It was cool in the shade as well, he noticed. Maybe twenty degrees' difference in temperature. Now, he thought, looking around impatiently, where the hell is that horse?

Wandering deeper into the trees, he suddenly yanked his reins, bringing his horse to an abrupt stop.

"Holy Mother of God!" he exclaimed. Not a dozen yards in front of him were two venerable cottonwoods, rooted majestically in the moist riverbank fifty feet or so apart. By the size of their trunks, Benoit knew they had been there long before the Spanish arrived, perhaps even before the mysterious people the Pueblo tribes called the *anazazi*, the ancient ones, had wandered through the surrounding mountains and across the flat-topped mesas. But it was not the trees that caught Benoit's attention. Affixed to their trunks as securely as the rough bark were the bodies of two men.

Resisting the urge to turn his head away, Benoit

made himself look. Instinctively he knew that one of
the men was Porcopio Sandoval, the other Panfilo
Lucero. It was difficult, however, to tell who was
who. Each man was naked except for a white cloth
wrapped around the loins. At least Benoit assumed
the cloths were white, but it was hard to tell for sure
because they were soaked by blood that had run
down their bodies like water down the nearby river,
staining the tree trunks and soaking into the sandy
ground. It was difficult to believe, Benoit told himself
not for the first time, that a human body could contain
so much blood.

But it was more than the blood that made Benoit feel
as if he were going to be sick. Calling upon his reserve of
willpower to keep from riding out of the *bosque* as
quickly as he could, he forced himself to note the man-
ner of death, striving for a clinical objectivity that would
permit him later to accurately recount the details.

Both men were spread-eagle, their outstretched
arms nailed to the trees by large spikes driven through
their wrists. An additional spike had been pounded
through their overlapped feet, which pointed downward like silent arrows. Each man, Benoit saw, also
had been viciously scourged. In some spots the thongs
had bitten so deeply that the underlying bone was
exposed so that it gleamed whitely in maroon caverns
of raw flesh. Around each man's head was a crudely
fashioned wreath of leather through which sturdy
spines from a prickly pear cactus had been rammed.
The faces of both men were contorted in pain, their
mouths open in silent screams, their eyes wide, the
irises rolled upward, almost invisible. Attached to the
trees above each man's head was a scrap of paper with
a few words clearly legible. Benoit knew enough

Spanish to interpret it easily. The words said, "This man killed a priest."

Gulping, Benoit turned away. He had seen enough. Turning to go, he was surprised to find his path blocked. Planted squarely across the trail was a large bay, the horse he had heard earlier, the sound that had brought him into the *bosque*. Atop the bay was a man clad only in a pair of white trunks. Over his head, completely masking his identity, was a black hood with slits for the eyes and mouth. In his hand was a whip from which a dark liquid still dripped.

Benoit reached for his pistol. But before he could get it clear of the holster, another black-hooded man appeared from nowhere and, with a grip like a vise, seized his wrist and twisted. Grunting in pain, Benoit felt his hand go numb. Out of the corner of his eye, he saw another hooded figure emerge from the trees to his left and move swiftly to his side. Then another materialized. And another. Before Benoit could dig his heels into his horse's side, one of the men grabbed his shirt and yanked him to the ground.

They never spoke a word, Benoit marveled later. But, acting like a well-rehearsed troupe, they methodically began to beat him with the whips. Not lashing him, but using the wooden handles like cudgels. Trying to regain his feet, Benoit was sent sprawling when one of the men hit him a blow on the thigh, knocking his leg from under him. Another cracked him across the shoulders. A third, using the whip handle like a poker, struck him in the kidney, causing Benoit to bellow in pain. In less than two minutes it was over. As he slumped into welcome unconsciousness, Benoit's last thought was the hope that they would not crucify him as they had done the others.

Benoit looked straight into the eyes of the Virgin
Mary. He was not surprised to see that they were
black.

"Am I in heaven?" he croaked through cracked
lips.

"Not hardly," said a male voice.

Benoit blinked. The Holy Mother spoke like a
man? What kind of cruel joke was this? Staring at the
image, he realized it was not the Madonna after all,
only a very realistic looking, life-size portrait artfully
painted on the snow white ceiling.

"Do you honestly think you deserve to go straight
to your reward without at least a couple of centuries in
purgatory?" the voice asked.

"Dammit, Alejo, are you trying to drive me
crazy?" Benoit whispered. With an effort that sent a
thunderbolt of pain crashing through his brain, he
turned his head. Alejo was leaning close, an anxious
iook on his face.

"How do you feel?" he asked, trying to keep his
voice calm.

"Water!" Benoit rasped.

"Just like a captain," Alejo said, grinning. "You
wake up giving orders." After pouring fresh water
into a crystal glass, he put his arm under Benoit's
shoulders and lifted him upright. "Not too fast," he
cautioned, holding the glass to his friend's lips.

Benoit gulped like a thirsty horse. "More!" he
gasped, surprised at his own hoarseness.

"Not right now," Alejo said, shaking his head.
"Too much will make you puke. Take a *siesta*, then
you can have some more."

"What—"

"Later," Alejo said. "Right now the important thing is that you rest. Everything's all right. I'll explain it all to you later."

"Okay," Benoit mumbled, feeling his eyelids closing. "I guess a little nap won't hurt."

"How long did you say I was out?" Benoit asked, lifting the cup to his lips. Inhaling deeply, he sighed in satisfaction, thinking that coffee had never tasted quite so good.

"I guess I need to know what you mean by 'out,'" Alejo said, pouring a fresh cup for himself. "You were definitely unconscious when you were dumped unceremoniously at our front gate."

"And that was when?"

"A week ago today."

Benoit shook his head. "You don't know how strange it feels to completely lose a week out of your life."

"Oh, yes, I do," Alejo added emphatically.

"That was a stupid thing for me to say." Benoit blushed. "Of course you do. But why was I unconscious for so long?"

"That's what I was getting ready to explain. You weren't really so much unconscious as drugged."

"Drugged?"

Alejo nodded. "You looked pretty ragged. As soon as my father saw the shape you were in, he sent for the *curandera*, the old lady who helped me so much. After she examined you, she decided that the best therapy was sleep. So she started feeding you some potion she mixed up especially for the occasion. It kept you quiet while your body healed."

"But there's nothing broken," Benoit said, wiggling his fingers and toes experimentally and running his hands across his chest to check for broken ribs. "In fact, I'm surprised I'm alive after what the *Penitentes* did to Sandoval and Lucero. Did you find the bodies?" he asked urgently.

"Yes." Alejo nodded. "And they've been properly buried. Padre Romero performed the requiem."

"Padre Romero! How ironic."

"Almost everyone from the valley was there, including Melquiares Nuñez."

Benoit shivered in spite of himself. "Why did they attack me? And why did they let me live?"

"They didn't intend to kill you, or even leave you permanently marked," Alejo replied. "The beating, as painful and traumatic as it was, was meant only as a warning."

"A warning to do what?"

"Keep your nose out of *Penitente* business."

"They don't have to worry about *that*," Benoit said forcefully. "If I never hear of the *Penitentes* again, I'll be happy. While I was drifting in and out of . . . what shall I say, awareness?"

"Awareness is a good word."

"I kept having nightmares about those men. Sandoval and Lucero. God, they must have suffered."

"This is not an excuse," Alejo said carefully, "but the Indians do a lot worse."

"I guess so," Benoit conceded. "It just looked awfully vicious to me."

"It was. It was supposed to be. In a way, it was a warning to everyone in the valley that the murder of a priest will not be tolerated."

"Have you put it all together?" Benoit asked.

"Have you figured out why Padre Rabalais was murdered?"

"Some of it will never be known, but I am certain that Padre Rabalais, as we had more or less concluded earlier, was an accidental victim."

"So the real target was Padre Romero?"

"Yes."

"But why?"

"That's a little more complicated, but I've come up with a theory. Remember how Reina's sister told us that Lucero was furious with Padre Romero, but we didn't know why?"

"Uh-huh." Benoit nodded.

"From talking to some of Lucero's friends, it appears that Padre Romero, after he was called to Reina's deathbed, refused to hear her confession or administer the last rites unless she renounced her lover."

"Renounced him? On her deathbed? That sounds strange."

"It *is* strange, but it's the way the old priest's mind works. In his view Reina was nothing but a whore. Remember when we talked to him how he said he had given the last rites to a *puta*. . . ."

"Oh, yeah, but it didn't mean anything at the time."

"Padre Romero made Reina repudiate Panfilo to his face. I really can't say I blame her. She knew she was dying, and the priest held the key for her to get into heaven. I might well have done the same thing myself."

"And Lucero didn't understand that?"

"I guess he was too overcome with grief to think clearly. All he could do was condemn Padre Romero for insulting him. I'm assuming, of course, that he took it as an insult. In his mind, the priest may even have been responsible for Reina's death."

"Okay," Benoit said slowly. "I can understand Lucero's anger and frustration. But how did Sandoval get involved?"

"Ah-hah! That's really very odd. Sandoval had been gone for so long that nobody remembered, except perhaps him, but he was Reina's *padrino*. Her father, who was killed in the revolt, had been Sandoval's best friend."

"He was her *godfather*?"

"Yes, but you have to understand that being a godfather means much more to a Hispano than it does to a *gringo*. It's a much more serious obligation. The tie can be as strong as that between father and child. So Sandoval, even though he had been gone for a decade, undoubtedly felt this very emotional bond to Reina. He may even have been in touch with her directly. Since both of them are now dead, we'll never know about that. Also, I don't know how Sandoval and Lucero got together, but I figure it had to be through Reina. Maybe it was at Reina's wake, which Sandoval could have attended incognito, but I have a feeling it was earlier, maybe several months ago. After Reina's death, they put their heads together and decided that they both hated Padre Romero. So they hatched a plot to kill him."

"I see," Benoit said. "They both had what they figured were strong motives for wanting the priest dead."

"¡Es verdad! That's for sure. The best I can figure is that Sandoval supplied the poison and maybe drew up the plan while Lucero carried it out."

"Lucero must have been near panic when he saw that Padre Rabalais was celebrating the Mass rather than Padre Romero."

"I think perhaps Pol underestimated a bit when he described the degree to which Lucero was upset when he tried to help Padre Rabalais. But he may have been so upset himself that it didn't sink in."

"All in all, a very sorry business."

"Yes, one that's well done with. But it's a great lesson in how powerful the *Penitentes* are."

"Will any of them ever be brought to trial for murdering Lucero and Sandoval?"

Alejo shook his head. "Who would bring them to trial? In the Mora Valley, as in many other areas of New Mexico, they *are* the justice system. At least for now. Personally, I don't know if that's all bad."

"How can you say that?" Benoit asked, surprised. "Killing Sandoval and Lucero was an act of savagery."

"This is still a savage land, *mi amigo*, despite the veneer of civilization. The people of the Mora Valley, as you saw in Pol's village—after years of being theoretically under the protection of the Spanish, the Mexicans, and the Americhanos—are still only a heartbeat removed from savagery. When *los Indios* attacked the village ten days ago, who was there to help them? The nearest army post is Fort Union, a day's ride away. They were no help, just as the Spanish and the Mexicans in the past had been no help. Instead, Moreños have learned to rely upon each other for protection not only from the Apaches, but from murderers like Sandoval and Lucero. If there had been a civilian court here, they would have been tried and executed. Since there was no official court, the *Penitentes* court tried and executed them.

From the perspective of a Moreño, the ends justify the means."

"That's very close to vigilantism," Benoit argued.

"No!" Alejo replied intensely. "It's survival."

Benoit was silent, considering how to respond. "You have a point," he said after several moments. "I guess it's all a matter of perspective. I know that people like your father are decent human beings; they want to do the right thing."

"Are Nuñez and his followers any less decent, to use your word, than my father because they also are doing what they think is right?"

"I don't know the answer to that," said Benoit. "Maybe when the territory becomes more settled and law is established, things will change."

"Perhaps," said Alejo. "But until that happens we must continue as we have for generations. I will tell you in all honesty that Bishop Lamy and Don José, who in my opinion also are decent men, are fighting a losing battle when they go against the *Penitentes*. They may drive them into hiding, but they are not going to eradicate them, not as long as the Brotherhood represents the only law we have. Speaking of Don José," he added, trying to change the subject, "he sends you his greetings."

"What?" Benoit asked. "I don't understand."

"A letter." Alejo smiled. "Hand delivered from Santa Fe. When it was apparent that you were not going to die but might be incapacitated for some time, my father rode to the capital to explain the situation face-to-face to Don José and General Barksdale. He just returned last night. He brought back a packet for you. By the way, he feels very badly about what happened to you, although it was completely beyond his control."

"He shouldn't," said Benoit. "I never for a moment thought that he had anything to do with the attack. But what about this packet?"

Alejo grinned. "Here," he said, handing Benoit a stack of envelopes he had been concealing in his lap. "After you've caught up on your reading, why don't you join us on the patio. My father's anxious to talk to you. He wants to make sure there are no hard feelings."

"Okay," Benoit said, snatching the envelopes. Even before Alejo was out of the room, he was ripping open the letter from Inge.

She sounds in good spirits, he thought, skimming through it hurriedly, then rereading it more carefully. He felt a lump in his throat when he got to the part in which she described what a thrill it was to feel the baby kicking. Erich's condition was unchanged, she reported, but Jim had gotten himself under control and his drinking had tapered off considerably.

"You should see poor Jace," she wrote. "He mopes around like someone who has lost his best friend, which I imagine he has. I feel I have lost both a friend and a husband and am so looking forward to the day when we can be reunited—you, me, and our new son."

Benoit smiled and carefully folded the paper along its original creases. After tucking it under his pillow where he could read it again later, he looked at the other envelopes Alejo had given him.

The one on the top contained a short note, in French, from Don José, expressing his gratitude for Benoit's help.

"You stepped into a delicate and difficult situation, but you responded like a true Christian," he wrote. "I am greatly disturbed by the physical inconvenience and pain it caused you, but please understand that both the Bishop and I are eternally in your debt. We are praying for your speedy recovery and hope that you will be back among us soon."

Who knows, Benoit thought, putting it aside. Maybe one day I'll need a friend high in the Church.

Barksdale's note was even more abbreviated: "Well done. Get back when you can."

Not for another week, at least, Benoit thought, tossing it on the floor.

He picked up the fourth envelope, weighing it thoughtfully in his hand. For several moments, staring at the familiar return address, he considered pitching it away unopened. Only the fear that *not* reading it might be worse made him change his mind. Sighing, he ripped off the end of the envelope and extracted the two sheets of expensive stationery. At least it's brief, he thought, glaring at the small but perfectly formed letters and flowing penmanship. At the sight, he felt his stomach tighten into a knot. Preparing for bad news—and Clement Couvillion had never let him down before—he began to read:

Washington
13 July 1858

My Dear t-Jean,

The situation here, as you may have read, is getting increasingly tense by the day, what with *solons* from the South and the North openly sniping at each other, neither side ever passing up the opportunity for a jab at his opponent. This, I fear, is but a prelude to the war that draws nearer by the hour. My colleague from South Carolina, the Honorable James Henry Hammond, threw down a gauntlet recently in a speech on the Senate floor. "Cotton is king," he bellowed dramatically, thereby challenging those who think the South is toothless. "You dare not make war upon cotton," he proudly proclaimed. "No power on earth dares make war upon it." Unfortunately, I fear his warning will not be seriously regarded by those who feel it is their destiny to change the South. A good example is that misguided mischief-maker from Illinois who appears determined to cause trouble. You know of whom I speak. That fanciful failure, Abraham Lincoln, the Republican candidate for Senator against the Honorable Stephen A. Douglas. What could be more war-baiting than his words to his party earlier this summer. "A house divided against itself cannot stand." Have you ever heard such claptrap? To the contrary, there are many who feel that *separate* houses represent the best solution, one for the South, another for the North.

On a more personal note, I had the pleasure of dining with your family while I was in New Orleans during the summer recess. I have to compliment you, my friend, your mother has never looked better. If only I were twenty years older. Your sister has the bloom of the new bride upon her, a condition she wears very well, I must say. In the library later, over brandy and cigars, I had a most enjoyable conversation with your brother and your new brother-in-law. Two more staunch and loyal allies for the Southern cause are hard to find. Your brother is so anxious to join our little contingent that it took quite a bit of persuasion on my part to convince him to remain at the Naval Academy and get all the free education he can absorb. It will be of inestimable value to us when the time comes.

In that regard, Jefferson Davis is hard at work on his plans for a quick strike once war is declared. As I mentioned to you in my last correspondence, your assistance in this instance will be invaluable since the New Mexico Territory is one of our top objectives. To be honest, I am a little disappointed in the lack of enthusiasm Maurice has shown so far for his task. Perhaps there are extenuating circumstances, but his reports have been few and far between. In view of this, it is imperative that you begin immediately to take a more active role. Our most pressing need is to begin making a list of officers we know we will be able to depend upon once the hostilities begin. And this is where I need—shall I say demand?—your prompt assistance. In your present position you are undoubtedly required to be in contact with those in posts throughout the territory. Your assignment is to begin quietly sounding them out, one at a time, privately and as tactfully as possible. Find out who is sympathetic to our cause. Who will join us and who will take the other side. This is intelligence of the highest order, so do not commit it to the mail. Keep your information under close guard, either on your person or under lock and key. In the fall, Marie will be visiting Santa Fe under the guise of a pleasure trip to California via the new

Butterfield Route, with a side trip to make a personal call upon General Barksdale, whose middle daughter is a close personal friend of hers. Pass the information to her and she will deliver it to me. As usual, burn this letter at the first available opportunity. . . .

There was more, but Benoit could not bring himself to read it. Angrily he balled up the letter and tossed it as hard as he could across the room. "God*damn* you, Clement Couvillion!" he cursed. His voice was louder than he intended.

"Are you all right, Jean?" Alejo asked solicitously, poking his head in the door. "I was just coming to see if you needed some assistance. Do you feel strong enough to walk?"

Benoit, hoping his flushed cheeks did not betray him, looked at his friend and lied.

"Everything's fine, Alejo. I just had some unexpected news from"—he paused, hoping God would not strike him dead on the spot—"a *friend* in Washington."

Throwing back the light blanket that was becoming necessary in the mountains as summer departed, he put his feet on the floor and tried to compose himself. "As my brother, the naval cadet, would put it," he said as normally as he could manage, "let me see if I have my land legs yet."